Don't Forget

Other Books by AJ Adaire

Journey To You

I Love My Life

It's Complicated

One Day Longer Than Forever

Friend Series
Sunset Island - Book 1
The Interim (a novelette)
Awaiting My Assignment - Book 2
Anything Your Heart Desires - Book 3

Don't Forget

by

AJ Adaire

Desert Palm Press

Don't Forget
by AJ Adaire

© 2017 by AJ Adaire

(trade) ISBN: 9781942976301
(ebook) ISBN: 9781942976318
(pdf) ISBN: 9781942976325

Desert Palm Press
1961 Main Street, Suite 220
Watsonville, California 95076
www.desertpalmpress.com

Editor: CK King
(https://www.facebook.com/RavensEyeEditing)
Cover Design: AK Adaire (www.ajadaire.com)

Printed in the United States of America
First Edition March 2017

Acknowledgements

Thank you to my very first reader, Martha, who carefully read every word, a long time ago. When I read a book, I'm able to say, "I liked it," or "I didn't like it." She has the skill to pinpoint exactly which parts worked and which parts didn't. If not for her early encouragement, I might not be releasing my ninth book today. Her very astute and helpful suggestions resulted in a better book and my sincere gratitude.

Following a major rewrite of this story, my readers, Betty, Sally, Michelle, and Sue read my final draft for me prior to submission. Thank you, ladies, for catching my typos and other issues. Thanks, too, Lee and CK for polishing my words and making me a better writer.

Finally, thanks to my partner, who put up with me disappearing into the office, day after day, as I rewrote this story repeatedly. We are so fortunate to be able to share a then, a now, and a forever.

Preface: A Note To The Reader

This is a fictional work; however, many of the situations depicted in this book were all too realistic in the eighties when the majority of this story takes place.

To help put things in perspective for some too young to remember that time, I'll share with you the beginning of my teaching career. I started teaching in the seventies. Teachers were not allowed to wear pants. We had to wear dresses or skirts the length of which had to be below our knees, and we wore heels. My first mandatory social event was to attend a tea at the school superintendent's house. White gloves and a hat were required attire. Times were seriously different back then.

As you read Jamie and Val's story, it may seem that their characters are excessively concerned about the repercussions on their careers were their lesbian relationship to become known. Their problem is compounded by the fact that they both work in the same school district and live within the confines of its not very liberal community. It is important to understand and accept that their fears were realistic; many lesbian women and gay men faced similar fears in real life. Sadly, some still do today, despite the protections we have gained. With the recent election, some of the hard-gained rights are threatened again.

To those of you who were educators, or know someone who was in education during the time this story takes place, you will surely be able to identify with the issues these two women face as they struggle with their feelings and fears.

I hope all of you will enjoy meeting Jamie and Val, as they endeavor to be brave enough to master living their lives together in a loving relationship, despite societal disapproval.

Chapter One

Present Day

"DAMN IT, VAL. I can't believe we've got to clean out thirty years of crap from our attic and we're almost out of time. We'll never finish before the movers get here next week." Jamie navigated around the neatly stacked boxes containing the contents of their den. "We knew the day would come when we'd have to downsize and move. Why didn't we do this years ago?"

Val fixed Jamie with a tender gaze that smoothed the crinkles at the corners of her eyes. With her laugh lines relaxed, Val's face took on a more youthful appearance. "Are we done now? Of course, I mean 'we' in the royal sense."

On the wall behind her, the pendulum of the antique clock beat out a steady tick tock sound. Val's left hand rested on her hip, while her right index finger tapped out a matching rhythm to the clock against the leg of her jeans. Patience, born from years of experience with her lover, dictated that Val wait for Jamie's ire to pass.

As Jamie approached her partner, she blasted out a sharp breath through pursed lips. "I'm sorry, it's just that…"

"I know, you're feeling pressured." Val tilted her head and smiled. "Don't worry, we'll get it done. The attic is the last thing we have to do." Val closed the gap between them and wrapped her arms loosely around Jamie's waist. "Have I told you yet today that I'm glad it's you?"

Jamie made a show of glancing at the ceiling as if trying to recall. "I think you may have told me you love me, but not that." She slid her hands up her lover's arms to her shoulders.

"Oh my, then I have been quite remiss." Val pulled Jamie closer. "You know that I do both, right?"

"I'm sorry." Jamie closed her eyes and shook her head. "It's…well…"

"I know." Val chuckled and kissed each of Jamie's cheeks. "Now, how about you go get the rest of the stuff in the attic organized, while I go downstairs and get a cloth? I'm sure the boxes are dirty after all those years squirreled away up there. If you stack them by the top of the steps, we can get them down together."

Jamie gave the love of her life a quick kiss before releasing her from their hug. A smile graced her lips as she watched Val turn toward the basement. "Don't forget," she called.

Val waved over her shoulder. "I won't."

Jamie chuckled. They'd been saying 'don't forget' to each other for years. She watched Val until she disappeared around the corner. Jamie pivoted, climbed the stairs, and headed to the attic to set about her task.

A bead of sweat tracked its way down the middle of her forehead. She used her hand to wipe her brow before she ran it over the leg of her sweat-soaked shorts. *How the hell did I get this old?* Her green eyes flashed in frustration, as she ran her fingers through her short, mostly white hair, pushing it away from her face where it adhered to her forehead. On her third attempt to rise from her position on one knee, she met with success. A groan punctuated her struggle to her feet. She bent over slightly as she stood up, careful not to bang her head on the roof rafter. To stretch out her screaming muscles, she stood under the main beam, bent back at the hips, and rolled her shoulders. Her eyes scanned the remaining boxes that held a collection of souvenirs and other memorabilia accumulated over the years. Neatly lettered lists taped to the lids identified their contents.

She wiped her forehead and bent to her task again. A grunt preceded the sound of the cardboard box scraping across the floor, as it followed the trail in the light coating of dust left by the previous cartons. Box after box, she repeated the same routine until she had them lined up at the top of the stairs. *Phew! Thank God...last one. Where the hell is Val with that rag?* Working her way down the steps backwards, she reached for and lifted the first banker's box. Stopping to rest every couple of steps, she backed down the narrow winding stairs and set the container on the floor of their second-floor den. *At this rate, we'll never get this done in time.* Releasing a grunt, she lifted the box onto the chest by the sofa, blew the dust from the lid, and dropped it to the floor. *Uh oh.* Her lips formed into a grimace, as she stared at the dirt on the carpet. *Val will have a fit. Where is she anyway?*

Jamie reached for the lid and brushed the dust away. In Val's neat hand, the label read *Jamie Parker – 2/3/85*. Inside, on top of a stack of letters, a picture of Bly as she'd looked when they first met stared back at her. The picture failed to do justice to the woman's magnetic eyes. The same eyes that attracted her so many years ago, that belonged to the first woman she'd made love with. It was so like Val to have set these things aside to save. Her partner had generously embraced her former lover as a friend, even after she knew the history they'd shared. Tears welled in her eyes, as a wave of emotion washed over her. *How lucky was I to find Val and have her love me in return? Considering everything, I'm still amazed that we got together at all, and I don't know why we saved all this stuff.*

"Hey, sweetheart, where's that rag?" Jamie closed the box and pushed it toward the discard pile.

Silence. Jamie's brows furrowed. "Val?" she bellowed. *I bet she doesn't have her hearing aids on.*

Jamie made her way downstairs and shouted Val's name again. Silence. *Now what? Where'd she go?* She glanced in the direction of the back door. *Nope. Locked.* "Val? Where are you?" The sweat on her heated body turned cold. Heart thumping, Jamie hurried around the corner and peered down the cellar stairway. What she saw there caused her blood to run cold. "Oh my God, Val." Jamie careened down the stairs to her partner, who lay crumpled at the bottom of the stairs.

Val's leg, bent under her at an awkward angle, was already swelling and turning blue. It was obvious that her ankle was either broken or sprained, although the more immediate concern was the blood pooling beneath her head. There was no response when Jamie touched her arm and called Val's name. Jamie hurried back up the stairs to call the EMTs. Breathing fast, she gave the address and other requested information the dispatcher requested.

"I know this will be hard," the calm female voice on the phone instructed. "It's important that you don't move her. The ambulance is on the way. Just a few minutes and they'll be there."

As instructed, Jamie went to unlock the front door. She took some comfort from the fact that before she turned to go back to Val, she could hear the sirens wailing in the distance.

The first person to hurry down the stairs was a tall, well built, Amazon of a woman. "Hi, I'm Kelly."

"Jamie."

"What's her name?"

"Val."

Kelly made a quick and thorough assessment of the injured

woman's condition. "Val, can you hear me?"

Val's eyes fluttered open. "Jamie…"

"I'm right here, sweetheart. Everything will be okay."

Kelly's eyes flashed from one woman to the other. "My teammates are bringing a stretcher. Please, let me get on that side there so I can prepare her for transport." The medic's face softened before she reached out her hand to Jamie. "We'll take good care of her." She patted her arm before setting about her medical assessment.

Jamie put a hand over her heart and tried to massage away the pounding in her chest, as the woman worked on her partner.

Kelly barely raised her eyes when the rest of the crew started down the stairs with the stretcher. She nodded, sought eye contact with the older woman, and reached over to place a hand on Jamie's shoulder. "I know it's hard. Please, try not to worry. Now, listen carefully. You'll need her medical cards and a book or something to help pass the time while you wait for her at the hospital. Don't forget a sweater, the hospital is always cold. So, go gather what you need and let us see to her."

Kelly allowed Jamie to ride in the front seat of the ambulance, as her coworkers attended to Val in the back of the van. Jamie gazed out the window and sniffed, wringing the tissue in her hands. Kelly reached up and turned on the lights before she pulled away from the house. "No siren unless people don't move. She'll be okay. Have faith."

Jamie smiled in Kelly's direction, her eyes bright and glistening. "I don't know what I'd do without her."

"I understand." The ambulance wheeled into the designated space at the hospital. "You'll go in that door and sign her in, and we'll take care of her from here." Kelly turned off the van and hurried toward the rear of the ambulance, as Jamie slid out of the tall vehicle. Jamie did as directed, while Kelly whisked Val away through a different door.

In reception, Jamie provided all the requested information asked of her. The woman behind the desk asked a myriad of questions with a practiced indifference. She seemed either unable or unwilling to remove her eyes from her computer screen.

Jamie shuffled through the Medicare, insurance, and prescription cards, as she answered the questions. She raised her eyes in a silent prayer of thanks to Kelly. She was the one who'd reminded her to get the wallet where they kept all their medical cards. Jamie pulled the last document, their medical power of attorney from the case. Although they were legally married, Jamie unfolded the medical power of attorney they had drawn up for each other years before. "You might want this as well," she said, handing over the legal document.

The efficient woman finally faced Jamie. "Oh good. It never hurts to have that." She disappeared for a brief time to make a copy and returned the document. "Would you like me to have someone escort you to the waiting room?"

"Yes, thank you. I'd appreciate that." Jamie felt like a pull toy, as she scurried along behind the hospital volunteer. With a relentless pace and long strides, he navigated the convoluted hospital hallways. She was out of breath by the time they arrived at their destination, and she wondered if she'd ever again find her way back to Val's room.

Before he hurried away, the blue-clad man pointed to a small room. "You can sit and wait there. I'll let the nurse know you're here. She'll come get you once they know more about your friend's condition."

"Thank you." She wanted to shout that Val was more than a friend. Her hesitation made the point moot, because the guy was already out of earshot as he rounded the corner.

The small and quiet lounge was so unlike the main emergency room that always seemed to hum with activity. Jamie, alone in the waiting area, sat in one of the mauve chairs like those that lined the basic-gray wall on the far side of the room. Barely minutes later, her screaming muscles demanded that she shift position yet again. *How does anyone manage to survive sitting in these chairs?* She smiled as she thought of Lily Tomlin's *Laugh-In* character, Edith Ann. *I'm just like her. If I sit back in the chair like she did, my feet dangle, and if I sit forward so my feet touch the floor, my back aches from no support.* Her discomfort made each painful second she waited for news about her partner seem at least twice as long.

Her eyes scanned the wall and stopped at the clock. As the second hand made its way around the clock face, she watched it pause on contact with the minute hand. It issued an annoying sound as it scraped its way free and leaped forward for its journey around again. Each annoying click marked the passage of one small increment of time. The overhead fluorescent hummed and flickered at will, alternately casting either a deep shadow or glaring sun-like brightness over the room. Her restless toes tapped on the floor, and her fingers drummed on the seat of the chair next to her. The clock's minute hand circled around to tally the passing of one hour.

Again, her eyes drifted to the dog-eared and outdated magazines on the coffee table. There was no reason to assume there would be anything of more interest in them this time around than there was the other two times she'd paged through them. Jamie closed her eyes and raised a silent prayer for her partner's safekeeping. Her eyes snapped open when a soft touch to her shoulder startled her.

"You forgot your jacket." Kelly draped the coat around Jamie's shoulders. "Any news yet?"

"No, not yet." Jamie pulled the jacket tighter around her. "You were so right, it is chilly in here. Thanks very much, I appreciate you bringing it to me."

Kelly shifted and checked the clock.

Noticing the action, Jamie said, "Don't let me detain you. You must have somewhere you need to be. What about…"

"No, I'm off work. I start my vacation tomorrow. I finished my shift, and I'm a free woman. I don't think you should be alone right now. There should be some news any time now. Would you like me to wait with you or call someone?"

"That's so kind of you. I don't want to take advantage. You've been so helpful already. I'm sure you have more important things to do."

"I'm sorry to say I don't." Kelly settled her tall frame into one of the chairs.

It surprised Jamie to see that the tall woman seemed to feel no more at ease in the seat than she did.

"You'd think that they could make this room more comfortable. Since so many people have to wait here for word of their loved ones, it could be more hospitable." Kelly stretched out her long legs and crossed them at the ankle.

"I thought it was because I'm short."

Kelly shook her head. "Nope." She shifted again, this time crossing one long leg over the other. She grasped her ankle with her left hand. "Do you have anyone coming to wait with you?"

Jamie shook her head. "I haven't called anyone yet. I thought I'd wait till I know what the situation is. There's no sense in worrying anyone before we know what we're dealing with."

The electronic door hummed, and the emergency room doctor rushed in and looked around. "I'm looking for Jamie Parker?"

Jamie leaped to her feet. "Yes, that's me. I'm Jamie."

The doctor extended his hand. "I'm Doctor Prada." He looked in Kelly's direction.

Kelly stood and started to back away. Jamie stopped her with a hand to her wrist. "How is Val?"

"We stitched the head wound and determined she has a concussion. Although she's feeling a little queasy and has a headache, she's awake and communicative. We also determined she has a fracture of her right ankle. We're going to take her into surgery to set it as soon as we can get an operating room available. It's a lot for a woman of her age, and I want to err on the side of caution. Once we set her ankle, we'll keep her here for observation for a day or so, then she'll have physical therapy." He put a hand on Jamie's shoulder. "Don't worry. The observation is to be sure she doesn't develop any serious complications. I checked the list of medications you provided, and it appears she's not on any blood thinners, so we're not too concerned. It's always best to be safe." He squeezed out a flash of a smile.

"What about her ankle? Will she be able to come home?"

"Upon her release from here, we'll assess her condition. At that time, we'll determine if she needs to go to a facility for physical therapy. Depending on how she's doing, she may be able to go home and have therapy there. We'll firm up all those details as soon as we know her head wound won't complicate anything. For now, we'll keep an eye on her." The doctor's face softened at Jamie's concerned expression. "I don't think there's anything serious to worry about. We just want to be cautious. We should know more by morning."

"Can I see her?"

"They're prepping her for surgery right now. They'll take her up soon, and it'll be a couple of hours afterwards before we get her into a room. You can visit her then, as soon as we get her settled. I'll send someone out to let you know the room number." He gave her a quick smile. "Don't worry, she's in good hands." Despite being at least forty years her junior, he gave her a fatherly pat on the shoulder before he rushed off.

Kelly put a protective arm around Jamie's shoulders and gave her a little squeeze. "You have a bit of a wait. I'm starving. Let's go get something warm to drink, and maybe a bite to eat."

"I need to be here for when..."

"I'll take care of that." Kelly disappeared behind the employees' only door and returned a few minutes later, a smile on her face. She tapped the pager attached to her belt. "My friend will let me know when they have Val settled. Come on, let's find somewhere more comfortable." She patted her stomach and grinned. "Preferably, somewhere with food."

7

They paid at the register for a sandwich for Kelly and some hot chocolate for Jamie. At Kelly's behest Jamie followed her down a short hallway to a small meeting room. "This will be a little quieter and more comfortable while we wait for news." Kelly took a hearty bite of her sandwich and gave Jamie a grin.

Jamie warmed her hands around her paper cup of chocolate. "Thank you. Are you always this kind?"

"It's my nature to help people." Kelly shrugged. "I guess it's why I do what I do. Anyway, I've no place I'd rather be than here with you." Kelly looked away. "I lost my mom recently, and when I saw you sitting there alone, I couldn't help but think of her. I wouldn't have wanted her to face a hospital crisis on her own, so…"

"So you took pity on this grateful old lady."

"I hope you won't mind my asking this. How long have you and Val been together?"

"Twenty-nine years. It'll be thirty in a few months."

"That's amazing." Kelly took another bite of her sandwich and chewed. "I hope one day I'll find a woman who'll love me as much as you love Val."

Jamie turned her full gaze on her companion. "My wish for you is that you find someone who can make you as happy as Val has made me all these years." Jamie studied the woman across from her. Blonde hair, trimmed short, fell in short curls around her face. Bright-blue eyes with darker than expected lashes sat above a straight nose. Full lips punctuated by deep dimples on either side softened her square jaw. "Someone as lovely and kind as you shouldn't have a hard time."

"You'd think, right?" Kelly swiped the napkin across her lips. "It's seems hard these days to find someone who wants a forever. Everyone seems so shallow, focused on their own selfish agenda. Although, I'd guess it's easier for me than it was for you and Val. Times have changed and society is so much more accepting today."

"You have no idea." Jamie shook her head.

"Tell me about how you met. Did you know right away that she was 'the one?'"

Jamie placed her chin in the palm of her hand. "Well, that's a long story."

"We have nothing but time."

"I guess that's true." Jamie pushed her sleeve up and glanced at her watch. "Okay, we met at the school where we both taught. It's amazing to think that we ever got together in that environment. Being gay back then, in the early eighties, especially in education, was nowhere near as accepted as it is today. Think about it, even today there are still teachers who fear loss of their jobs if someone discovers they're gay or lesbian. Not only was our superintendent a bigot in general, he was a well-known homophobe as well."

"So how do two people who work in that kind of environment find and come out to each other?"

"Very carefully." Jamie chuckled. "It was interesting how our friendship developed into something deeper. At first, we had a cordial and casual relationship. We never saw each other outside of school or did social things together. Mostly, we'd see each other at teachers' meetings where we'd exchange pleasantries. A few years after I started work there, Val got promoted to Vice Principal of the preschool program. Several years later, I became Vice Principal of the middle school program. I was thirty-two then. Val was four years older. Once we both had administrative positions, we began to see each other more often at meetings, although the relationship was still only professional.

"About three years later, money became an issue for the district, so the state took over management of the school system. As part of the take-over, they undertook what they described as a reorganization inquiry. The state team tasked with the project held meetings and interviewed every member of the staff in small groups. Rumors flew about a study done to identify new money sources. When the interviews concluded, the team announced that there would be a reorganization of the administration and some staff cuts.

"In October, they promised that a new organizational chart would be forthcoming. Fall became winter and we continued to hear whispers about the reorganization. Word was that the vice principals were to be the 'sacrificial lambs.' We endured that speculation for months, fearing the abolishment of our positions. It gave new meaning to the phrase 'tense working environment.'"

"So how did you move from that tense situation to a hot romance?"

Jamie laughed at the surprising question. "That, like the reorganization, was a long project that took months. One day, while shopping, I bumped into Val at this little gift shop. I showed her a desk plaque that listed *The Six Phases of a Project*. I suggested we were somewhere between steps four and five."

"What do you think?"

"Hm, search for the guilty and punishment of the innocent. That sounds about right." She smirked and pointed to the little coffee shop next door. *"Let's get something to drink and figure it out."*

"We went to the little coffee shop and spent nearly two hours talking. I remember that I kept ordering more tea so we could stay there talking. My teeth were floating by the time we left. We commiserated with each other over the situation at work and what would happen if we both lost our jobs, before the conversation took on a lighter tone." Jamie glanced at the clock.

"No news yet." Kelly tapped her pager. "So, that was it? Love at first sight?"

"Hardly. You have no idea."

"So, tell me about it. It'll help pass the time till we hear that Val is out of recovery and in her room."

Jamie's mind's eye drifted back to their beginning, and she started the story.

Chapter Two

Reflections

JAMIE GLANCED AT THE mirror on her way to the bathroom. Her reflection showed a woman in her thirties. Her current weight of one hundred and ten, toned pounds looked good on her five-foot-two-inch frame. She had good posture, a result of her father's nagging in childhood. Short, dark hair framed her high cheekbones, full lips, and bright green eyes. She'd grown to love her naturally wavy hair, something she'd viewed as a curse when she was younger.

If there could be a perfect scenario for relaxing in her heated pool on a late-spring day, this would be it. The forecast called for abundant sunshine, a light breeze, and warmer than normal temperatures. She tucked her sunscreen and towel under her arm and grabbed an apple from the fridge before heading for the pool.

Jamie organized her belongings on the deck, before she turned on the filter. There was a delicate balance between silence and the annoying hum of the pump as it circulated and filtered the water. Sacrificing quiet, she opted for the motor. It gave her pleasure to pass from full sun to cooling shade with each sweep around the pool. Jamie loved to lie on the floating pillow and just drift with the current created by the output of the skimmer.

Jamie slid into the pool. She covered her nipples with her hands to reduce the shock of the water on that sensitive area. She shivered once, and then swam several laps. Now positioned on the floating raft, she let out a slow sigh and swung the float around to face the sun. She let her mind drift. Val would be arriving before too long.

It was mere minutes later, when Val's arrival interrupted Jamie's reminiscences. "Hello, I'm here. I brought you a cold drink." She came up on the deck, dumped her bags, and lifted the cooler lid. "Look, I brought our favorite soda." She held up an icy cold bottle of Boylan's creamy birch beer.

Jamie paddled over to the edge and climbed onto the deck. Val popped open the top of the bottle and handed the frosty beverage to Jamie.

"You spoil me." Jamie sucked some of the frothy foam from the bottle.

"You know I enjoy doing it." Val took another sip. Her warm brown eyes scanned Jamie's face. "You're always doing for someone else. I enjoy doing little things for you. It gives me pleasure."

Jamie leaned back in the deck chair and propped her feet on the railing. "So, what's up?"

"Now that I'm here," Val shrugged, "I plan to forget about the purge at work and enjoy myself today. What about you?"

"I arrived at the same conclusion earlier today. I'm not going to let the situation at work ruin my weekend. It's bad enough it rules my world from seven a.m. to seven p.m. all week."

Thus began their day together. They talked and frittered away the time, as they floated around the pool. Around five thirty, Jamie pulled the towel around her shoulders and rubbed her arm. "Shower?" She watched Val stand and let her eyes roam, as Val gathered her belongings.

"Umm. Sounds good," Val said over her shoulder. "Then dinner. I'm starving."

Val showered first. When she finished, Jamie used the bathroom for her shower. She dried off, dressed in her underwear, and wrapped the towel around herself. Entering the bedroom, she found Val sitting on the bed looking at her arms and legs.

"I've seen medium-rare steaks about the same color as you are." Jamie put her arm next to Val's to compare burns. "Looks like the first burn of the season."

"One problem with that, I'm Italian. I don't burn in the traditional sense. Even though this looks like I'm really red, it means nothing. In a day or two, I'll be nice and tan if I put some cream on when I get home."

"You don't have to wait that long." To be heard, Jamie raised her voice as she headed for the bathroom. "I have some great after-sun cream that really reduces the peeling. I'll get it, and we can take turns applying it." She returned and handed the cream to Val who made quick work of applying it to Jamie's back.

Val handed the tube to Jamie and turned her back. Lowering the towel to her waist in the back, she kept her breasts covered as best she could.

Jamie wouldn't be able to deny that she was enjoying the smooth feel of Val's skin against her palm. "You're so lucky that you don't peel. I have no doubt that I will."

Jamie watched Val in the mirror as she applied the cream. Val, who would be turning forty in the fall, was four years older than Jamie. Her beautiful, collar-length, dark hair had natural, reddish highlights and a slight curl. The color of her hair and naturally olive complexion combined to give the appearance that she was glowing. Standing a couple of inches taller than Jamie, she was of medium build with large breasts and a small waist. She truly did have an hourglass figure. Val looked up as Jamie finished applying the lotion, and their eyes met in the mirror. Val's smile was quick and warm.

Jamie could feel the pulse in her neck pick up its pace, as her mind worked overtime. She returned the smile. *Her mouth is her best feature. That mouth. Just looking at it makes me want to press my lips right there on the corner where it turns up.* She licked her lips. *It's not polite to drool on your guest.* She stepped away. "I think that'll do it." Jamie gathered her clothes and left Val to dress in privacy.

In the bathroom, Jamie dressed and applied some light makeup. *I wonder what would happen to our friendship if Val actually knew the real me and that I could step over there and kiss her silly with very little provocation. I don't dare reveal my true thoughts and feelings.* Jamie worried more for fear of reprisals at work than fear of losing the friendship, although both concerned her.

They finished dressing and left in Jamie's car and headed for the restaurant that was about a half hour away. As they started out, Jamie turned on the radio and adjusted the volume to a low level. Willie Nelson was crooning *You Are Always On My Mind*. Jamie shrugged one eyebrow. *How appropriate.*

Val shifted toward Jamie. "So, is this restaurant a favorite of yours?"

"I first came here with my ex-husband, Josh, years ago. Although the building has changed a bit, it's still a great restaurant with a nice selection of food. It's cute and quaint, with about six tables inside the restored mill plus about four on the patio. I understand that they've added an additional dining area recently."

Jamie pulled the car into a parking space near the front door. As they entered the restaurant, Val exclaimed, "Oh, this is perfect. Look at the tables overlooking the waterwheel. I wonder if we could sit there?"

The host granted their request to sit overlooking the scenic wheel.

Val's eyes sparkled as she struggled to hold back her laughter. "What? Is something wrong?"

"Not at all." A blush of red crept up from Val's neck to the top of her forehead, making her radiant. "It's the water. You know, I'm glad we're not that far from the restroom. I'll probably need it several times tonight after listening to the water trickle."

The waiter interrupted their conversation to deliver menus and read the list of additional choices. Following his departure, there was a flurry of activity. Someone brought them a basket of warm, yeasty rolls, and another server filled their water glasses. Their waiter scurried back to take their order when he saw they looked ready. They ordered a bottle of wine and the prime rib with house salad. Dinner was a continuation of the enjoyable day they'd spent at the pool.

"To you." Val held up her glass. "Thanks for bringing me here. I love it. "

"My pleasure." Jamie clinked her glass against Val's. "It's always been a favorite of mine."

"You mentioned earlier that Josh and you used to come here. Do you still miss him?"

"Yes, but I'm taking lessons, and my aim is getting better all the time."

Jamie laughed at Val when she gulped the swallow of wine she'd sipped a second before. "I'm sorry. I guess I shouldn't make fun. I can't say I miss him specifically. It would probably be fairer to say I miss being paired. Being alone isn't fun."

"Sometimes I'm lonely, too." Val averted her eyes to her plate and cut off a piece of her meat. She raised her eyes and met Jamie's gaze. "I've never been married, so I don't know what it must be like to leave a committed relationship. Since we're here, I guess it doesn't bother you to come to somewhere you came with him."

"Not anymore. I've completely resolved my feelings about him. I will admit that right after the divorce, it used to bother me when he brought a date to one of our favorite places and then told me about it. These days, I hardly ever think of Josh any more. Before and during our marriage I thought of him as my best friend, in addition to being my husband, so the divorce cost me both. We were such kids when we got married. We kind of grew up together and we both changed. At the time, when our marriage ended, I wanted us to remain friends. I felt very sad when that friendship never really came to fruition following our divorce. I saw him a couple of years ago. It was a strange feeling seeing him, someone I used to be intimate with for so many years. He was, in essence, a stranger. When I looked at him, I felt nothing."

"Nothing?"

"Yeah, I remember being shocked by that. I gave it a lot of thought. I remember that it came as a shock to me when I recognized that I no longer loved him. Truth was that I had no feelings about him... I realized that he was a stranger. I no longer knew who he had become, and I was a decidedly different person. After that, things were easier for me. Counseling helped, too."

"That's an interesting way to view it."

The waiter showed up, removed their dishes, and returned with two "doggie bags."

The waiter placed a dessert menu on the table. "I recommend the gelato. It's made here. Would you like some coffee, tea, or an after-dinner drink?"

Val ordered coffee, and they agreed to split a scoop of the homemade hazelnut gelato. "Bring two spoons please," Val said with a wink in the waiter's direction.

Jamie put her spoon down. "Phew! I'm stuffed."

"You don't look like a teddy bear."

Jamie's brows knit together. "What?"

"You never heard that joke?"

"I guess not. Tell me."

Val leaned forward and smiled. "Ok, but promise not to throw something at me. Why couldn't the teddy bear finish his dessert?"

Jamie shrugged.

"Because he was already stuffed."

Jamie shook her head. "Okay, here's one back at you. When you see a heart carved in a tree, don't think 'oh my, how sweet,' think about how many people bring a knife on a date."

Val chuckled and opened her mouth to counter, but the waiter brought the check.

On the way home in the car, Jamie glanced over at Val. "Tonight was fun. However, other than learning that you like dumb jokes, I didn't discover much about you. You're always asking me questions about my past, yet you never reveal much about yourself or your relationships."

"That's because there's not much to tell. I'll also have to admit that secrecy is a Scorpio trait." Val played with the clasp on her purse.

"There you go changing the subject again. How am I ever to get to know you better if you keep avoiding my questions?" Jamie reached over and turned off the music, softening her criticism with a warm smile.

"I'm being honest when I say there's not much to tell. I was pinned to a guy I started dating in high school. We dated all through college. I went to an all-girls school, and he went to a college a couple of hours' drive from the school I attended. Because of the distance, I only saw him a few times a year when he came home for semester breaks"

"Didn't you go out to see him at his school?"

"No." Val cocked her head. "How stupid I was. He always told me he was too busy with his studies at medical school. Later, I found out that he must have gotten the pins mass-produced. He was pinned to another girl at his college at the same time, so I guess he was busy all right." Val inhaled a deep breath and shifted in her seat. Her palm brushed across her forehead.

"I'm sorry, Val. I'm sure that hurt."

"If you want to call it such, losing him was not the most painful part. A friend of his slipped up, and I found out about the other girl. When he came home for Christmas break and I confronted him, he turned nasty and accused me of some hateful things. The worst was that he needed her because I was frigid. I haven't dated anyone since him."

Jamie looked over at Val who was looking out the window. "He was angry and hurtful, because you caught him. It's clear he didn't deserve someone like you. You shouldn't give up because of the hurtful things he said."

"I know. It wasn't really because of him. Truth is, I didn't have time for dating. My dad had a stroke the year after I graduated, so I helped my mom with Dad's care for twelve years. After work, I'd go home to relieve Mom."

"I thought you traveled a lot, because I remember you telling me about your trips to Italy."

"I would go to Italy for a week or two, in the summer, if I could get away. Several times, I had to cancel scheduled trips, because either my mom or dad would get sick. I think the stress of me not being there would bring on a health crisis in one or the other of them. I was never sure if it was real or imagined."

"I'm sure having to cancel plans was a huge disappointment."

Val shrugged. "We all have responsibilities. I loved my parents, so it didn't seem like a sacrifice. I just kept putting one foot in front of the other. Since Dad died, I've never gotten back into the dating scene.

Between then and now, I haven't found myself wanting to spend much time with anyone. Val looked at Jamie. "So, like I said before, no deep, dark secrets...there's nothing much to reveal. What about you, dating anyone?"

"No, I dated someone for a while after my divorce." Jamie shrugged one shoulder. "It didn't last too long, and it ended up being an experience that didn't go where I'd hoped it might. We parted as friends, and it helped me to learn a lot about what I really need and want in my life."

The remainder of the ride was quiet, as each woman's thoughts turned inward. Jamie pulled the car into her driveway and walked Val to her car, where it felt natural to give her a quick hug good-bye. She could feel Val stiffen up. It had been a surprise, earlier, when Val allowed her to apply the lotion and had applied it to Jamie in return. Raising her hand, Jamie waved a quick good-bye, and watched until Val's taillights disappeared.

Chapter Three

Reflections

EARLY IN MAY, THE school calendar gave the students two days off for faculty in-service meetings. Teachers mumbled and groaned, as they left their classrooms and headed for their compulsory workshops. Administrators from the nursery/elementary level, the middle school, and high school gathered together, class rosters in hand, to project staff needs for the upcoming school year.

Val entered the room and glanced around. Jamie waved and gestured for her to come over. "I saved you a seat, Val."

"Thanks. What's new?" Val placed her papers on the table in front of her. "It would seem there's got to be an easier way to do this than by hand."

"I don't know why they don't create a database for all the students. They could be sorted and grouped that way. Although I've never investigated it, I would think that some enterprising company must have developed a computerized scheduling program by now."

Val laughed out loud. "Computers in this district? We had to be the last school system in the state to get rid of dial phones. We only recently got push-button models with the new intercom system."

"Tell me about it. I'm the only one in my building who can program the phones to answer the proper line."

Val's brow furrowed. "What do you mean?"

"The installer was a nice guy. I ate lunch with him on the days he was working in my building. He was telling me about what a neat system he was installing for us. I remember him shaking his head and saying that it was ridiculous that the district hadn't bought the programming package for the phones."

"So, he told you how to do it?"

"No." Jamie shook her head. "The day the installer finished up the install, I asked him if he had a manual I could have. Even though he had to go out to his van, he was able to find one to give me. I took it home to read it and learned that you don't have to have all lines that come into the building ring on every phone. So, I fooled around with the phones in our office. I fixed it so that if a call comes in to Bill's direct number, the phone rings in his office. My line rings in my office. All of the lines ring on the secretary's phone and blink on ours. She can pick up on any of the lines and announce the name of who is calling by using the intercom. It's how they're supposed to work."

"Really? That's amazing. How hard is it to do?"

Jamie grinned. "Like anything else, it's simple once you know how."

"Would I have to promise you my first born to get you to fix the phones in our department so they ring, right?"

"Hm. I'd consider it a pleasure. We can do it on our lunch break." Jamie tapped her class lists on the table to line them up, before placing them back in front of her. "It still boggles my mind that they didn't have them programmed for us. It's like buying glasses without lenses or radios without batteries."

Their conversation was interrupted by the arrival of the superintendent. "Ladies. Gentlemen. Let's get started. It's no secret that we're in a dire financial situation this year. We need to be sure each class holds the maximum number of students allowed by law." Several hands shot up. "I don't want to hear it. I know you all feel you have special circumstances. I'm here to tell you there are none that will cause me to hire even one additional teacher. Now, let's begin with the high school. How many students will you be graduating?"

The high school principal gave his number.

"Marie and Val, how many students do you anticipate you'll send over to the middle school?"

And thus it went until, in the end, they had an idea about student population for each building, including new student enrollees. The superintendent took the floor again. "Okay, now that you have an idea of which students and how many you'll have, please prepare tentative rosters and have them in to my office within the next week."

The superintendent cleared his throat. "Now, there's one more thing. Rumors will spread faster than ice cream melts on a hundred-degree day. Your staff will be asking questions of you before the end of school today. The high school coach, Barry Hyde, has been suspended, pending an investigation into a concern raised by one of the teachers. She saw him embrace a high school boy and has questioned the nature of their relationship. The student is especially vulnerable, as he recently lost his family and is in foster care. Coach claims it was an innocent demonstration of affection. I suspect that is what they *all* say. Child Protective Services is involved, and I guarantee that we will get to the bottom of this as soon as possible. You can assure the other teachers that any inappropriate behavior like that will not be tolerated in our district."

The superintendent pointed to the high school principal. "Jack?"

"What is the official position that we tell the staff?"

"Simply say that the situation is being reviewed and there will be a press release when there is more information available. You can add that anyone who has any information about the situation should come see me personally." The superintendent glanced around the stunned administrative staff and hurried out the door.

Jamie swallowed the lump in her throat and glanced at Val.

Val raised an eyebrow and leaned over to whisper a comment. "I know Barry and his wife personally. I can't believe he had anything other than honorable intentions toward that boy. I hope that this matter is settled, and he's reinstated with an apology as soon as possible."

"Me too. It makes everyone uncomfortable." Jamie sighed. "Come on. Let's go see if we can set up your phones."

AJ Adaire

Chapter Four

Reflections

JAMIE SIPPED HER TEA and considered her options for the day. *Maybe I'll hang out around the pool for a while. Before fun, though, there are some chores to do.* She set about the task of doing the laundry. Before going to the pool, she unlocked the deadbolt on the front door and rang the upstairs bell.

Robbie stuck his head over the banister and yelled an upbeat greeting to his landlady. "Hey, do you come in peace?"

"Always."

He looked down at Jamie standing in their shared downstairs entryway. "I'm in a hurry to get to the bank before it closes. I'll be back in a bit. Can we visit then?"

"Sure," replied Jamie. "I'm spending the day at the pool. Maybe you'd like to join me when you get back?"

Robbie thumped down the stairs with his knapsack over his shoulder. "Sounds good. I'll catch up with you later at the pool." He draped a long arm over her shoulder and gave Jamie a quick hug and a kiss on the cheek before he left the house.

Jamie closed the outer door and re-entered her apartment. She played with the cats until they lost interest and flopped on the floor to stare at her. *Wonder what's keeping Robbie.* Her toe tapped, as she glanced around her apartment. The minute she was idle, her mind drifted and, of course, settled on Val. Recalling the enjoyable day they'd spent together the prior weekend, she picked up the phone and punched in the numbers from memory. Val answered on the third ring, causing Jamie to smile at the sound of her voice.

Val's voice sounded like warm syrup. "I tried to call you on Wednesday, so I could tell you how much fun I had with you at the pool and at dinner."

One of Jamie's cats jumped up and settled on her lap. "Really? I had fun too. This week has been a busy one. I played racquetball with a friend one night, worked late another. I thought of calling or stopping in to see you several times. Something always popped up to delay me, and then I worried it was too late to call."

"What are you doing today?" Val's voice sounded hopeful. "Maybe we could get together and do something?"

"Well," replied Jamie dragging out the L sound at the end of the word. "If it's Saturday and the sun is shining, then it must be pool time. You up for a dip in the pool?"

"Think it'll be warm enough?"

"Should be. I'm running the heater and the sun is warm, so I think you'll be comfortable. We were okay last week."

"I'd love to, although I have one condition. Next weekend is Memorial Day weekend, and I'm opening my house at the lake. I'd like it very much if you'd join me for the weekend. Can you?"

"That sounds like fun. I'll double-check the calendar while you're on your way over. I don't think I have anything on for next weekend."

"Great. I'll see you in a few. Need anything?"

"No, Val, just your company. Robbie said he'd stop down later, and I plan to invite him too."

"Oh good. I haven't seen him in a while, so I'll have a chance to find out what he's been up to. I'll see you shortly."

Jamie put on her bathing suit and went outside to settle on one of the pool deck chairs to wait for her friends.

Robbie popped around the corner, sat in the chair next to Jamie, and lit a cigarette. "And how are you, Miss Thing?" Jamie loved Robbie's youthful good looks, deep dimples, and short, copper-colored hair. The sprinkling of freckles across his nose made him look too young to smoke.

"Those things will cause you an early death." Jamie waved a hand at the cloud of smoke.

Robbie responded with a warm, throaty laugh and nodded his agreement. "You may be quite correct. I'm still waiting for you to answer my question though."

"I'm good.

He exhaled in Jamie's direction. Reconsidering, Robbie waved the smoke away when he saw the look of displeasure on his friend's face. "Have you heard from Bly?"

"Off and on. We keep in touch." Jamie sighed. "I'm lonely without her around. It's hard sometimes. Fortunately, the longer she's gone, the easier it's becoming. I suppose, since everything was so new to me, I allowed it to become all consuming." She rubbed the back of her neck, as she considered that idea. "Bly moving to California helped us truly become friends again. In many ways, after we stopped being lovers, we actually remained a couple who weren't having sex. I'm comfortable with and feel good about where we are now."

"So what's next? Think you might ever consider dating anyone again?" Robbie moved his chair so he could more easily make eye contact with Jamie.

Jamie's brow furrowed. "What do you mean?"

"You know what I mean. It's been what, six or seven months since Bly left? Bly is history, so it's time to move along." Robbie took another drag on his cigarette. "You haven't shown the faintest interest in anyone since you and Bly ended your romantic relationship. How are you going to meet someone to date if you don't make yourself socially available?"

"Robbie..." Jamie's tone said it all. "I don't care what you say, I'm not rushing into anything."

Robbie turned his head away and arched his eyebrow. They fell silent for a bit. "Want to come to a party with me?" Robbie often asked Jamie to join him when he went to a party or to the local gay bar. "Come on, come with me. Maybe you'll meet someone. Be serious. In your wildest imagination, what are the chances someone from our school will be there?"

Jamie exhaled a tight breath.

"Come on, girlfriend." Robbie slipped into a more flamboyant style. "Some friends of mine are having a small party. Afterwards, we'll probably end up at the bar. Come with me." His eyes sparkled, as he poked her in the arm. "Pretty please?"

Jamie shook her head and stifled a laugh. "Stop. In the first place, I'm not looking to meet anybody yet, and in the second place, you know how I feel about coming out with you. I just can't deal with living my life as openly as you do."

"Open...who me? That's not the way I see it. Although I do go to bars or to a party now and then, most people have no idea I'm gay. You have to remember that anybody there has the same 'secret' I do." Robbie emphasized the word secret by making quotation marks in the air with his fingers. "I don't understand what you're so damned worried about."

"I know you don't understand it, Robbie. You have to remember that, as a teacher, you have something that I don't have as a school administrator...tenure. Besides, you've always known you're gay and have been comfortable with it since you were a teenager. I'm just figuring it out now in my thirties." Jamie sought understanding in Robbie's eyes. "I have to live my life in a way that makes me feel comfortable. I do appreciate the offer to join you. I'm sorry, I just can't. Meeting a friend or two that you might introduce me to, or meeting some of Bly's friends, is different. They are, for want of a better term, prescreened. Going to a bar or a party where I have no idea who might show up is something I'm just not comfortable doing." Jamie heard a car door slam and said, "I think Val just arrived." She knew that Robbie would interpret her statement as 'watch what you say.'

Val hurried in. As usual, she was laden with several bags containing her towel, lotion, drinks, and snacks. She never came empty handed. "Hello there, sun worshipers," she called, as she climbed the stairs to the deck. She set her things down, stuck a toe in the water, and grinned her approval. Val directed a special smile at Jamie and waved in Robbie's direction.

"Did you see the newspaper this morning? Coach Hyde was cleared of all charges against him. The articles said that the accusations were completely unfounded. You know that the student involved is an orphan. It seems that Coach and his wife had applied to adopt him. The day the teacher saw them hugging was the day Coach told him their application was accepted and they had a court date. Apparently, documentation was easy to obtain that proved what the boy and Coach had claimed."

Nearly in unison, Jamie and Robbie expressed positive reactions. Jamie looked at her companions. "I'm so relieved for the coach and his family."

"The administration rushed to a judgment. The superintendent is a bigot and looking to make an example of somebody. He's on a witch hunt." Robbie made no effort to hide his disgust. "I know someone in the high school who overheard him refer to another teacher as a 'light-in-the-loafers' fairy.'"

"Oh my." Val's hand covered her mouth. "That's terrible. I know the superintendent was obligated to investigate the claim and report it to child services. Still, I'm not sure it had to be handled the way it was, so publicly. Until proven, it should have remained private."

Robbie nodded. "Maybe whoever turned him in started spreading the rumors. That was unfair to everyone involved."

The conversation drifted to other topics until Robbie stood and announced he was getting in the water. He jumped in the deep end, while Val and Jamie eased their way in on the stairs. After some initial good-natured splashing, they settled on separate rafts. Robbie slipped on his sunglasses and, within minutes, he seemed to drift off to sleep on his raft. The two women paddled toward the opposite end of the pool, so they could talk quietly without disturbing their sleeping friend. They turned their mats to face each other, and each held the other's float to keep them from drifting apart.

An hour or so later, Robbie slid off his mat into the water and climbed out of the pool. "I've gotta boogie." He dried off with his towel, waved to Val, and winked at Jamie. "Catch you later, ladies."

As the women waved back, their floats separated. They quickly reached for each other's hand to pull the rafts back together. The mats moved toward each other, and Val and Jamie regained their hold on them. As they did so, their arms brushed, and Jamie felt her face redden. *Get a grip, girl. This is one situation that you don't want to let get out of control. Val is a straight woman who would be shocked to know of your 'other life.'*

"Are you okay? You look like you might be getting sunburned already."

"No, I should be okay." Jamie checked by pressing down on the skin on her arm. "I put sunscreen on, although, the sun is pretty warm today."

Settled back on their rafts, both sighed and let the sun lull them back into total relaxation. The breeze blew a few strands of Val's hair across her face, and she brushed them aside. "I don't know which I enjoy more, your pool or my house at the lake."

"I expect each has its own charm," Jamie responded, lids still closed.

"Are you okay? You seem very quiet today. Has something upset you?"

Jamie glanced over at Val before closing her eyes again. "No, not really. I guess the stress from school is getting to me. I feel like I'm worn out. Besides, I talked to my friend Bly from California this morning, too. After we hang up, I always feel a little sad. I do miss her."

"You're such a good friend to have. You're good to all of us. I don't think I've ever heard one bad word about you, Jamie."

Opening her eyes, Jamie glanced over at Val. "It's because you don't know the real me that you feel that way."

"So tell me what's to know that I don't know already? I can't think of one thing I'd change about you if it were up to me." Val began to push and pull gently on Jamie's raft, creating a rocking sensation.

"If it were up to me to change one thing about myself, I think I'd like to be stronger...emotionally stronger. I'd like to have more strength of my convictions and to be more capable of standing up for what I feel and what I believe in. Maybe, in a way, to be able to be more honest with people."

"How can you say that? I don't know anyone who lives their life more fairly or honestly than you do."

Jamie fought to control her expression, squashing the cringe that threatened to emerge. The two friends floated around the pool for the rest of the afternoon. As the temperature cooled, they closed up the pool, showered, and changed into comfortable clothes.

"Let's stay in for dinner." Val picked up her pocketbook. "I'll go get a pizza."

Jamie phoned in the order, and Val left to get the pie. Val's car was barely out of view down the drive, when there was a knock at the door. Jamie pulled open the door, surprised to find Robbie standing in the hallway.

"Hi. I'm on my way out. I thought I'd just double-check with you and see if you'd changed your mind about coming with us tonight. It should be an interesting group of people. I'm pretty sure there won't be anyone there you need to worry about. Come on, you'll have fun."

Jamie stepped aside to offer Robbie entrance. "No. Thanks anyway, Robbie. I think I'm just going to stay home and relax. Val is coming back soon with a pizza we ordered, and we'll just hang out here."

With a shake of his head, Robbie grabbed the handle of the door preparing for a fast escape. Robbie wiggled his eyebrows up and down and gave Jamie a sly smile. "Oh, just the two of you alone, huh?"

"Oh, come off it. She's a co-worker, terminally straight, and would have apoplexy if I so much as sat on the same sofa with her."

"No, Jamie, I think you're wrong about that. I was watching the two of you together while you thought I was asleep this afternoon. There's a chemistry developing between you that permeates the air like electricity before a storm. I think the woman has feelings for you."

"Well, I think you're certifiable. Anyway, I'm not ready for chemistry, it's too hard."

"I know you're thinking about your relationship with Bly, although you said you've moved past that."

"I am. We should have remained friends instead of allowing the attraction to get the best of us. I don't want the same thing to happen with Val."

"Hiding away like you've been doing is only prolonging the agony. Someday, you'll have to face the fact that you're a lesbian and figure out how you plan to deal with it." Robbie adjusted the backpack to his other shoulder. "Don't get me wrong. I'm the first to admit that being gay or lesbian isn't easy. There's no doubt that my life would have been easier if I was straight with two point five kids, a wife, a mortgage, and last, although certainly not least, a happy mother."

Jamie chuckled. Robbie had come out to his mother in high school. Now, over ten years later, his mother still hoped Robbie's attraction to men was a phase.

"At some point, you'll have to deal with your feelings. Dating women or getting married is simply not for me and, from what you say, dating men is not for you either."

"I know you're right. Still, I can't see myself involved in the bar and party scene. So many relationships initiated there seem transient and shallow. They develop in an instant and then just as quickly end; and people move on to the next before the sheets in the bed are cold." Not wanting to be insulting, Jamie thought seriously about whether she should verbalize her next thought. "Put a local group of lesbians in a room together, and half of them have slept with each other. Although it terrifies me, and I don't know how to achieve it, I know I want more than a series of relationships that fizzle out before the change of address labels are ordered. It seems that here, when there's a breakup, each partner is replaced by the next woman who happens to be single at the same time. It's like a lesbian version of musical chairs or maybe musical beds. I don't want my life to be an endless series of short-term relationships like that."

"Neither do I, nor do most of the others. Maybe that's why they all keep trying. Anyway, don't believe everything you read. There are many long-term gay and lesbian relationships out there. Too bad they're not the ones you notice nor, for the most part, the ones you see at the bars." Robbie wrapped an arm over Jamie's shoulder and gave a squeeze. "I've gotta run. I'll catch up with you sometime this week. By the way, I envy you the rest of your evening with foxy Val, who looks great with her new tan. You can take it to the bank when I tell you that she's attracted to you."

"Stop stirring the pot and get out of here." Jamie chuckled, as she hugged and kissed Robbie good-bye. "Have a great time, and by the way, you look smashing," Jamie tossed a final wave in his direction and closed the door.

A short time later, Val juggled the pizza through the front door. "Here, take this bag, I have a surprise for you in there. I hope you like beer with your pizza."

"Oooh, after a day in the sun, it should put me right under the table." The two moved into the TV room, where Val put the pizza on the coffee table. They sat down on the rug to watch the evening news as they ate. While Val was in the bathroom, Jamie went to the kitchen and returned with two more cans of beer. Jamie sat on the love seat and adjusted the TV, fully expecting Val to come in and sit on the sofa across the room from her. She blinked away her surprise, as Val plopped down on the love seat next to her.

"I...I uh...picked up a video today." Jamie handed the box to Val. "A friend told me about it. She thought the beginning was one of the funniest scenes she's seen in a while."

Val read the title out loud. *The Gods Must Be Crazy.*

"Have you seen it?"

"No, I'm up for a comedy though."

Jamie grunted as she tried to reach a spot on her back. "I hate it when I peel. It itches so much."

Val leaned forward and clasped her hands together. "Can I peel you, please? It's something I love to do."

Jamie wasn't wearing a bra. She turned around and slipped her shirt over her head, using it to cover her breasts, as she exposed her back. "Be my guest."

Val started to peel sheets of skin from Jamie's back, placing them into a tissue she produced from her pocket.

"I don't know how you can do that." Jamie cringed. "The sound alone gives me the willies. I have to admit, though, that it feels very good." *And just a little intimate.* "If I didn't think I'd injure myself, I'd take a bottle brush to my itchy back. I've been unable to pass a door frame for most of the past week."

Val peeled all the loose skin and then started to scratch Jamie's back.

"Umm," Jamie purred. "That feels so good. I'll give you a lifetime to stop." She had to fight to keep herself from covering her mouth with her hand.

Val ended up applying some after-sun lotion to a grateful Jamie.

Her touch was slower and more sensual than it was the first time she'd applied it. She prolonged the task, as she massaged the slippery lotion into Jamie's skin.

Jamie felt herself warm to Val's touch. After only a couple of minutes of the sweet torture, she popped up and pulled her shirt down, ignoring the surprise on Val's face. "Thank you. Maybe we should get this movie going before it gets too late to see the whole thing."

They spent the rest of the evening watching and laughing at the movie. Jamie grabbed the pizza box, and Val collected the cutlery and the plates. They carried everything to the kitchen, where they washed up the few dishes they'd dirtied. Val wiped the last dish.

"I think I'd better get going. I enjoyed the movie a lot. I can't remember the last time I laughed so hard. Thanks for picking it up for us."

"I had a fun time, too."

The women walked to the door, where they exchanged a brief hug. Val was the one to initiate the quick embrace, and Jamie noted that this time, she seemed more relaxed about their affectionate exchange. Jamie checked the cats' water and locked up before sliding into bed. Barely settled, the phone rang and she plucked the receiver from the cradle on the night table.

"Hi, it's me again. Val. What are you doing?"

"Not much. I just got into bed." Jamie pulled the blankets around her, as the cats snuggled in place between her knees. What's up?" She adjusted the pillow behind her and leaned back against the headboard.

"I wanted to tell you again how much I enjoyed myself today. I can't believe I drank that much beer. I should sleep the sleep of the innocent tonight."

"Perhaps, more like the sleep of the guilty." They both chuckled.

"Anyway, we forgot to talk about the weekend at my cabin. Did you check if you're able to come up to the lake?"

"Oh sorry, it slipped my mind to tell you. Yes, I'm looking forward to it."

A half hour passed before the two women said their final good-night and hung up the phone. Jamie snuggled lower into the covers. *We never seem to run out of things to say to each other.* Jamie let her thoughts drift back over the day. It was some time before Jamie finally drifted off to sleep, a smile curling her lips as she remembered.

Chapter Five

Reflections

AT WORK ON MONDAY morning, Jamie got a call from Val. "Have you gotten any notice about a meeting? I've heard rumors circulating among the staff that the new organizational chart will be announced at a Thursday meeting."

"No, however, I haven't read the internal mail yet." Holding the phone to her ear with her shoulder, Jamie reached for her *In* basket and rummaged through the stack, looking for a memo. "Nope, nothing here. Once again, the rumors seem to be false."

"I'm about to scream. I wish this would end. I can't stand it. We've been dangling for five months now. I try not to worry about how I'll support myself if I lose my job…"

Hearing those words caused Jamie's stomach to roll. "I know, I feel the same way. I only hope that if they cut all of us, they'll put us back in the classroom in September. Maybe there'll be vacancies we can slip into. I don't want anyone else to lose his or her position so I can have a job. The one thing I'm sure of is that I'll be glad when all this speculation is over and I can sleep again. I think even my bags have bags." Jamie loved it that Val laughed at her joke.

"Mmm, I know what you mean. Ugh! I've made up my mind that I'm not going to think about it anymore. I'm glad we have plans for the weekend and something to look forward to."

"I know. Every morning, when I wake up, I promise myself that I'm going to push it out of my mind. It pains me to admit that my resolve usually has disappeared by the time I get into the shower." Jamie could feel Val smiling on the other end of the line. "I agree with you, that it'll be good for us both to get away and forget all about this place for the weekend."

Val heaved a heavy sigh. "I'm having a very difficult time being here today."

"I know, I'm worse than the kids. Funny, they think they're the only ones who want to cut school or play hooky."

"I feel exactly like Mr. Jones."

Jamie searched her mind to recall the name. "Who's that?"

A warm chuckle set up the joke for Val. "You haven't heard of Mr. Jones?"

"I can't say I have."

"So, Mrs. Jones woke her son by saying, 'Get up John. You have to go to school.' He rolled over and refused. 'No, I don't want to go to school today.' Mrs. Jones said, even more forcefully, 'Come on. Get up. You have to go.' John pulled up the blankets over his head and whined, 'No. I don't wanna go.' Mrs. Jones ripped the covers from her son. "John Jones. Get out of that bed this instant. You have to go to school. You're forty-five years old and you're the principal." Val chuckled.

"Ha! So you and Mr. Jones have a thing going on, huh?"

Their shared laughter left them both feeling better.

"Hey, Jamie. Do you have any comp time accrued?"

"Yeah, I do. Why?

"What if we request comp time off for Friday afternoon after lunch? If we get an early start for the cabin by lunchtime, instead of at the end of the day, maybe we can beat some of the Memorial Day traffic."

"That's a great idea, Val. I'll go talk to the boss right now."

"Me too. Check with you later."

On Friday, benefitting from an early departure, everything went smoothly on the drive up to the mountains. The two women arrived at the lake around two on Friday afternoon. They dropped their bags in the bedroom before doing the chores associated with being in the cabin for the first time for the season. Despite Val's protests, Jamie insisted on helping clean the cabin, carrying in, and storing the supplies from Val's car. She took directions about what she could do to be most helpful. The women worked well together, accomplishing all of the tasks required in less than two hours.

"This is great, we're done. You were a huge help, Jamie. I think we still have time to walk to the restaurant. It should be a nice stroll."

They walked down the slope, through the trees, to the path that led around the lake. They took a break to sit and enjoy the warm afternoon sun when they came upon two flat rocks near the water's edge.

Val pointed at the brightly colored bird. "Look, there's the first bluebird I've seen this season, over there, on the bush."

"Wow! Wish I'd brought my camera with me. I won't forget next time."

They walked the-half mile to Belle's Lakeside Tavern to get dinner. Jamie raised an eyebrow at the seedy exterior appearance of the restaurant and cast a questioning glance toward Val.

"Trust me, I know what I'm doing." Val smiled at Jamie's concern. "Get the spaghetti. It costs just seven dollars and it's all you can eat. Price aside, the food is really good."

They walked through the half-empty bar and settled at a table in the back dining room where the two ordered the spaghetti. "We're lucky it's early. We won't be able to get in here tomorrow without a reservation."

"Do you ever use the cabin in the winter?" Jamie plucked a roll from the basket and buttered it.

"Not any more. Dad used it for hunting. Why?"

"I wondered if you ski."

A frown line appeared between Val's brows. "Snow ski? Jamie nodded.

"No, I've never tried it. Do you?"

"I can ski, although, you'd have held little hope for me the first time I tried it." Jamie chuckled. "Josh, my ex-husband, was an avid skier. On our first Christmas together, he bought me everything I'd need for skiing. First, the pants had a bib and suspenders and were fully insulated. On top of that, there was a down jacket and mittens, all designed for below-zero conditions. Oh yeah, don't forget the silk underwear. We had a small mountain a short drive from us. In truth, it was more like a hill that he thought would be a perfect place to give me my first lesson."

"Bowden's Mountain. I know where that is."

"Well, there's an 'advanced slope.'" Jamie used her fingers to put quotation marks around 'advanced slope.' It's very short, but quite steep. The temperature was about thirty-eight degrees, as we parked the car and sat below it, watching the skiers. I was dressed from head to toe in all my below-zero gear...the insulated down jacket, the bibbed pants, and don't forget the full set of thermal underwear."

"Mittens too?" Val grinned.

"Down-filled, of course."

"Were you melting?"

"That's the understatement of the night. I was so hot by the time I got out of the car, I think I made squishy noises when I moved." Jamie set down her fork, as she got into the story. "I watched the advanced skiers swish their way down the steep hill. It looked so easy."

"He didn't start you on the advanced slope did he?"

"No. He taught me how to cast the skis at an angle so I could climb, and he made me climb the beginner's slope. There was a rope lift there. I don't know why he thought I was ready to careen off the side of a hill, yet at the same time thought I wasn't ready to use the lift. Anyway, I herringboned up the hill to the top of the beginner's slope. The slope was gentle from the top to the bottom, at a straight angle. Instead of showing me how to snowplow, he stood me at the top of the hill and demonstrated a simple turn. He said, 'the way to turn is to lean and weight.'"

By now, Val had also put her fork down and had her chin resting on her hands, eyes twinkling.

"It looked so easy." Jamie rubbed her hands together. "I was ready. He said 'lean and *weight*.' I heard lean and *wait*," Jamie spelled the two critical words.

"Oh no. What happened?"

Jamie shook her head. "It wasn't pretty. I pushed off, and I leaned and w a i t e d." Jamie raised her arm and pointed to her watch. "I took off on one ski and careened down the hill. Eventually, I veered off toward the cow pasture on the right side of the slope. I tore straight down the hill, headed toward the bottom, totally out of control. I finally got the second ski on the ground and headed downhill at an even faster velocity. I must have looked like a cartoon character in one of those animated movies. That's about when I hit the snow fence."

"Oh my God! Were you hurt?"

"You mean hurt as in having done damage to anything other than my ego?" Jamie chuckled. "No, there was no permanent damage done, thanks to all my padded clothing. Unfortunately, I was wedged under the fence. My boobs stopped me from passing completely beneath it. My skis rested in the drainage ditch on the downhill side of the fence and my upper torso was wedged on the uphill side. I couldn't get out with my skis on, and couldn't slide down any further because my boobs wouldn't fit beneath the fence. How my skis managed to pass beneath there, I never did figure out."

Val threw her head back and burst out laughing.

"Shh." Jamie put her hand over her mouth to stifle her own

laughter.

"How did you get out?"

"I had to wait for Josh to ski around the fence. That meant he needed to ski back to the advanced slope and come back toward the beginner's slope to me. I lay there wedged in until he came around and got my skis off. By the time I squidgied my butt out from under the fence and stood up, I was soaked from the inside to the outside and more than past pissed when he laughed at me. I must have looked like a drowned rat."

Val dabbed at the tears running from the corner of her eyes. "I'd have divorced him on the spot."

"I had a three cylinder hissy fit and stormed back to the car. For our anniversary, I went to Camelback for their ski camp. I spent a week alone there learning how to ski and learning how to love skiing."

"Did you ever forgive Josh?"

Jamie looked toward the candle on the table. "I'm not sure I ever did." She grinned, and they shared a moment of laughter together.

For dessert, they shared a piece of homemade, blueberry cobbler.

"Oh, my God, I'm stuffed," groaned Jamie. "And now you expect me to walk home?"

Laughing, Val stood up and gestured for Jamie to follow. "Come on, wimp! I'll take you the long way around the lake so we can work off some of those calories. It'll be good for you. There's a lovely place to sit not far from the cabin, and we can wait for the sunset."

The two circled the perimeter of the lake and found a large rock to sit on at the edge of the water. At first, they sat silently, side by side. Jamie absorbed the beauty of the lake and surrounding scenery. The surface of the water was smooth as glass, and the sun, just beginning to dip behind the mountains, cast long shadows across the surface of the water in the shape of the surrounding pine trees. With every breath she inhaled of the fresh pine scent, Jamie could feel some of her stress drain away. There was little activity around the lake, because not many people had arrived for the weekend, yet. Jamie assumed that the waterfront would become more crowded the next day, as people began opening their cabins for another season.

While they sat, they talked about the problems at work and what they would do if they lost their jobs. The longer they talked, the more outrageous they became with their potential future professions. "Jamie, you'd never starve, because you could become a contractor. You love to build things and work with wood."

"Ha! That's probably an option." Jamie laughed. "What about you? Oh, I know. I think you should go into the convent and become a Mother Superior. You could whip those nuns into shape with your excellent leadership qualities and angelic disposition."

Val held up her index finger and wiggled it back and forth. "No, no, no…that's not a possibility. I look terrible in black."

"Oh, stop. You made me snort."

Val put her hands on her thighs and tapped them up and down. "Ready to head back to the cabin? The sun will be setting soon."

Jamie nodded and stood. "Thank you, I feel better already, even after only a couple of hours here."

"Me too. It's so restful, and your company only adds to the enjoyment."

As they walked, Val drew Jamie's attention to various points of interest, while she shared stories about the people who lived on the lake.

Back at the cabin, each got a book and went out to sit on the Adirondack chairs on the deck, which overlooked the mountains and forest on one side and the lake on the other. They watched the sun dip below the mountains and read until the last light from the sunset dimmed enough to make reading impossible. In the fading light, they watched the ducks paddle serenely across the lake. The quiet was barely broken when a fish jumped, concentric circles growing on the surface of the water where it landed. A soft, pine-scented breeze drifted across the lake, barely rustling the branches. The peepers started to chirp, and Jamie felt herself relax as she absorbed the tranquil beauty, scents, and sounds around her. The large, orange moon loomed above the trees, as the sun disappeared below the horizon.

"Look at that." Jamie pointed at the night sky. "It's magnificent here. Thank you for inviting me to join you. I'm really enjoying myself."

"Good." Val put her book on the table. "I'm lucky. It is surely a beautiful location. Before this area started to be developed, my dad bought the land and built this place as a hunting cabin. After he died, I put some money into the cabin and fixed it up. I added insulation and wallboard, winterized it, and added a few modern conveniences in the kitchen." Val's eyes softened and a smile danced on her lips, as she scanned the breathtaking scene below them. "My dream is to retire up here one day. Between here on the weekends, and your pool during the week, you and I could have the best of both worlds. I hope you'll come here often with me this summer."

Jamie nodded her agreement. "That's a deal."

Val rubbed her palms together. "I'm freezing, and the mosquitoes are biting. Do you mind if we go back inside?"

"Sure, no problem." Jamie picked up Val's book and tucked it and her own under her arm. "I'm sorry, I was enjoying myself so much, I didn't realize how cool it became. Now that you mention it, it is chilly out here. Must be my climate control."

"Climate control? What's that?"

"Well, when everyone else is hot, I'm usually comfortable and when everyone else is cold, my body seems to pump out heat." Jamie smiled, "Climate control."

"Oh, I get it. Unfortunately, I don't have it, so let's go back indoors and get me warm."

They raced back to the cabin, laughing and jostling each other like children. Once inside the cabin, Jamie built a small fire in the Franklin stove, just big enough to take the dampness and chill out of the air. She left the stove's door open, so they could watch the flames lick up between the logs. Jamie joined Val on the sofa opposite the stove where they sat watching the fire. Val got a blanket from the back of the chair and threw it across her legs. "The fire is mesmerizing, isn't it?"

"Um hmm. You know, I'm surprised how much cooler it is here than at home. I guess I didn't realize how much higher this place is. The altitude really makes a difference in temperature."

Jamie's eyes traveled around the room, noting details of the objects Val displayed to decorate her home. The eat-in kitchen occupied the right, back corner of the cabin where the back door exited to a large screened-in porch. The living room overlooked the lake. The open design of the living area allowed a view of the lake through the large, kitchen windows in the back, through the porch, as well as through the picture windows on the right side of the house. The one bedroom sat to the right of the front door and faced the street. The bath was down a short hallway that also contained a large closet holding the washer and dryer, a linen closet, and storage closets for outerwear.

Thanks to the open floor plan and the cathedral ceiling over the living room, the compact cabin had a roomy appearance. The area above the bedroom, now closed in, appeared as if it might have been a loft at one time. To either side of the chimney and the stove were shelves filled with books and games. White, slatted shutters covered the windows. Collected treasures occupied the shelves, and a pewter oil lamp with a milk glass shade sat on the wider countertop of the lower cabinets. The white shutter-slatted doors of the cabinets below matched the white shutters covering the windows. The white wall unit provided a pleasant contrast to the nearly navy walls.

The charming room exuded a feeling of comfort and warmth. The women sat watching the fire and making small talk for about a half hour and then decided it was time to go to bed. Jamie closed the doors on the stove and banked the fire with ash to keep a slow burn in the stove overnight. The fire made it cozy in the cabin, despite the cooling temperature outside.

The large bedroom contained one double plus a single bed. "Jamie, you take the double." Val paused at the door. "If you don't mind, I'll leave the bedroom door open so we can benefit from the heat of the fire."

They each changed into nightclothes and got into bed. Jamie watched in the firelight as, within moments of snuggling in, Val got up to retrieve another blanket from the living room. She added it to the pile on her bed, wriggled back under the covers, and pulled them around her chin. "Brr. I don't know what's wrong with me, I can't seem to get warm."

"I don't know either. I'm nice and toasty over here. If you can't get warm, you can jump in here with me. I guarantee that you'll be warm in no time. Don't forget that I'm climate controlled." Jamie noted Val's hesitation, as she seemed to struggle with her decision. "Really, I don't mind," encouraged Jamie.

Hesitantly, Val came over and got into bed with Jamie. "Umm, you're right, it's lots warmer in here with you. You've got the bed warm already. I'll just stay long enough to get warmed up and then will go back to my bed. I've never been able to sleep with anyone. I guess it's because I'm an only child and didn't have the experience of sleeping with any siblings. I always slept alone."

"Suit yourself. You won't bother me at all if you stay, honest."

Val pulled the covers up under her chin and laid stiffly at the edge of the bed, doing an excellent imitation of a board.

In the semidarkness, Jamie struggled to hold back a smile. *If I yell 'Boo!' I guarantee she'd bolt for the door. I'd bet my full week's paycheck that she'll last ten minutes here in bed with me.* She closed her eyes and enjoyed the comfort of being close to Val.

The sunbeam came across the room and crept slowly closer to the bed where the two women slept. Jamie awoke first and smiled as she became aware of Val breathing rhythmically next to her in bed. *Ha! And this one said she couldn't sleep with anyone.* Jamie studied Val's peaceful features as she slept. Her mouth was relaxed and looked sexier than ever. *Get a grip*, she admonished herself. She held her position, barely breathing, before she sighed and turned away. *You'd better stop thinking those thoughts and remember exactly who this is you're dealing with.*

Val opened her eyes as though she sensed Jamie's appraisal.

"Good morning."

"Oh, don't look at me." Val shielded her face with her hand. "I look terrible in the morning,"

Rising up on one elbow, Jamie laughed as she teased Val with a smirk and a raised eyebrow. "No, not terrible, I think you look adorable. How'd you sleep, Miss I Can't Sleep With Anyone?"

Val paused, as if considering her response. "Like a baby. The last thing I remember was thinking I would get up soon. I just got so warm and cozy. I recall considering that I didn't want to get up and go get in that cold bed over there," Val gestured toward the single bed on the opposite side of the room, "and I guess I fell asleep. Your climate control kept me cozy and toasty all night."

"Glad I could be of service." Jamie threw back the covers and padded barefoot out to the wood stove. Opening the doors, she was pleased to see some embers still inside the chamber. With a few small pieces of kindling and some torn newspaper, accompanied by a bit of puffing and blowing, it wasn't long before a small fire sufficient to take away the morning chill crackled in the stove. She visited the bathroom before returning to the bedroom to pull on the pants to her sweat suit. "I'm going to make breakfast while you get dressed," she said, before heading into the kitchen. She fussed with the fire and started gathering ingredients.

By the time Val emerged, Jamie had breakfast well under way. "Umm, what are you making that smells so good?"

"It's called camper's breakfast. It has sausage, peppers, onions, potatoes, and tomatoes all sautéed together. When they are all nice and caramelized, the eggs get scrambled in. It smells great, looks terrible, and tastes absolutely amazing."

After tasting her first forkful of the savory meal, Val wiped her chin. "This is really good. I could get used to you being here."

Was that a blush I saw on Val's face?

"You build a great fire and make a wonderful breakfast. What other hidden talents do you have?"

Enjoying their playful banter, Jamie winked. "All that is hidden will one day be revealed, but you have to look." Jamie chuckled. "I think I heard that in a Charlie Chan movie."

"Okay, inscrutable one...you more likely saw it in the Bible. Regardless of the source, I'll keep my eyes open for clues." Val mopped her plate with the last of her toast and returned Jamie's grin. "What? It was really good."

Although close enough to walk to the store, they drove into town to get supplies for dinner and breakfast the next morning, thinking they might have too much to carry on foot. Val wanted to stock up on staples for the rest of the season. By the time they returned, the sun had warmed up the morning air and drew the women to the water. They paddled the length of the lake and back in Val's canoe, enjoying the sunshine. Sitting in the Adirondack chairs, they read, talked, and relaxed the remainder of the day away in easy companionship.

Val cooked a delicious chicken recipe for dinner. That evening, after they cleaned up, they played Scrabble and munched chips in front of a small fire. Jamie changed her clothes and got into bed, while Val changed in the bathroom. She returned around the corner and stopped at the bedroom door. "Do you mind if I sleep with you again? You were so warm last night that I'd like to take advantage of your climate control again tonight."

Jamie simply threw back the covers. Her welcoming smile offered an unspoken invitation.

Once settled, Val seemed more relaxed this time, and they chatted for a short while in the semidarkness before they both drifted off to sleep. It was the last time that Val ever asked permission to join Jamie in bed. Although it seemed a given, neither of them was brave enough to begin a discussion about the unusual sleeping arrangements.

The next morning, they repeated the prior morning's routine and spent the rest of the day in much the same manner as the day before, albeit without the canoe trip.

Monday morning, rain threatened to fall any minute. Val stood on the back porch. "It's so gray out. It leaves out doing anything outside for anyone but the ducks."

"I wouldn't mind reading and relaxing indoors, would you?"

"Not at all. I might even take a short catnap before we have to drive home."

Lunchtime arrived before they knew it. Val went into the kitchen and opened the door to the refrigerator. "Let's pick on whatever is left in the fridge."

"Sounds good. If you'll fix us something, I'll start the packing. Other than cleaning out the woodstove, are there any other chores I can do?

"Can you make sure everything is secure?"

Jamie checked to be sure all the windows were locked and the house was buttoned up tight. She cleaned out the woodstove and filled the wood box. As she washed her hands in the sink, she told Val, "The fire is all set for next time. All you need do is strike a match."

"Thanks, that's a great idea. I'm about finished here." Val added the last item to the cooler she'd filled with perishables she wouldn't be leaving at the cabin. They ate lunch and loaded up the car, hoping to beat some of the traffic.

About ready to leave, they found themselves looking out the back porch door toward the lake. The two Adirondack chairs looked lonely and forlorn sitting on the deck.

They both sighed. "This is my least favorite time here, when I have to leave." Val, her eyes bright, turned toward Jamie and shrugged. "Ready?"

"Not really. There's not much choice though, if we don't want to be stuck in all the traffic."

A little more than two hours later, they pulled into Jamie's driveway. Jamie got her bag out of the back seat and came around to Val's side of the car.

"I had a wonderful time, Val."

"Me too. I loved being with you at the cabin and look forward to the next time."

"Well, I guess I had better get inside. Thanks for the weekend. See ya." Their eyes held until Val put the car in gear and had to turn away. Jamie sighed, her hand waving good-bye. She stood there until after Val's car disappeared around the corner. With slow feet, she carried her bag to the house.

Chapter Six

Reflections

THE MINUTE JAMIE OPENED the door to her apartment, the cats ran to her, meowing their welcome home. "Hi boys." Dropping her bag, she sat down on the floor so that they could each take turns being scratched. Robbie tromped down the stairs to also welcome Jamie back. "How was your trip to the cabin?"

"Really fun. Thanks for taking care of my boys. Did they behave?"

Robbie grinned. "Always. Besides, you know I'm known for my ability to herd kitties."

"I do." Jamie's laughter blended with her friend's. "We had a great weekend. I really appreciate that you cared for the guys so I could go.

"It was a true pleasure. I can't stay and chat, because I have a date."

Jamie gave her friend a thumbs-up sign and a hopeful expression.

Robbie held his hand out and wiggled it back and forth. "Meh. I'm not too optimistic. I've gotta get ready." He tossed her a grin and ran up the stairs two at a time.

Once the cats were content with the amount of affection Jamie provided, they wandered off, tails high in the air. She finished unpacking and organized her clothes for the upcoming week. There were four and a half weeks of work left until the end of June and the start of summer break.

Some of her friends were envious of her two-month vacation. The thing they forgot was that vacation also meant two months without pay. Being the daughter of a depression-era mother, Jamie always budgeted carefully. She saved over the winter months so she could weather the summer months without working. Owning the two-family house and having the income from her upstairs tenant helped pay the mortgage. All that remained was to make sure she saved enough money for her food, car payments, and spending money. To supplement her savings, she sometimes accepted small repair or painting jobs from her friends, or friends of friends. Along with saving for the summer, it was her habit to put some money into her investment fund, demonstrating that she took to heart her mother's advice to always save for a rainy day.

The phone rang, and she plopped down on the sofa to answer it.

Without even a hello, Bly began, "Okay, enough about me, what have you been up to? Heard anything about the job yet? How's the love life? Do ya miss me?"

Jamie laughed. "Well, hello to you, too. Of course I miss you. No news yet about the job. Thought we'd hear about it last week. Sadly, that never happened."

Jamie wondered what exactly she should tell Bly about the weekend with Val. "The upside of not hearing any bad news was that Val and I took Friday afternoon off, headed up to her cabin in the Poconos, and spent a fantastic weekend there." Jamie related a few more of the significant details of her trip to the lake, including the platonic sleeping arrangements.

"Sounds to me like you're smitten by this Val woman."

"Yes, I'm afraid that's true. Although, I think you need to keep your horses firmly in check. For several reasons, there's no potential for anything more than a friendship. You know all of them too well."

"Humph. Your life is clearly more complicated than mine." Bly's throaty chuckle made Jamie miss her company. "Some counselor I am. I don't have any advice for you. From everything you've told me, she seems interested in, even receptive to you. It's obvious that she enjoys spending time with you. Then there are those sleeping arrangements you told me about."

"Yes, remember, it was purely to keep warm," Jamie cautioned.

"Yeah, right. Ever hear of blankets?" Bly cleared her throat. "And as far as her being straight is concerned, don't let that stop you. Don't forget, so were you, once. Straight, I mean."

"I know. I don't know what's wrong with me. I think it's partially all the upheaval at work. I feel so tentative about my future there. Anyway, thanks for listening."

Their conversation concluded after Bly shared the highlights of her life that seemed to mainly center on work and the friends she was making there. When they hung up, Jamie didn't even have time to think about their conversation before the phone rang again. It was Val. "Let's not let the weekend end yet. How about we do something tonight?"

"Sure. Want to go listen to some music? My friend Bly introduced me to the members of this band one night when we went to hear them play. I've followed them ever since and try to catch them when they're in town."

Although the bar was a straight bar, the band members were all lesbians. They drew a mixed crowd, including a large number of gay women in the area.

As Jamie drove down the highway, she leaned on the armrest between the bucket seats. Her arm brushed against Val's, and it amazed her when Val didn't pull away. Jamie cracked the window as her skin warmed with pleasure. They rode the next several miles with their arms touching, and Jamie could feel her pulse in her neck increase from the contact. She took a stronger grip on the steering wheel to help resist the urge to take Val's hand. Risking a quick glance over at Val, she hoped for a clue about what her companion was thinking. Val smiled back. *Could it be possible that Val was enjoying their contact as much as she was? Was Val just becoming more comfortable with her? Maybe she wasn't feeling an attraction after all.*

Jamie glanced over at her passenger. *Does she think about what happens between us as much as I do? I remember once I recognized that I was a lesbian, I almost felt like a stranger in the straight world. Despite that, I wasn't prepared to completely embrace the gay world as my own. For me there were other worries as well. The dissolution of my marriage, followed by my breakup with Bly, left me uneasy and wondering about my ability to sustain a relationship. Even now, I'm afraid to risk my heart, and to love without reservation. Will I be able to give the relationship the energy and depth of emotion a new love deserves?* Her stomach grew queasy, as she worried about her worthiness as a partner. She shook her head to shrug off the heavy feelings. To Val she said, "Hey! We're almost there. The restaurant is just down the end of this street."

Jamie wheeled into a parking spot. Inside the bar, they found a table near the band and ordered drinks from the waitress. Jamie noticed two of the women that she and Bly went to P-town with. They waved to Jamie, as she and Val sat down. After the first set Val excused herself to go to the restroom, and Jamie seized the opportunity to go say hello to Sandy and Liz. She invited them to stop over for a visit. "It seems we've all been too busy to socialize. I promise, I'll call soon so we can make definite arrangements to get together."

Jamie returned to their table. Although Val offered a questioning look, she didn't ask anything. There was no opportunity for discussion, because the music started again. They listened to the band until the end of their second set, when Jamie looked at her watch. "Do you think we should leave so we can function at work tomorrow?"

Val checked the time and nodded her agreement.

As Jamie maneuvered her car into the sparse traffic, Val asked, "Jamie, do you know those two women from coming here to listen to the band?"

"No. I met them through my friend, Bly. They were her friends. I vacationed with Bly and them and some others, for a weekend up in Massachusetts." Jamie maneuvered the car around a slower vehicle and set her cruise control for three miles per hour over the limit.

"Where'd you stay in Massachusetts?"

Jamie hesitated, as she tried to decide whether to be honest or vague. "Um...we stayed in Provincetown. Have you ever been there?"

"Yes, once, a long time ago with my family. It was beautiful. I remember the great shopping, with all the crafts and other interesting items for sale. Dad and Mom wanted to leave soon after we arrived because there were so many gay people there."

Jamie felt her heartbeat increase. "How about you? Did it bother you?"

Val shook her head. "I can't remember thinking about it much. I don't think I've ever known anyone who was gay. What about you?"

Jamie's mind raced. She wasn't sure that she was comfortable with the direction the conversation was taking. Still, she couldn't think of a graceful way to avoid answering the direct question. An abrupt change of topic might raise Val's curiosity, so she mustered her courage. With a voice indicating a calm she didn't feel, Jamie replied. "Yes, I do. My best friend, Bly, is gay." Bly never hid her identity as a lesbian from anyone, so she wasn't telling a secret or breaking a confidence. Still, she felt a little uncomfortable outing Bly. She would have preferred to let Bly tell Val herself.

Val made no comment, so Jamie rushed forward. "When Josh and I got married, we tended to socialize with other married couples. My single friends drifted away because we no longer shared similar interests."

Jamie paused while she clicked off her cruise control and passed the slower moving car in front of her. "After my divorce, I shared with Bly that I realized I had no single friends. Although I still socialize with my married friends, sometimes it can be a little awkward. Bly and her friends took pity on me and invited me to go on vacation with them.

They went to Provincetown to meet some people they know there. In the end, I decided to go along and enjoyed myself very much. It was an interesting, very diverse, and enjoyable group of people."

Jamie reached out, punched the radio on, and tuned in a local station, ending the discussion. The rest of the ride passed with little conversation while they enjoyed the music. Jamie lowered the volume, as she pulled up in front of Val's house. Their parting turned from talk about work the next day to good night. On her way home, Jamie hoped that she hadn't said too much. Val had seemed nonplussed by the revelations.

Jamie settled in bed and exhaled a tired breath. She knew that the last couple weeks of school would be difficult, because the kids were normally on their worst behavior at the end of the year. She replaced the negative thought with a positive one. Her last thought before she drifted off to sleep was about Val and how she looked forward to the rest of the summer and spending some time at the cabin with her. Jamie closed her eyes and fell asleep, warmed by the recollection of sleeping with Val at the cabin.

Chapter Seven

Reflections

TUESDAY MORNING, WHEN THE alarm blared, Jamie wasn't ready to be awake. Despite her unwillingness to get up, she dislodged the cats and threw back the covers. She arrived early, as she usually did, and the day went along smoothly until lunchtime, when the secretary informed her that there would be a meeting at four. Jamie suspected this meeting might reveal the decision that everyone had been waiting for since the fall.

Jamie's boss stuck his head in her office door. "I'm heading over to the meeting, Jamie."

"If it's okay with you, Bill, I think I'll hang in here until you get back."

Bill returned from the meeting less than an hour later. Jamie could tell from the look on his face that the news wasn't good. She followed him into his office and took a seat across the desk from the man she'd worked closely with for many years. His boyish good looks, kind face, warm gray eyes, and gentle manner made him a pleasure to be around. He'd been her supervisor through her entire career, first when she was a teacher and later as his assistant. They shared a mutual respect and a warm working relationship.

"I have bad news, Jamie. They plan to abolish all the vice principal positions effective at the end of the school year. Your position, as well as Val and Jennie's positions, will be abolished effective on June thirtieth. You'll all return to teaching positions based on what openings are available. Because of Regina Porter's retirement, we know there will be an opening in this department. I don't know how you'd feel about coming back to the same department you used to supervise. If you agree, I can arrange to place you in that position, otherwise, I'll find another vacancy for you within the district. It's my hope you'll stay in this department, and I'm sure the rest of the staff shares my opinion. I tried to have your salary frozen at your current level. Unfortunately, you'll have to drop back to teacher's pay."

"Let me think about it Bill. I'll let you know in a few days, if that's okay." Jamie stood and turned to leave. Her limbs felt heavy, and forming a coherent sentence was a struggle. She managed to say, "At least the wait is over, and I won't lose my job," before she stood up. She mustered up a weak smile. "Thanks, boss. I appreciate all you've done. I'd like to think about the position over the weekend and will let you know what I decide on Monday."

In the parking lot, she sat in her car until the tears cleared enough for her to drive home. She called Val the minute her briefcase touched the floor. "I can't deny it's a disappointment to be demoted through no fault of my own. However, even though we'll all suffer a demotion, at least there's no more suspense. It's a definite relief knowing we no longer have to worry about unemployment." She took some comfort from petting her cats who had both managed to find room on her lap.

"Yes, I feel exactly the same."

"The hard part is the cut in pay associated with the demotion. It's lucky the change in salary won't start until fall. I've already saved up for this summer. During next school year, I might try to pick up some extra money by doing some painting or other odd jobs for friends. Or maybe I can pick up some tutoring. The extra money will help me make ends meet next summer."

Although it was a short week, it seemed like it lasted forever. Friday finally arrived, but work was too busy for them to make an early departure. Because they ended up working the full day, they arrived at the lake a couple of hours later than they had the week before. Jamie and Val tossed their bags in the bedroom. With fewer chores than the previous weekend, they wasted no time walking to Belle's for dinner. "I think a cocktail is in order tonight," Jamie said, as she flopped down in her chair.

"I couldn't agree more." During dinner, Val responded to Jamie's questions about the lake area and some of the people who occupied the cabins there.

They split the check and started for the cabin. Jamie patted her tummy. "Once again, a great meal. I know I ate too much. Somehow I couldn't resist that dessert."

Back at the cabin, Jamie volunteered to make drinks and received an enthusiastic reception from Val. They brought their glasses to the back porch and settled in. On their third cocktail, they were past mellow. Val's cheeks were flushed, as she put her empty glass on the table.

"Want another?"

"Oh no, thanks. I think I'd better beheave." Val put her fingertips to her lips. "Did I say beheave? I meant behave, of course."

"I know what you meant." Jamie winked.

"You know, I once read that almost everything that's enjoyable in life is either illegal, immoral, or fattening. We covered fattening with our dinner; we took care of illegal by speeding all the way here. I guess the only thing left is immoral."

"So what would you consider immoral?" Jamie smiled, hoping for a clue about what Val was driving at.

"Almost nothing, I guess, as long as it didn't hurt anyone else." Val kept her tone light and teasing. "So what about immoral, come on, make me an offer I can't refuse." She wiggled her eyebrows.

Jamie turned her face toward the lake, hoping her facial expression didn't reveal her first thought. She didn't know how to respond and was thankful that Val seemed unaware of her red face and tied tongue. She glanced at Val and decided to pass the whole conversation off as a joke. Pushing up to her feet, she picked up their empty glasses. "I think I'm too exhausted to come up with any original, sinful ideas right now. I think I'm going to turn in for the night. Do you want me to help you close up, or are you going to stay here for a while?"

Val looked up and smiled. "No, it's okay, I can close up. I'll be in soon. I think I want to stay here just a little longer."

Jamie got ready for bed, slid between the crisp sheets, and soon fell asleep. She awoke when she heard Val come into the bedroom to get her clothes and then leave. Val finished her shower and returned, as Jamie was again drifting off to sleep. Jamie could sense, more than see, Val hesitate at the doorway as she entered the room and stood between the beds. She held her breath, as Val lifted the covers and slid into bed.

Jamie could feel the warmth from Val's shower and smell the fresh scent from the soap and shampoo she'd used. The temptation was strong to roll over and sink into Val's neck to inhale the sweet, warm aroma. Instead, she held still and tried to continue her regular breathing pattern. She felt her brows furrow, as she considered Val's decision to sleep with her again. The prior weekend, Val justified the sleeping arrangements because she was cold. Temperatures several degrees warmer than last week's, made this a pleasant night for sleeping. In the darkness, Jamie could hear Val breathing and soon drifted off to sleep. She awoke about two hours later when Val got out of bed and left the room.

Jamie lay there listening and heard Val go out onto the back porch. About fifteen minutes later, Val re-entered the room and slipped back into bed. On her right side, Jamie was facing away from Val. She didn't move when Val rolled on her side and moved a bit closer in a spooning position. She felt a tentative hand on her waist.

Jamie's mind raced. *Maybe she's just cold from being on the porch, or maybe Robbie is right about Val being attracted to me.* She tried to quiet her pounding heart and force herself to sleep. She was unsuccessful, and when the room began to lighten, she decided to get up and watch the sun rise over the lake. As she turned over, she noticed that Val was awake too. "What's the matter, can't you sleep either?

"No. I feel like I haven't slept a wink all night. I was so restless last night. I hope I didn't keep you awake. I don't know what's wrong with me."

I think I might know what's wrong, at least I hope I do. Am I wishful thinking to hope that Val is beginning to have feelings for me? Is it possible Val is feeling the same disquiet I felt the first time I recognized my attraction to another woman?

They passed the morning reading and spent the afternoon on the beach. The water was still too cool for them to swim, so they walked along the water's edge, getting wet to their knees, and later rested in the sunshine. They ate their meal on the porch and afterwards walked to town and bought some magazines. Jamie found one with a quiz in it. She bought the magazine and, when they returned to the cabin, she sat down and began reading the quiz. Val sat down next to her and looked over her shoulder.

Val grabbed a pencil and paper from the coffee table. "Let's take the quiz." She numbered the paper and poised with her pencil in hand, waiting. "You can read the questions any time."

They progressed with relative ease, taking turns responding to the questions. Each revealed little details of their lives. Both picked blue as their favorite color and Italian as the most liked food. For dislikes, Val said she hated Brussels sprouts, and Jamie turned her nose up at asparagus and fish.

"Okay, next is your favorite article of clothing." Jamie rested her head against the back of the loveseat and thought back. "I remember that I got a pair of jeans when I was about eight or nine. They were new and stiff. I loved how they smelled. I cried when my mother washed them." Jamie smiled in remembrance. "Even today, I can still smell them. What about you?"

"I got a mauve colored sweater from Italy, in my twenties. I think it was cashmere. I loved it." Val tapped the pencil on the paper. "I wore it until my elbows poked through the sleeves. I couldn't bring myself to part with it and kept it in the drawer long after I'd stopped wearing it."

"Did you finally throw it away?"

"I did. I kept a piece of it in my jewelry box for years after so I could remember it."

The next question asked them to name their favorite memory as a child. "I grew up on a farm. Out beyond the chicken coops was a field of peonies and daffodils. I loved the gorgeous color display...and the smell." Jamie closed her eyes. "I remember lying on my back in the grass and watching the clouds scud across the sky as the heavenly aroma wafted over me." Green eyes popped open and turned toward Val. "What about you?"

"Coming here, of course. I loved the time I spent here with my parents, but especially that spent with my dad." Val looked at the last question. "Uh oh. They saved a sad one for last. Who would do that?"

"What is it?"

"Your saddest memory as an adult."

"That's easy for me, it was my divorce. I felt like such a failure."

"I'm sorry."

"Don't be, it's old news." Jamie waited for Val to tell her memory.

"Come on, let's take a walk by the lake. I'll tell you my saddest memory later."

They strolled near the water's edge. On the way back to the cabin, Val started to tell Jamie about her father's illness and death. They sat on the porch sofa, as Val related her saddest memory. "My father had a stroke. After twelve years of our caring for him at home, my mom wasn't able to manage him alone during the day. We made the painful decision to put him in a care facility. One night, he must have tried to get out of bed to go to the bathroom. He fell and hit his head. Later, we discovered that no one bothered to check on him after midnight. Rules dictated that the nurses were to make rounds to check the patients every hour. No one found him on the floor until shift change at six a.m. It was too late for treatment for his head injury to be effective. He suffered for nearly a month before he succumbed to his injuries."

Jamie reached out her hand to Val, resting it on her arm. "Oh God, that's horrible. I'm so sorry."

"We couldn't believe something like that could happen. Before his accident, my mother and I traveled to the nursing home every day to feed Dad dinner and to help his roommate with his meal. His roommate's wife came every day at lunchtime to feed her husband and help my dad. We stayed most of the day on the weekends to visit with him and help in the snack shop." Val paused and trembled in a deep breath before she was able to continue.

"My mom tried to sue them for negligence. My dad was seventy-three when he died. The jury seemed to feel that, at that age, he had outlived his worth as a human being. They awarded her a small settlement of a few thousand dollars, and the lawyer got a large chunk of that. It wasn't about the money, although with Dad gone, there's no doubt that Mom could have used the funds. We wanted to draw attention to the fact that the staff there weren't following the guidelines and were putting peoples' lives at risk. Shortly after my dad's incident, another patient died at that facility, and the state closed them up. It was unfortunate that it was too late for my father and the other poor man who died." After she finished the story, Val fell silent and studied her hands. A few seconds later, she gave a deep sigh and raised her head. "My mom died of a broken heart, shortly after he passed away." Val blinked, breaking the tenuous grasp of the tears brimming in her eyes. Two large tears flooded over and rolled down her cheeks.

Wiping her eyes with her sleeve, Val apologized. "Sorry, this is the first time I've told anyone this story since he died over three years ago. I closed his business, paid all of their bills and debts, and just pushed on."

Jamie could see the tears running down Val's cheeks. In a natural effort to comfort her companion, she put her arm around her back. Val seemed to welcome the comfort, as she leaned her head on Jamie's shoulder and relaxed into her embrace. "Go ahead, Val, cry and let it out. It sounds like your life was pretty rough for a long time. I'm glad you're finally letting go of some of those feelings you've been carrying around with you for so long. More than that, I'm glad I could be here for you." Jamie plucked a bouquet of tissues from the box next to her and handed them to Val.

Val dabbed her eyes and gave her nose a good blow.

"If we get into bed, do you think you can sleep?"

Val nodded and stood up.

They changed their clothes and settled in the double bed. There was no expectation of Val sleeping in the single bed alone. After several minutes, Val reached for Jamie's hand. "Thanks."

Jamie tightened her grasp in response, fully expecting Val to let go. Instead, Val held fast and they fell asleep with their fingers entwined. During the night, Val rolled on her side and rested her head on Jamie's upper arm, cuddling against her.

Awakened by Val's change of position and touch, Jamie felt conflicted. She wanted to turn toward Val, to hold and give her the comfort that it appeared she needed and wanted. Inhaling and exhaling in a steady rhythm, she remained unmoving. She hated that she lacked the courage to express her feelings for Val.

A few seconds passed. Val's hand remained on Jamie's arm. A millimeter at a time, Jamie pulled her arm toward her side, until Val's hand rested against her torso. The contact of Val's hand touching her breast warmed her from her center to the perimeter of her body. Soon they both drifted off to sleep. She'd never before experienced anything that felt so right to her.

Sunday morning found Val facing away from Jamie. Upon awakening, neither mentioned the intimacy of the night before, as they made the bed and dressed. During the remainder of the day, the two women talked about safe subjects.

The conversation in the car on the way home focused on the subject of work. Jamie told Val that she'd decided to take the teaching position in the middle school. "At first I had mixed feelings about going back to teach in the same area where I'm currently an administrator. As a supervisor, I've always enjoyed a positive working relationship with the teachers in my building. I don't anticipate too much difficulty transitioning back to coworker from supervisor."

"I envy that you'll finish up soon. I have to stick it out through summer school. I still don't know at which grade level I'll be placed."

Jamie was a ten-month employee and only worked the summer if she was needed for a special project. Her work year concluded when all the reports and scheduling for the following year were complete. Val's position was twelve months, because she ran the summer school. Even though summer school ended at the end of July, Val worked through, preparing schedules and curriculum until she took her vacation in August.

"I plan to take vacation after summer school ends. How would you feel about joining me here at the lake?"

"You know I'd love to do that, because I love it here. I've got a problem though, because I can't leave the cats for that long. It wouldn't be fair to leave them for a two week stretch with Robbie just coming to feed them twice a day. I can't afford to put them in a boarding facility for that long, and I know they'd hate it."

"Oh."

Jamie reached and patted Val's arm. "I'll see what I can do."

Val dropped Jamie off and headed home. As she pushed the front door open, she almost collided with Robbie coming down the steps. "Oh, hi. I was just coming down to check on the cats. You're a little later than you expected, and I figured the boys might be hungry."

"Can you come in for a visit?" After an affirming nod from Robbie, Jamie opened the door to her apartment. The complaining meows of her cats greeted her. "I know, I know, I'm a terrible mother." She greeted them with scratches. They followed her to the kitchen, where she served up portions of wet food in two separate bowls."

Robbie patted his shirt pocket, searching for a cigarette. He seemed to remember Jamie didn't like him to smoke in her apartment. He settled for opening a bag of pretzels from a basket on the counter and helping himself to a pretzel rod. Between crunches, he asked, "So how was the weekend?"

"Terrific and terrible." She related the highlights of the weekend. "If I don't work up the courage to clarify things soon, I'm afraid I'm going to go crazy."

Robbie came over and put his arms around Jamie, giving her a warm embrace. "Just be patient and continue to respond to her as you have been and let things unfold. If she has feelings for you and wants more, she'll let you know one way or another in due time. Things like this have a way of working themselves out."

"I know you're right. Sometimes, I can't help myself...I'm feeling so much for her. I don't want to just have a fling with her."

Robbie's chuckle lightened the moment. "You don't? And you're sure about that?"

Responding in kind, Jamie paused and smiled back. "Well, yeah, I do." She grinned. "It seems though, that my physical attraction has intensified into something more than your ordinary, garden-variety lust. I want it all. I want to be with her. Despite my own doubts about everything, I can't deny wanting something deeper and more permanent with her. The minute she leaves, I can't wait to see her again. Sometimes, I have an almost overwhelming need to wrap her up and fend off the world for her. I want to keep any potential pain from touching her, and I want to share everything I'm capable of giving her.

Some days, I could use the same from her."

"You know, if Val is as important to you as she seems, maybe it would be best to be patient. If it's meant to be, she'll work it out and come to you. Besides, what's your hurry? Relax and enjoy the process. The only urgency is the one you're creating for yourself. Once you open your mouth, you can't ever take those words back, so be certain before you say anything."

"I know. You're right." Jamie sighed with the exertion of verbalizing her thoughts. "My mother is coming to visit next weekend, and I won't get much alone time with Val for a couple of weeks, at least not while Mom is here. Maybe things will fall into perspective with a little distance. Enough about me, Robbie, what's new in your life?"

"Nothing much. I'm obviously still looking for love in all the wrong places." He grinned. "I'd better go. You need to unpack, and I have some papers to grade." Jamie walked him to the door, where they exchanged hugs and a kiss good night. She trusted and valued their ability to share secrets without worry of broken confidences.

After Robbie left, Jamie locked the door and changed her clothes. She was looking forward to getting into bed to read a while before she turned off the light.

The phone rang. "Hi, I just wanted to say good night to you."

"Thanks, Val, it's good to hear your voice after such a long interval." They both laughed and talked for almost an hour. Finally, both were sleepy, so they wished each other a good night's sleep and hung up.

Chapter Eight

Present Day

JAMIE AND KELLY BOTH jumped when her hospital beeper buzzed and dragged them into the present. Her story immediately forgotten, Jamie jumped up to watch, as Kelly used the hospital phone to check the message. "Jamie, Val is out of recovery and in her room. Come on, I'll take you up. You owe me the rest of the story, though."

"I promise."

Kelly navigated her way through the convoluted hallways of the hospital. Jamie's strides were about half as long as Kelly's, so she was out of breath by the time they arrived at Val's room.

"I'll stay in the waiting room." Kelly pointed in the general direction of the lounge. "It's just down the hall there."

Jamie paused at the doorway and looked at her lover. Val's eyes were closed, and her face was so pale it nearly matched the white pillow cover. Jamie brushed away the tears that brimmed in her eyes and crept in, hoping to avoid waking her partner.

"I know you're here, sweetheart. It hurts to open my eyes though."

Jamie approached the bed and quickly glanced around before placing a light kiss on Val's lips. "Thank God, you have a hard head."

Val winced, as her eyes snapped open to glare at her lover. "Hmm, not even a few minutes of sympathy?" Her eyes slammed shut, as she again winced in pain.

"I'm sympathetic." Jamie brushed Val's forehead, smoothing the furrow between her brows. "And sincerely grateful you didn't do more damage to yourself than you did."

"Mmm. Feels good. Bad headache." Val sighed. "I'm sleepy."

"Are you allowed to sleep?"

As if on cue, the nurse, Nancy, came in, wrapped a fresh ice pack around Val's ankle, and checked her vital signs.

Nancy smiled at Jamie. "Try not to worry. She's going to be okay.

She'll hate me by the end of the shift, because I'll have to come in every hour or so to take her vitals and make sure she's able to wake up." Turning back to her patient, she hung a new bag of meds. "This is a mild pain reliever that should make you feel more comfortable in a few minutes."

Jamie settled into the chair next to Val's bed. Taking Val's hand into her own, she smoothed and caressed the age spots she found there. They'd shared so many years together. Her eyes filled, as she pushed the thought from her mind that someday, one of them would have to face the world alone.

Val peered at Jamie through the slit she'd opened in her right eye. "Don't cry, I'm not going anywhere." Val squeezed Jamie's hand.

"I know that. It just kind of, you know, hit me. You scared the bejesus out of me." Jamie exhaled a shaky sigh. "Whatever would I do without you?"

The nurse came back into the room, interrupting their conversation. "Hi, I'm Joanne. You must be Jamie. I'll be Val's other nurse tonight. Surgery went as planned, and she's stable for now. They installed a plate to stabilize her ankle. Because of her head injury, they want to monitor her a little longer, although expectations are that there will be no complications. She'll probably sleep for a couple of hours now. The lounge around the corner has some recliners, a phone, and some snacks."

"Honey, I'm feeling so sleepy. Why don't you go to the lounge and get some rest while you can? Better still, go home."

"Not a chance," Jamie said. Val gave her hand a squeeze and closed her eyes. "Sleep well. I'll see you in a few."

Jamie gathered her belongings and then watched as Val drifted into a sound sleep. Kelly stood up when Jamie entered the waiting room and made her way to the chair next to her.

"You're still here. Although I appreciate the company, I hope you know that I don't expect you to stay."

"I know." Flashing a wide grin, Kelly sat down and patted the chair next to her. "I don't want to miss the rest of the story if you feel up to talking some more."

Jamie slumped into the chair. "Aaah. This is the most comfortable chair I've sat in all day."

"Do you want me to run you home?"

"No, I want to stick it out for a while to make sure everything is okay. I do want to make a call first, to be sure my friend takes care of my cats." She dialed Robbie's number.

"I'm at the hospital. Val fell." She waited for the person on the other end to breathe. "No, I'm fine." She tried to continue. No luck. "Stop. Here's what happened." Jamie told Robbie about Val's accident. She reassured her friend that both she and Val would be better served if he took care of the house and the cats. "Yes, I promise I'll call if there are any changes."

Jamie replaced the phone receiver into the cradle. She smiled at her companion. "Robbie's one of my best friends. I've known him for years. His friendship brings all the advantages of having a husband, and none of the disadvantages."

Kelly chuckled. "I'm sure there is a whole evening of rich conversation about that topic. I hope you'll forgive me wanting to save it for another time, though. If you're ready, I'd love to hear the rest of your and Val's story."

Jamie leaned back in her soft chair and continued telling her story.

Chapter Nine

Reflections

THE FINAL WEEKS OF school dragged by. Jamie began to clean out her desk and sort through her files in preparation for her move back to the classroom. She read through, then shredded or filed the stack of papers on her desk. As she worked, she found herself mentally drifting back to the weekends at the lake, thinking of Val and the enjoyable hours they'd spent together over the past few months. Almost as if on cue, the phone rang. Jamie felt her spirits lift and her pulse quicken when she heard Val's voice. "It's nice you called. I was just thinking of you."

"You were?"

"Um hmm. I was being sentimental and wishing that we were at the cabin."

"I'm afraid I'll be missing my cabin this weekend myself. Some friends rented it out for the weekend and the week following. I'd prefer not to have to rent it at all. To help defray expenses, I only rent it to friends or people I know and try to limit the rental occasions to two or three times a year."

"Well, now at least I feel better knowing it's not available, so I can't miss it too much." Jamie tossed a pile of old papers into the recycle bin. "Oops! Listen to me. Here I'm ready to invade your cabin again for yet another weekend, and I don't recall an invitation." Jamie thumbed through another of the folders on her desk as they talked.

"What do you mean? I told you that you have a standing invitation. You're welcome any time that you want to come. I love your company, and I don't know how I'd stay warm without you there."

Jamie's eyes widened. She could feel herself flush red. Her head snapped around, as she checked her surroundings, unable to believe Val had said that on a school phone. *Don't panic. Be rational. Val could have meant that I usually take care of the wood stove when I go to the cabin with her.* "Um...yeah. Well, I'm sure you can build as good a fire as I do, although I admit that I'm happy that my scout training pleases you."

"That's not exactly what I meant. We can talk more about that later tonight when I give you a call. Oh no, look at the time. I have to run, or I'll be late for a meeting. Bye." Val hung up, leaving Jamie sitting at her desk with the dead phone still at her ear.

The phone rang as the day finally drew to an end and Jamie prepared to leave for home. She frowned at the unusual, after-hours call. "Oh, Robbie. What's up? Is something wrong?"

"I'm sorry for the last-minute request. I'm glad you're still at your office. My car acted up on the way home from work. Do you think you could come pick me up at the car dealer on your way back to the house? In exchange for the favor, how about I treat you to dinner and a movie?"

"Ooh. That sounds like a good plan. I'll check to see what's playing at the theater."

"Check to see if *Top Gun* is showing. I'd love to see that."

"I bet you would." Jamie laughed. "It'll be fun to spend some time with you when neither of us has to rush off somewhere. I'll pick you up at the repair shop."

On the way home, Robbie gushed about how hunky Tom Cruise was in the film. Jamie countered with how hot Kelly McGillis was. They stopped in at the club to listen to the band. By the time she arrived home and bid Robbie good night, it was after midnight. As she prepared for bed, the phone rang. Expecting Val, she snapped up the phone.

Bly didn't even say hello. "Finally! Where've you been? I've been trying to get you all night. My aunt died, and I have to come back to New York on Thursday. The funeral will take up a good bit of the day on Friday. The good thing is that I'm not scheduled to fly out until Sunday morning. So, I wondered if you'd be available to spend some time with me? Maybe we could spend the day together in the city on Saturday, catching up. If it's not too much trouble, you could drop me at the Newark airport on your way home. What do you think?"

"Oh, fun. It'll be wonderful to see you. I didn't expect to see you until Christmas. I'm sorry to hear about your aunt."

"Thanks. She was a wonderful woman. I am glad that, now, the whole visit won't be for a sad reason."

"I can't believe how well this works out. I have to pick my mom up at the airport on Sunday afternoon. She's flying in from Florida. Do you have anything specific in mind for Saturday, or do you want to play it by ear?"

"I have reservations at the Midtown, where we stayed last time when we went in to see that show, remember?

"Yes." Jamie scratched Chips as he joined her on the bed. "It's not far from the theater district, so maybe we could see a play? I don't care what we see as long as it's lighthearted and fun."

The two women talked for a few more minutes and finalized their arrangements to meet each other. Jamie smiled at the prospect of seeing Bly again.

On Tuesday morning, just before lunch, Jamie called Val at her office.

"Hey there. I called you last night. Hope you were having fun."

"I'm sorry, I should have told you I'd be out. She explained about Robbie's car trouble and their spur of the moment plans. "Can I make it up to you by buying you dinner tonight?"

True to form, Val was gracious. "Why are you even apologizing? It's not like we made definite plans. Although I'd love to take advantage of your unwarranted guilt to get you to treat me to dinner, you're too late. I already have a dinner invitation."

Feeling a momentary and unexpected pang of emotion, Jamie bit her lip? "Oh? Anyone I know?" The strength of her reaction surprised her. As a general rule, she didn't consider herself to be a jealous person.

"I'm getting together with my boss. Marie asked me to join her for dinner at her home. I have a feeling that she wants to discuss something with me, and it seems she doesn't want to do it at work. We don't get together outside of school all that often. When we do, it's usually for a movie or dinner out."

Jamie sighed and shifted in her seat. "Nice, I'm glad you're getting together with her. You always enjoy it." *You have no idea how glad I am it's her you're seeing.* She hurried to change the subject. "Oh, I almost forgot to tell you I'm going away this weekend, well Saturday, anyway. Bly, my friend from California, called me last night. She's flying in for a funeral on Friday. I'm going to visit her in the city on Saturday, then I'll stay over and pick up my mom at the airport on Sunday afternoon." They compared calendars for the remainder of the week trying to find time to get together. Jamie had long-promised plans for Wednesday. Thursday was out for Val because of prior commitments with another friend.

"Oh." Val was quiet for a moment. "What about Friday?"

Jamie begged off for Friday. "I need to prepare for my mom's visit. Before she shows up, I want to clean up the house and get the guest room ready for her, go shopping and all of that. After that, there's laundry, ironing, and packing for my trip to the city to meet Bly."

"Oh, darn, I hoped we might find time to get together before you left. Unfortunately, we both seem to have a busy week ahead of us, so I guess we'll be in touch on the phone before you leave."

"I'll talk to you soon." Jamie placed the receiver in the cradle. She sat for a few moments trying to analyze her reaction to Val's dinner plans. *Did I really feel worried? I was, no doubt, relieved when I discovered the identity of Val's dinner companion was her boss and longtime friend.* Jamie shook her head. *Oh boy, I'm in trouble here. I hope it's good trouble. I have to see her before I go away this weekend.*

In case she couldn't finish everything she needed to do before the weekend, Jamie didn't say anything to Val about her plan. She decided to do the food shopping after work on her way home. After putting the groceries away, instead of giving in to her desire to put her feet up, she began cleaning and tidying the house. She put fresh sheets on the beds in the guest room and her bedroom. She tossed in a load of laundry and hung fresh towels on the second rack in the bathroom. One final check of the house proved that all was as it should be. The sound of the clock striking ten times reinforced that she was ready to call it a night.

Her sense of pleasure about her accomplishments helped to offset her tiredness. Almost everything she needed to do to prepare the house for company was done. Despite the fact that the packing still remained, she felt pleased with her better-than-expected progress. She debated whether to go to bed or prepare a nice cup of tea. Tea won, and she sat down at the kitchen table to read the paper as she sipped. Simon, her sleek tuxedo cat, plopped down on top of the article she was trying to read. "Hello there. You never met a newspaper you didn't think was made for you to sit on, have you?" Chips, as always curled up on her lap. The unexpected ring of the phone made all three of them jump.

"Hi, Jamie, it's Val. Do you have a few minutes to talk?"

"For you, always. Is something wrong?

"Wrong? No, nothing's wrong per se." Val hesitated. "Umm...look, I have something I want to share with you, something that I'm excited about...

"Except..."

"Well, the timing is poor for me to be telling you my good news."

Jamie felt the frown line between her eyes deepen. "So, come on. Out with it. If you have good news I want to hear it. Honest."

"Okay, you know I told you that tonight I had dinner plans with

Marie. Jamie, I...I...damn it Jamie, I have mixed feelings about telling you this."

"You're starting to worry me. Just tell me."

"Sorry. Okay, this evening Marie confided that she's resigning as Principal."

"Wow! That's news. When?"

"At the end of this school year." The next few sentences poured from Val in a rush. "She's recommended me as her successor. It won't be official until the school board approves my promotion at their next meeting. Marie said there shouldn't be a problem. Jamie, I'm being promoted to Principal."

"Oh, Val, that's fantastic news."

"I'm really excited about this opportunity. At the same time, I'm sad that I'm having such good fortune at the same time you're about to lose your position. It doesn't seem fair that I'll end up with a promotion and you have to go back to the classroom."

Jamie exhaled a long breath she hadn't realized she'd been holding "Look. I can't think of anyone better qualified, or more experienced, who could do as good a job as you will. As Marie's assistant, you've been training for that job for years. I think they've made a wise choice. Please, don't worry about my feelings about going back to the classroom. You know that I preferred teaching to being an administrator. The only advantage to being a vice principal is the money. Teaching is much more rewarding. My biggest problem with the loss of our positions was the manner in which they handled the situation. I don't think that change is inherently negative. It's the adjustment to something new that's difficult. Despite everything else going on, please believe that I'm thrilled for you. I couldn't be happier. Honest."

She waited for Val to process the fact that her excitement regarding Val's promotion was sincere.

"You'll never know what it means that you are happy for me."

"So, I have some good news of my own to share."

"Wonderful." Val's voice brightened. "What is it? Tell me."

"Hmm...I think it's good news." Jamie paused. "Yeah, I'm sure it'll be good news. I worked hard tonight and should be able to finish everything else I need to do before I leave, except pack. How about if I take you out Friday night for a drink to celebrate your promotion? What do you think?"

"Oh, that would be perfect. Yes, that's definitely good news. It's too bad you can't see the big grin on my face."

Jamie pictured Val's luscious mouth turned up at the corners. As if her tongue had a mind of its own, it moistened her lips.

"Please, don't tell anyone from school the reason for the celebration. They should make a decision in a few days. If I'm approved by the board, they'll formally announce my appointment after the meeting."

"My lips are sealed." Jamie made a clicking sound. "That was the lock closing my lips." She got the reward she wanted when Val laughed.

"I'm thrilled we can get together before you leave on Saturday. Thanks for being glad for me. I was worried about how you'd feel." Val exhaled.

Forgetting to filter what she said, Jamie blurted, "I can't wait to see you on Friday." It felt like forever until Val responded.

"Me too. I'll pick you up at around six thirty."

Jamie hoped Val's smile was as big as her own.

Chapter Ten

Reflections

ON FRIDAY, AT SIX thirty sharp, Jamie answered the doorbell with a welcoming smile. As Val entered the living room, she gave Jamie a quick hug. The pleasing scent of Val's perfume made Jamie want to bury her nose in Val's neck to enjoy the fragrance in a much more personal way. She breathed in the aroma and settled for stating, "Mmm, you smell good."

Val smiled, and Jamie thought she saw a hint of red blush on Val's face as a result of the compliment. When Jamie offered a drink, Val shook her head. "I'll wait, thanks."

Jamie risked allowing her eyes to drift over Val's body. She looked even more attractive than usual. Her golden tan accented her gold-flecked eyes. She was dressed all in white. The contrast of the light clothes against her tan skin made Jamie bite her lip to stop the expression of her feelings from tumbling out of her mouth. Jamie made her face a blank and picked off a piece of lint from Val's sleeve. "Wow! You look amazing." As she pulled her hand away, their fingers brushed together. *Was it by accident, or did Val engineer the casual caress?*

This time, Val drove on their way to the bistro. Jamie reached over and squeezed Val's shoulder. "I saw the official notice of your appointment as Interim Principal got posted today. Congratulations."

A beautiful smile spread on Val's lips. *God, that mouth.* Jamie felt her pulse quicken. She turned away and ran her hand over the smooth leather in Val's Mercedes. "This car is so comfortable."

"Thanks. I love it." The cherished car, chocolate-brown outside with a rich tan inside, was now five years old. Val caressed the leather steering wheel and gave Jamie a halfhearted smile. "I know I'll have to sell her soon. It was a onetime extravagance I'll never be able to afford again." Val's shoulders dropped and her voice slowed. "When my father was ill for so long, I lived with my folks, so I was able to save enough to buy the car of my dreams."

Jamie smiled thinking about how different their tastes were in cars, in music, and other unimportant areas. It surprised her that the differences never mattered. In truth, their differences seemed to broaden and enrich their relationship rather than stifle its growth. Val loved classical music and opera, while Jamie was more eclectic in her tastes. Over the past months, Val had begun to appreciate some of the current songs on the radio. She'd even accompanied Jamie to see the Pointer Sisters in concert. *I know she tolerates my pop-country music favorites like Charlie Daniels and Juice Newton. The allure I feel for Jimmy Reed remains a mystery to her, I'm sure.*

As for Jamie, she was still trying to develop an appreciation for opera.

Val reached for the radio. "Maybe a compromise station...easy listening?"

An instrumental version of "Love Me Tender" began to play. Jamie sang the words.

"If you're making up those words, you should be a song writer."

"Oh wait, you're serious." Jamie just smiled. "No, they're the real words from a number one hit by Elvis. I can't believe you don't know that song."

Val humphed. "I'm sure I can hum several arias or songs from operas you won't know the words to."

"No doubt about that. No sane person would ever bet against that."

To prove her point, Val hummed "The Toreador Song" from *Carmen*.

"Wait, I know that one." Jamie sang, "Toreador, oh don't spit on the floor."

"Oh please! Stop." Val smacked Jamie's leg. "Where did you ever hear that?"

Jamie touched the corner of Val's mouth with her finger. "I see it, that little smile you're holding back. Come on, let it go."

"You're impossible." Unable to control herself any longer, Val gave in. "Thank goodness we're here."

They were both still chuckling as they got out of the car.

Inside the bar, they found a table. The wine they'd ordered arrived, and Jamie raised her glass. "To your new position." Their glasses clinked.

"Thank you." Val's eyes softened as they met Jamie's. "How are you feeling about packing up your office?"

Jamie shrugged. "I think the first few months might be a little awkward. After that, it'll be as if I was always a teacher."

"I admire your calmness. You always seem able to accept and adjust to conditions around you. It's seems like you fit no matter where you are." Val took a sip of her wine.

"Thanks." Jamie studied her drink. "I hate to burst your bubble though. You see it like no matter the situation I'm able to adapt and appear comfortable. Truth is, inside, I never feel that I belong anywhere, even though it may appear that I do. It's a subtle difference I guess, belonging or appearing to belong. Know what I mean?"

Val nodded.

The waiter interrupted the conversation to ask if they wanted another glass of wine. The topic was left unfinished as Jamie declined the waiter's offer for another round of drinks. "Can you bring me the check instead?" They returned to Jamie's house where she put the water on to boil. She opened the cabinet and took down a jar of coffee. "I'm sorry, I only have instant."

"That's okay. I don't mind it." Val sat at the table, while Jamie prepared their drinks. "So, tell me about your weekend plans."

Jamie told her about her arrangements to meet with Bly. "We have a lot of catching up to do. I admit that I'm curious to learn more details about Bly's life in California. It's different talking on the phone than having a conversation in person. Even if we don't do anything other than sit around and gossip, I'm sure we'll enjoy our time together."

Jamie rinsed the cups and loaded them in the dishwasher. "I'll be right back." A moment later, she returned with a gift box wrapped in soft, blue paper and handed it to her guest.

Val looked up in surprise, questioning Jamie with her glance.

"It's a little congratulation, thank-you, etc., gift. I thought it would fit with the decor up in the cabin. Go on. Open it. I hope you like it."

"What did you go and do this for? It wasn't necessary." Opening the wrapping carefully, Val removed the card from the box first and read it aloud. "I treasure every moment we spend together. Thank you for sharing your life with me. Your friendship means so much."

That day, Jamie had argued with herself about what to write. She wanted to write that she was falling in love with Val and that she desired more than a friendship with her. In the end, she made the decision to stress their friendship in the note. Friendship would always be there.

Val looked up with tears in her eyes.

"Jamie, the sentiment is beautiful, thank you." Val removed a small hurricane lamp from the box. The base was pewter, with a delicate glass shade on top. Jamie had also included a Wedgwood-blue candle for Val to use the first time she burned it. "Oh, this is gorgeous, and you're right, it's perfect gift to coordinate with the one at the cabin. It was my mother's."

"I tried to find one that matched as closely as possible. I thought it would look pretty on the bookshelves, opposite the one you have. I'm glad you like it."

Val put the lamp and the card back in the box and stood up. "I guess I'd better go. I'm sure you have a few things to do before you leave for the weekend. Do you need me to feed the boys or do anything with the pool?"

"No, Robbie is taking care of them." Jamie smiled. "Thanks for asking."

Jamie walked Val to the foyer and unlocked the outside door for her. Val turned and put her arms around Jamie. "Thank you for everything, for the drinks and the gift. Most of all, thank you for being who you are." Before she released Jamie's arms, she brushed her lips against Jamie's cheek. "Have a good time tomorrow. I'll miss you."

Before Jamie could say or do anything, Val left her standing in the hallway staring at the door. Jamie closed her eyes and reached her fingers up to her cheek to touch the still tingling spot. She exhaled and tried to quash her sudden feeling of emptiness. Val hurried down the sidewalk and got in her car. Jamie's eyes glistened, tears threatening to spill over, as she watched Val's taillights disappear around the corner. *If only*. She shook her head and headed inside.

Jamie did some last-minute chores around the house then packed a small suitcase, and then she got into bed to read. She finished her novel before she was ready to sleep and locked the book in the cedar chest with the others. Jamie recalled their conversation from earlier that evening. She knew that Val didn't understand her statement about honesty. Jamie sure did, as would many other lesbians living their lives in secret and in fear that others would disapprove. *I'm so tired of hiding my true feelings from people who are important to me.* Jamie was annoyed with herself and sad that she didn't have the courage to be more honest with Val. *I wish I had the inner strength to tell her that I'm in love with her. At least I'm finally able to be honest with myself about how I feel.* In bed, Jamie adjusted the cats and slid deeper under her covers. She turned out the light and felt tears of frustration well up within her. It was a long while before she could sleep.

Chapter Eleven

Reflections

THE CLOCK RADIO ON the headboard roared to life at six thirty, blaring the oldies hit, 'Oh What A Night.' "Ain't that the truth?" Jamie mumbled as she pushed the off button on the radio. "Ugh, I'm not ready to be awake yet." She flipped back her covers. "Come on boys...move. I've gotta get my show on the road." She dragged herself from the comfort of her bed to take a quick shower. Refreshed, she performed the rest of her morning ritual with alacrity. Finally, her mind came to life, as she thought about the day ahead. She started to hum *Lady Madonna*, one of her favorite Beatles tunes, as she applied a light coat of mascara to her eyes and dressed in tight fitting jeans and a soft blue shirt with an open collar. The final touch was a spray of musk before she slipped her sockless feet into her boat shoes.

Within twenty-five minutes of rolling out of bed, she was ready. She nodded her approval to the reflection in the mirror and zipped the last-minute toiletry items into her travel bag. In the kitchen, she tended to the cats. Robbie would feed and play with them again later in the afternoon. Jamie wolfed down some cereal and her vitamins, and then washed up the dishes. Finally, she grabbed her bag and headed for her car to begin the journey.

The morning was crisp and clear. The temperature was about sixty-five degrees. Propelled by a light breeze, the fluffy white clouds scudded across the vivid-blue sky. She pushed the button to open the convertible top and then snapped the tonneau cover in place. *That might be a little optimistic.* She turned up the collar of her coat and flipped on the heater switch. That should be enough to keep her comfortable till the air warms up. With the radio tuned to her favorite oldies station, she was set. It was a beautiful day for a drive, and the traffic was light.

As she drove, she allowed her mind to wander back more than two years to the day she met Bly in the cafeteria of the Veteran's Hospital where her father was. She'd paid for the food on her tray then turned toward the hum of the dining area. The dismal, faded paint and dim illumination of the small room did nothing to elevate her heavy mood. Glancing around, she forced her face to relax and conceal the pity she felt for the scrub-clad hospital staff and sad looking fellow visitors. *At least, someday, I'll not have to take my meals here anymore. These poor employees are doomed to suffer an interminable existence in this depressing place.* She squelched the thought, as she scanned for an empty seat in the overcrowded room. Two tables away to her left, an attractive brunette looked up and smiled. She gestured to Jamie to come and take the empty seat across from her at the small table. With no other option presenting itself, Jamie joined the stranger.

"Thank you. I was afraid I was going to have to eat this standing up. I'm Jamie, by the way."

"Bly." Her dining companion said, as she extended her hand and looked deep into Jamie's eyes.

The woman's hand felt smooth and warm as Jamie took it into her own. "Bly is an interesting name. It's different."

"It's a Native American name meaning tall. I guess my family had high hopes for me." Bly smiled and gave a quick tip of her head to the side. One perfectly shaped brow raised and lowered and a deep dimple appeared in her cheek. "It's rumored in my family that my great-great-great-grandmother was Native American, although it's never been confirmed."

The eyes that locked onto Jamie's were an interesting mixture of pale green and brown, with flecks of gold. In the play of light, there was a faint shade of blue sprinkled in as well. Jamie had never seen anything like them before and found herself mesmerized. She struggled to drag her eyes away. "You have such interesting eyes. They're an amazing color." She could feel the blush creeping up her neck to her face.

"Thank you, I get that comment often. They're definitely an ice breaker." Bly wiped her mouth with her paper napkin, grimacing at its coarseness. "I don't recall ever seeing you here before. Do you work here?"

"No, my father is here for treatment. Three-pack-a-day man since he was just a kid."

"Sorry. That's a difficult diagnosis to get." Elbow on the table, Bly rested her chin on her folded hand.

Jamie squirmed a bit in her seat, feeling like a subject under a microscope. She watched as Bly's glance slid down her arm and stopped on the bare ring finger of left hand. The indentation remained.

Bly blinked and raised her eyes to Jamie. "Is the treatment helping your dad?"

"No, they gave him three to four months, and he's already two months in from that prognosis. They just did a test on him to see if the cancer has spread to his brain. It's already traveled from his throat to his lungs." Jamie glanced away.

Striving for more subtlety than Bly demonstrated earlier, Jamie checked out Bly's ring finger as she looked down at her plate. *No ring. Now why in the world do I care if she's married?* Jamie forced a smile, as she returned her gaze to her dining companion. "What about you? Why are you here?"

"This is my own personal salt mine. I work here...Social Worker. What do you do?"

"I'm an administrator in a state-run school."

The din in the room made conversation difficult. Bly broke the comfortable silence between them. "How are you accepting your dad's prognosis?"

"Um, it's hard to say. I have my moments." Jamie took a swallow of water. "No real choice other than to accept it. The cancer was already spreading by the time they diagnosed him, so he seems pretty resigned to it. Still, fifty-nine is too young to be passing on. Our relationship was always a rocky one. Because I'm here with him now, I know I'll have no guilt when he's gone. I won't have to second guess whether I did the right thing where he's concerned." Jamie again sought brief eye contact with those fabulous eyes. She dragged her gaze away and forced herself not to stare. Exhaling a ragged sigh, she pushed the remainder of her meal around her plate.

Bly organized her plate and plastic silverware on the Styrofoam tray and prepared for disposal. She'd already been half way through her sandwich when Jamie sat down. Bly rummaged in her purse for a moment. "Ah. Here" She extended a slightly dog-eared business card. "I'm currently assisting patients with placement for rehab. If I follow the rules, it's not within my job description to help you on a formal, professional basis. Still, there's nothing saying I can't be a friend, should you need some support." Bly indicated the exit to the right of the cashier with a nod. "If you go out that door and turn right, my office is the third on the right. Do you come in to visit him every day?"

Jamie nodded. "I usually come in after work, stop in to see how he's doing, and talk or read to him for a while. Then I grab a quick bite before I go back to his room to sit with him for another hour or so until visiting hours end."

Bly smiled. Her expression softened. "I'm usually here every day just before six for dinner if you want to join me." Her eyes narrowed, as they swept three sides of the room. "Sometimes having a little company in these surroundings helps."

"I bet. I might just take you up on that offer." She looked around. "I'm sure it won't come as a shock to you if I tell you that dining alone in this place can be damaging to the spirit."

Bly stood up. "I'm going to refill my coffee. Want anything?"

Jamie's gaze followed Bly's progress over to the coffee machine, averting her eyes when Bly glanced over at her. The two women lingered over coffee and tea, making small talk common to virtual strangers. By the time they parted, they shared two goals in common. They both wanted to meet again, and they both wanted to know each other better.

After meeting the next three evenings in the cafeteria, Jamie again found herself at the table across from Bly. She glared at her plate and slumped in her seat. "How do you tolerate this? I don't think I can stand the hospital food one more night. How about I bring us some really good steak sandwiches tomorrow, from the outside world?"

"I suspect I have no taste buds remaining. They've all been killed off from eating here." Bly snickered. "Okay, you've got a deal. I'll supply beverages and will look forward to dinner tomorrow. Besides, there'll be more privacy and better acoustics in my office for us to talk." She glanced around. "For sure, the environment is a bit more cheerful than in here."

The next evening, Bly flung the door open to Jamie's knock. Laughing, she grabbed Jamie's wrist and pulled her into the office. "Thank God! Starvation was setting in." The aroma of fresh cheese steaks with fried onions immediately filled the room. "That smell is heavenly. You have no idea how I've been looking forward to this, I'm famished."

"Sorry, the line at the sandwich shop was out the door."

They devoured the sandwiches, as they chatted about their day. During a lull in the conversation, Jamie wiped her hands and stood up. "I'm going to say good night to my dad."

Bly walked her to the door. "I was wondering if you'd like to meet me for dinner at The Better Half on Saturday? You know, for some real food that doesn't get served on a Styrofoam tray or come in a plain, paper wrapper."

Meeting off the hospital grounds solidified the fact that theirs was no longer a professional relationship; they had become friends. Two days later, Bly picked up the phone.

Jamie didn't need to identify herself. "I just got a call. My dad..."

"Are you here at the hospital, Jamie?"

"On my way."

"I'll meet you upstairs at his room."

Jamie rushed in and found Bly already there waiting for her when she arrived at her father's bedside. Minutes after her arrival, the doctor met with them. Bly held Jamie's hand. "I'm sorry, Ms. Parker." Jamie turned into Bly's arms for solace as she cried.

At the viewing, Bly stood in line to pay her respects. Jamie pulled Bly into a quick embrace when she reached the front of the line. She held onto her long enough to whisper, "Thank you. You being here, made all the difference in the world. I don't know what I'd have done without your support through all this. Are you coming to the burial and luncheon?"

Bly stepped back and shook her head. "I have to go back to work. How about coming over to my house tomorrow night?"

Jamie nodded. "I'll call you when I get home, and we'll make plans."

***

Jamie peered at her reflection in the glass of the storm door. She smoothed her clothing and brushed her fingers through her hair. After a final a deep breath, she pushed the doorbell.

"Come in." Bly took the bottle of wine that Jamie extended and with her other arm pulled her into a quick embrace. She led Jamie into the kitchen, where she uncorked the wine and poured some for each of them. Bly swirled the wine in the glass, inhaling its fragrance before taking a sip. "Umm." She glanced at the bottle. "Mateus. Nice choice." She took Jamie's hand and led her into the living room. Her fingers found the previously noticed ridges on Jamie's ring finger. "How long?"

Jamie pulled her hand away and took a sip of her wine. Settling on the sofa, she exhaled a long breath. "Long enough that the evidence of my marriage should have been erased by now."

"Do you want to tell me what happened, or is that too personal?"

"We had different interests. I was interested in him, and he was interested in someone else."

"I'm sorry."

"What about you, Bly? You've never mentioned a date or that you're seeing someone. Were you ever married?"

Bly observed the light coming through the wine in her glass, as she swirled the liquid. "No, never married. It's not an option I've ever considered, Jamie. I'm a lesbian." Her eyes flashed up, studying Jamie's reaction.

"Oh."

"Is that a problem for you?"

"Problem? I, uh…I'm a little shocked, I guess. I had no idea." Jamie fiddled with her hair before she brushed it back. "What does that mean to our friendship? Does that change anything?"

"I hope we can still be friends. I very much enjoy your company."

Jamie's eyes swept the room. "So, do you have a girlfriend?"

Bly humphed. "I was seeing someone. I met her when she was separated from her abusive husband. I became involved with her despite my own misgivings. Cindy seemed to want me when she was with him, and she wanted him when she was with me." Bly studied her fingers, her brows furrowed. "Cindy has difficulties perceiving herself as a lesbian, and fears people will discover what, in her mind, is her shameful secret. She wanted us to be together, although she didn't want anyone to know about our involvement."

Bly stood up and went to the kitchen to get the bottle of wine. She continued her story as she returned to the living room. "Cindy just couldn't love me the way I needed her to, whatever her reasoning, which seemed to change from day to day." Bly uncorked the bottle and filled their glasses. "After her bruises healed, she left me and went back to him. She was only with him for a few weeks, when he beat her black and blue again. Following the second incident, she finally left him and got an apartment on her own. She asked me to wait for her until she could work out her issues. Like a fool, I agreed." Bly placed her shaking hand on her thigh and blinked back tears.

Jamie took a sip of her wine and looked away to give Bly an opportunity to regain her composure.

"Although Cindy and I were no longer seeing each other, she would call once or twice a week in tears. She'd cry and tell me that it was still me she loved. She just couldn't deal with being a lesbian and having everyone know about her."

"Did you want everyone to know about the two of you?"

Bly shrugged. "Maybe not everyone. There's no doubt that I wanted to be more open than she did. I've never been one to hide who I am." Bly leaned back into the sofa cushion and ran a finger down the seam, brushing at a nonexistent piece of lint. "I suggested counseling to her and she went. She swore to me that she was working hard there to accept her attraction to me so we could be together."

"So you're still waiting for her?"

Bly shook her head in denial. "No longer. That ended right around the time you and I met. A friend of mine, who worked at the same office as Cindy, mentioned that Cindy was dating a fellow from there." Tears welled in Bly's eyes. She blinked them away. "I couldn't believe how she betrayed me. I felt stupid for waiting, all the while thinking we might still have a chance. I cooled my heels for months, waiting for Cindy to resolve her issues. It devastated me to find out that she would be capable of treating me with such utter disregard. I mean, she didn't even tell me herself, I had to hear it from an acquaintance."

"I'm so sorry, Bly." Jamie touched Bly's arm in emphasis. "So, you're not seeing anyone now?"

Bly's fake smile didn't disguise her hurt. "No, still licking my wounds, I guess."

***

Late spring faded into summer. Bly extended an invitation. "Jamie, I was wondering. I'm planning on taking a trip to Provincetown with a few friends of mine. I'd love it if you'd come with me."

"Will your friends care that I'm not a lesbian?"

"Will it matter to you that they are?"

Without hesitation, Jamie answered. "No. Tell me more about the trip." In the end, Jamie agreed to join in on the fun.

They drove up as a group, Jamie, Bly, Amy, and Beck in one car, followed by Liz and Sandy in their own. The women reconnected at the guesthouse where they were all staying. During the daytime, they lay on the beach or spent time shopping. At night, they visited the bars to hear the lesbian singers and comedians. The trip was a lot of fun, and Jamie felt comfortable with Bly's friends.

"I never figured you would have a straight friend, Bly," Beck said when they were alone. "How long will it take you to turn your straight friend into your next girlfriend?"

"You're off base here, Beck. She's not interested in me that way. We're just friends."

Beck saw more than either Jamie or Bly did. "Uh huh." She patted Bly on the shoulder. "If you say so."

Bly dropped her friends at their place. She and Jamie returned to her house so Jamie could get her car keys she'd left there on the counter. Bly followed her to the door, where the two women exchanged a brief kiss and a hug, as usual. Jamie hesitated, then pulled Bly to her and rested her head on her friend's shoulder.

"Jamie, what's wrong? Tell me. Did the weekend upset you? You seemed fine earlier."

Jamie pulled away, trailing her hands down Bly's arms and finding her friend's hands. "Bly, I need to talk to you. I think I'm falling in love with you. I know you're not ready, especially for me, someone who's always dated men."

Bly pulled Jamie to her again and hugged her close. "Jamie, I'm not ready for anyone. If I were, it would be you. Although I won't deny that I'm attracted to you, you need to know that I'm not ready for a new relationship. I've been clear about that."

"I know." Jamie gave a wan smile and glanced up at Bly. "For the first time in my life, my heart tells me that I'm emotionally and sexually attracted to a woman. Clearly, I'm the last thing you need."

Bly kissed the top of Jamie's head. "Maybe you need to do some work before you make this leap. I can recommend a friend to you if you want to talk to someone about what you're feeling. I have her number in my office. I'll call you with it tomorrow."

"Thanks. And thanks for taking me with you. I had a fantastic time." She pulled Bly down and gave her a quick kiss on the cheek before leaving for home.

Jamie wasted no time making an appointment with the woman Bly recommended. She entered into counseling with the therapist, Ann Hannover. Jamie discussed the guilt she felt over ending her marriage, as well as her attraction to Bly. A number of sessions later, Jamie summed up their discussion. "So, it's possible that I repressed my attraction to women for years and that I wrote off my attraction to my ninth-grade teacher as a crush. Then there's the fact that I preferred the friendship of my best friend in school to a date with a guy. How could I be so unaware?"

Ann didn't react to Jamie's sarcasm. "So what's happening with you and Bly now?

"Other than my dreams of making love with Bly? Maybe I should tell you about how I lust for her as we sit opposite each other in her living room? Regardless of all that, our friendship continues on a platonic level although the sexual tension between us is palpable."

"She may not yet be ready for you, Jamie. Cindy hurt her deeply. Because she would be your first lesbian relationship, you may frighten her."

Two nights later, Bly came to Jamie's house for dinner. They hugged and exchanged a quick hello kiss at the door as usual. There was a moment when they looked at each other. Their second kiss became the tipping point where platonic ended and another whole dimension was added to their relationship. That first nonplatonic kiss sent unfamiliar waves of lust through Jamie. As they kissed passionately, hands slipped under shirts to explore. Locked together, they stumbled to the sofa. Bly's breathless, "Wait, please, wait, stop," brought Jamie to a reluctant awareness.

Jamie sat up and tugged on her clothing to straighten it. "What's wrong?

Bly whispered. "I'm sure you've heard that your first relationship with another woman never lasts. I hope that's not true. If it is, then maybe by being friends, we can manage to both emerge reasonably unscathed in the end. So, be sure, Jamie, and be careful with your heart."

Jamie knew she wanted Bly, although Bly's statement didn't ease the nagging doubts. She hoped there would end up being more between them than just sex or friends with benefits. She trusted Bly to keep her word that they would always remain friends in the end, no matter what. Committing to her decision, she leaned into Bly and raised her lips to accept Bly's kiss that set her afire.

The pair made the transition to the bedroom, as they lurched from wall to wall, lips refusing to separate. "Wait." Bly waited for Jamie to focus.

"What's wrong? Did I do something wrong?"

"No. Everything's fine. Let's slow this down a little. I want tonight to be something you'll always remember." Bly kissed Jamie, refusing to release her lips until she moaned. She found a hollow where Jamie's shoulder met her neck, and nuzzled and teased it with her tongue. When Jamie moaned, Bly reached behind her to unhook her bra. Jamie inhaled, as Bly slipped her sweater and bra off over her head.

Bly bent to pull Jamie's breast into her mouth. She then turned Jamie around and stood behind her so that she could look into the bureau mirror. Jamie's eyes met Bly's in the reflection. She watched Bly's hands slide around her waist then raise up to support each breast. Her eyes closed and her head fell back against the taller woman's shoulder, as Bly's thumbs stroked her already erect and sensitive nipples. "I want you to see me love you."

Jamie watched her breasts rise and fall in Bly's hands, as the tempo of her breathing increased. Bly stepped away for a brief moment, stripped her shirt off over her head, and removed her bra. She brushed her breasts against Jamie's back. Energy hummed between them, and they groaned in unison.

Jamie met Bly's eyes in the mirror. "I want more of your kisses." She pivoted around to face Bly and moaned when her breasts brushed against her lover's. Bly's hands moved to unfasten Jamie's slacks and slide them down her body to the floor. As Jamie stepped from the last of her clothing, Bly stripped off the rest of her own.

"You have a fantastic body." Bly licked her lips and leaned into Jamie. "Are you nervous?"

Jamie nodded and wrapped her arms around Bly. "Excited too."

"It's not too late to change your mind."

Jamie shook her head and sought Bly's lips.

***

Bly lay with her forearm over her eyes, her breath slowing. "Umm. You're a fast learner." Both sated for the time being, they remained facing each other with legs entwined. "So was it different for you with a woman?"

"Without a doubt. You were tender and giving, and certainly more focused on pleasing me than he ever was."

The next morning, tender hands roaming over her body awakened Jamie, bringing a smile to her lips. Again, the two women made love.

Chapter Twelve

Present Day

JAMIE INTERRUPTED HER STORY, as she glanced at the clock on the wall. It had taken a while to summarize parts of her history into a narrative that made sense, because she had to eliminate the more intimate details from her recollections. Privately, she cherished the more intimate memories as she recalled them and related the highlights of her life to her new friend.

"I see you're looking at the time. It shouldn't be too much longer." Kelly patted Jamie on the shoulder. "Can I get you anything? How about some hot chocolate?"

"That would be nice, thank you."

"I'll be right back." Kelly's long strides carried her down the hallway and out of sight.

"Here you go." Kelly handed Jamie her chocolate.

"Thank you. That tastes very good."

"So you and Bly obviously didn't make it."

"We did okay for a few months. At first, I thought that Bly and I might grow to love each other." Jamie chuckled. "I suspect my hope was based more on lust than on reality."

"That happens." Kelly chuckled. The sound indicated her comment was based on experience.

"We never fought, just started bickering about little things. You know, like which way the toilet paper should roll, under or over. I was neater than she was. Dishes left in the sink more than once caused a tiff. After some soul-searching, I came to the realization that, although I loved Bly, I wasn't in love with her. I think that our relationship worked in the beginning, because it was a safe and comfortable place for both of us to be."

"So you broke it off?"

Jamie looked down at her hands. "Technically, it was a joint decision. Our transition back to being friends was gradual. Despite being strained at first, we both worked to keep the promise we made each other in the beginning, and our friendship endured."

Jamie sipped her cocoa and again looked at the clock. "It's been an hour and a half. I'm going to go see if she's awake yet." She disappeared around the corner only to return a few minutes later. "Still sleeping. The nurse said to give her another hour or so. At least she looked a little better. She has more color and seems to be resting quietly."

Kelly reached over and squeezed Jamie's hand.

Jamie patted the kind woman's hand and smiled a sad smile. "I don't know what I'd have done without your company today. You've forced me to keep my mind on the past instead of the future. That was comforting in a way. I know the past, I fear the future." She patted Kelly's hand.

"She's getting the best of care and seems to be out of the woods. I don't think there's anything to worry about. Now, it's a waiting game to find out how bad her ankle is. You'll need to decide about her care after the hospital. The doctors will probably decide that rehab as an outpatient might be a good idea."

"Val will hate that, especially now, because we're moving to our place at the lake. That's what we were doing when she fell, sorting and packing. We're trying to finish before the movers come. The furniture is taken care of because the house is going furnished. We put an addition on the cabin, an office. Even with the extra space, we still have entirely too much stuff. That's why we have to sort out how much of the personal items we can keep and what we can bear to part with." Jamie's eyes filled. "Our friends have all volunteered to help. Most of them are our age or older, and although their minds are willing, their flesh is weak." Jamie made herself laugh. "Honestly, it's sorting and tossing. Nobody can do it but Val or me. I don't know how I'll finish it alone."

Palms turned up, Kelly gestured with her fingertips toward the length of her body raised. "Look at me, strrrong like bool," Kelly said, in her best Eastern European accent worthy of Uncle Tonoose. "I can help pack and carry things. You'll sort. Worst case, there's storage. If we need more help, I have some equally bull-like friends who will help us. Now don't worry."

Jamie applied pressure to Kelly's shoulder until the tall woman leaned forward and inquired, "What are you looking for?"

"Your wings. I'm sure someone up above must have sent you."

"No, I'm a mere mortal. Come on. Tell me more of your story. You were just leaving Val for the weekend to go visit with Bly in New York."

"Okay, let's see. Where was I? Oh right…"

"Bly and I had been over for a while. She'd already moved to California, so it was the first time we were seeing each other since she'd left."

AJ Adaore

Chapter Thirteen

Reflections

JAMIE'S WATCH READ NINE thirty, after she parked in a lot not far from her destination and walked the few blocks in the morning sunshine to Bly's hotel. She checked with the desk clerk to get the room number and was soon in the elevator on her way up. Softly, she tapped at the door of Bly's room.

Before she knew it, Bly jerked the door open and wrapped her in a bear hug. They stood there holding each other. "I'm so glad you could make it to the city this weekend."

"Yes, I'm glad to see you too. I'm so sorry about your aunt." Jamie threw her bag on one of the beds then looked around. Two double beds against one wall dominated the large room. Opposite the beds was a small table flanked by two comfortable looking chairs. To the left there was the bathroom and the closet. The room was bright and, because it was on the tenth floor, reasonably quiet.

Each woman took a chair and began to catch up on their lives. "So tell me what's happening at work. You haven't mentioned it in any of our phone calls." Bly slipped off her shoes and stretched her legs across the space between them resting her feet on the edge of the seat of Jamie's chair.

"I'm finishing up at the office. All of the vice principal positions were cut. The oldest woman decided to retire. The day they informed her that her position was being abolished, she walked out saying, 'If you don't need me doing this job in September, you don't need me doing it now.' That was it. She went straight to personnel, took her vacation time as her notice, and hasn't been back since."

"She more or less gave the figurative finger to the school board and higher-level administration."

"I'd say so." Jamie laughed. "The second is Val. Because her boss decided to retire, Val's being appointed Interim Principal and will most likely end up as Principal as soon as the board meets. Last is me." Jamie shrugged. "I'm the only one returning to the classroom. I don't mind that, really. I know I need something different in my life. Maybe a change in my work situation is what I'm looking for. So how is life in California?"

"I'm happy I moved." Bly crossed one shapely leg over her other. "I've grown to love my little apartment on the outskirts of San Francisco. I couldn't afford to live in the city proper. I've made some friends at work and in my apartment building. It's definitely a gay town and very easy to be oneself there."

"That's great for you. What about the job? You told me it was a difficult adjustment."

"The job has proven to be challenging and rewarding all at the same time. Some days are frustrating and exasperating, while other days are possibly the most rewarding, wonderful work situation I've ever been privileged to experience in my career. I love it. The people are nice." Bly's voice gained animation as she provided more details about the work situation and told Jamie about the new people she was meeting there. "The organization is large enough that I don't stick out, and small enough that I know enough of the staff to make me feel a part of the place. It was a good decision to move. Just as you feel the need for something different in your life, I had also felt that need. I miss you and your friendship, but everything else is really good. What are you doing socially?"

"Not much really. The usual." Jamie stood and looked out the window. "I've been tied up with school and finishing up there. At work, I'm sorting through and packing up files and doing as much as I can to help with the year-end reports. I'm still responsible for planning graduation, and all that is keeping me busy."

Jamie returned to sit opposite her friend. "I started spending a lot of time with Val. In the beginning, it was most often about lamenting the work situation. The more time we spent together, especially over the past few months or so, we started to become a lot closer. On weekends, we've been going to her cabin in the mountains, a couple of hours from home."

"Hmm...mountain cabin? That sounds nice."

"It is. The cabin is on a lake. It's really beautiful, cozy and private. There are only a few other cabins scattered around near hers, and town is a little less than a mile away. I've loved the time we've spent there. During the week and on off weekends when we don't go to the cabin, we've been spending time at the pool, having dinner, or playing games."

"Just what kind of games are you playing with her, Jamie?"

"Come on, Bly, don't be sarcastic. Board games. I'm struggling with this, because I think I've fallen in love with her, and I don't know how to handle it." Jamie spent the next ten minutes or so talking about Val and the times they'd shared together. She finished talking and looked away from Bly's penetrating eyes.

Bly reached over and took her hand. "Oh, Jamie, you've fallen in love, haven't you? I can hear it in your voice and sense it from the admiration in your words when you talk about her. I'm happy for you and at the same time concerned about the struggle you're going through."

"Thanks. It's the same old...you know, me being afraid to tell the truth about who I am."

"Do you think that if you tell her you find her very attractive she'd be offended? What's causing you to hold back so long?"

Jamie's eyes filled, and she looked down. "There's more than that. I'm concerned that I just don't have enough to offer her in a relationship. I failed with Josh. I failed with you. Val is so tender and unspoiled...I don't want to hurt her. I feel that she deserves more than I'm able to offer her. I'm so afraid of having my heart broken again that I might hold back too much of myself. I'm such a coward."

"Don't be so hard on yourself. Maybe it's not so much cowardice as it is self-preservation."

"Maybe." Jamie resettled herself in her chair pausing to organize her thoughts. "There's no doubt that you and I ended up involved for a couple of reasons. We were attracted to each other on several levels. There was also the fact that our relationship was safe...for both of us. We recognized, early on, that it would never work out for us on a permanent basis as lovers. Both of us were hiding in a safe harbor, using each other in the gentlest sort of way."

"I guess that's probably true. Have faith, Jamie, everything will work out. One of you will gather the courage to tell the truth about what you're feeling. I do wish you love and happiness with her. From what you've told me, she sounds like a great person. I hope I have the opportunity to get to know her."

Jamie stood. Taking Bly's hands to pull her to her feet, she encircled her friend in her arms. "You know, I love you very much. Thanks for listening. Now, how about we get out of here and see the sights and get some food."

They wandered awhile, poking around in some stores before heading for a small bar and grill called Charlie's. They ordered lunch and enjoyed a cocktail. After Bly's third drink, she said, "Hey, I have a great idea. Why don't you call Val and invite her to come to town to meet ush."

"Ush?" Jamie teased. She was sober enough to realize that was a crazy suggestion. Still, she did miss Val and wanted to place the call just to say hello. She didn't have enough change, so she placed the call collect.

Val accepted the charges. "Oh yes, absolutely. I'll take the call." At Jamie's hello, Val's words tumbled out. "Jamie! It's so good to hear from you. I was just thinking about you. I can't believe you called me."

"Neither can I," Jamie cleared her throat. "I, uh...I'm sorry about the collect thing. I didn't have any change, and I wanted to call. I'll pay you back."

"Don't worry about it. I'm just glad you called."

"I hope they were good thoughts."

"About you?" Val chuckled. "What else could they be?"

"You have a point there." The sound of Val's laughter made Jamie's grin widen from ear to ear. "So...um...I've been telling Bly what good times we've been having lately. She suggested that I call and invite you come into the city and join us. She wants to meet you." Inwardly, Jamie cringed. *What a coward. I'm crediting Bly with the idea.*

"I wish you'd called me earlier. It's too late to drive in now. Anyway, what would we do with two cars in the city?"

"I know. It's a crazy idea. I missed you, though, and it would be fun for you to join us. I really do understand that it's a long drive and too late. I'll be home early tomorrow. Maybe we could get together for dinner?"

"That sounds good. I'd like that."

"I can pick up some Chinese on my way home. It's been a long time since you met my mother. Tomorrow night would be a perfect opportunity for you to get reacquainted. I like her to meet and get to know my close friends, plus I'd get to see you for dinner."

"Can I make a different suggestion?"

Jamie switched the phone to her other ear and stuck her index finger in her free ear. "Sure. What's your idea?"

"Why don't you bring your mom here for dinner instead? I promise I won't make Swiss steak." The sound of Val's snicker made Jamie smile and miss her even more.

Swiss steak was a new recipe that Val, normally an excellent cook, had prepared for them one night several months back. The meal turned out to be barely edible. The steak could have been used to make the soles of a substantial pair of work boots, and the gravy tasted like wallpaper paste. Ever since that meal, if either of them tried to avoid being the one to prepare dinner, they'd always threatened to make Swiss steak. The threat always resulted with either going out to dinner or ordering takeout.

"That would be perfect," Jamie nearly jumped up and down. "I'll drop Bly at the airport, pick up my mom, and drive home. I should arrive home around four. How about dinner around six? I'll call you when I get home just to confirm I made it okay and there were no delays."

Val agreed to the plan. "I'm so glad you called. It was good to hear your voice. I've missed you this weekend. By the way, you never told me if you could come with me to the lake for vacation when I go in August. What do you say? It'll be fun."

"Robbie plans to be around and told me he can take care of the pool. My only problem is that I don't want to leave the boys for two weeks."

"Well, you could bring the cats with you. They would love the porch. Don't you think they could use a vacation, too?"

Jamie pumped her fist in the air and mouthed *yes*. "Val, you're amazing. That would eliminate the only thing holding me back. I promise they'll behave. We can talk more about it when I get home. I'll see you tomorrow and don't forget, no Swiss steak." They were both laughing when they hung up.

"Well?" Bly greeted Jamie with a satisfied grin when she returned to the table. "Judging from your body language during the phone call, she was happy to hear from you. Is she coming?"

Jamie shook her head. "She thinks it's too late to drive into the city and I agreed." Jamie's face flushed a light shade of pink. "She told me she missed me, too."

"Ah. That's nice."

"She and I arranged to get together tomorrow for dinner. I'll bring Mom, too." Jamie finished the last of her drink and glanced toward the door. "Want to go?"

The pair walked back to the hotel, stopping to look in the windows but not buying anything. They walked through Times Square and debated about seeing a show, but decided they'd rather head back to the hotel. They used the hotel pool and the exercise room, then went out for dinner, stopping for a nightcap at a small lesbian bar Bly knew about. They were back at the hotel before midnight. When they hugged good night, Jamie marveled that she felt no sexual response to Bly and sensed no desire on Bly's part. She smiled, as she pulled the covers up in her bed and rolled to her side.

Chapter Fourteen

Reflections

JAMIE LAY IN BED listening to Bly breathe. Trying not to move, she craned her neck to see her watch on the night table next to the bed. It read six thirty-nine when she slid out of bed and slipped into the bathroom. She closed the door as silently as possible and did her morning grooming. Wrapped in a robe, she returned to the bedroom. Bly, capable of snoozing through anything, was still asleep. Jamie sat down at the desk, put her feet up on the opposite chair, and began to read yesterday's newspaper. At seven fifteen, the phone on the night table buzzed with an annoying persistence. Bly sprung to a sitting position and reached for the phone, immediately awake. Able to hear only half of the conversation, Jamie's curiosity was piqued by the time Bly hung up the phone.

Bly slid to the bottom of the bed, nearer to where Jamie was sitting. "Guess what?" The rhetorical question went unanswered, as Bly blurted out, "That was Mitch, my boss. There's a seminar here, in the city, all day Tuesday and Wednesday, and Thursday morning. A guy I work with had plans to fly here tomorrow to attend. Unfortunately, he's ill. His wife called the boss in the middle of the night to say the guy was just admitted to the hospital for an emergency appendectomy. Poor guy. He held on till the last minute, thinking he'd improve and feel good enough to make the seminar."

"So, Mitch wants you to go?"

"Yup. He remembered I was here due to the family emergency and asked if I would mind going to the conference. They added a day for travel time on Friday, so I don't have to go back to work until the following Monday. That means I have a couple more days to spend with you, assuming you're willing to have an extra houseguest."

"That's wonderful."

"If it's okay with you, I'll come home with you today. I can get the train into the city Monday evening or early Tuesday morning."

"Wonderful, we'll get to spend some unexpected time together. Will you come back to my place on Thursday or fly home?"

"I'm not sure. I'll have to call and see what transportation arrangements I can make and let you know." Bly jumped out of bed and gathered her clothes. "I'll take a quick shower and we can grab some breakfast before we go to the airport to pick up your mother. "Yay!" She shot a quick grin in Jamie's direction. "This will be fun."

While Bly showered, Jamie called Val to tell her about the sudden change in Bly's plans. "That means I'll have an extra guest with me. I'm sorry about the short notice. I'd be happy to take everyone out for dinner if there isn't enough food for an extra person."

"Stop," Val said with a chuckle. "Enough. Take a breath. There's no reason to change plans. I'll have plenty of food here for everyone. Oh, by the way, we're having chicken, not Swiss steak."

"There is a God!"

"You're fresh." Val snickered. "And I'd love to meet your friend Bly. I'll add one more place setting to the table. Voila…problem solved. Dinner will be ready around six. However, you can come whenever you want, okay?"

Jamie exhaled an audible sigh. "Thanks, Val. Need anything? I could get some wine if you'd like."

"No. Everything's taken care of. Come whenever you and your guests are ready. I'm looking forward to seeing you and Katherine and meeting Bly."

"Okay, thanks. We'll all see you later."

With Jamie's call ended and Bly dressed and packed, they went to the front desk and checked out. They stopped in the garage to put the bags in the car and grabbed a quick breakfast. One uneventful drive to the airport later, Jamie parked in short-term parking. There was an hour-long wait before Katherine's flight was due to arrive. They passed time in the coffee shop, reading the Sunday newspaper. As Katherine came walking down the hallway to the baggage area where Bly and Jamie were waiting, her pace belied her age. When she saw her daughter, Katherine gave a jaunty wave.

Jamie watched her mother approach and smiled to herself as she noticed that she needed a haircut. Before Katherine moved to Florida, Jamie was the one who cut her mother's naturally curly hair. Her mother usually made the journey up to visit at least twice a year, and each time she would request a haircut from Jamie, because no one could be found in Florida who did as nice a job as her daughter did. She usually only needed to get her hair cut by 'those Florida hair butchers' twice a year.

The mother and daughter exchanged big hugs. "Hi Mom. This is my friend, Bly. Her plans to fly back to California today changed when her boss extended her time here, so she'll be coming home with us."

"The more the merrier, I always say." Katherine gave Bly a hug, while Jamie picked up her bag from the carousel. Soon the three were chatting away about the flight and Katherine began to tell them all the Florida news. She talked rapid fire and nearly nonstop on the trip home.

"Hey Mom! If you don't let us get a word in occasionally, you're going to run out of news. Then we'll have nothing to talk about for the rest of your visit."

Everyone, including Katherine, laughed at Jamie's joke. "Oh hush! You're not too old to have me take a broom to you."

Undaunted by Jamie's teasing, Katherine's soliloquy continued, supported by Bly's occasional comments or questions. Jamie settled deeper into her seat and let her mind drift. She felt herself smile at the thought of seeing Val soon. It wasn't long before Jamie pulled into her driveway at home. She dropped her mother's bag in her bedroom and used the phone there to call Val to say they were home and would be there on time.

"I'm set. You can come over when everyone's ready."

Jamie hung up and went to see how the other two were doing in the kitchen. Bly and Katherine were chattering away like old friends.

Jamie related the plans for the evening to her guests. "Why don't you unpack and then we'll go." Jamie picked up her suitcase. "You take my room, Mom. Bly and I will share the guest room." Jamie saw to it that her mother had everything she needed then went out to the kitchen to wait for her guests. Soon, everyone appeared, and they drove to Val's apartment.

Val's smile lit up her face as she swung the door open.

Jamie glanced down at her watch. "Thanks for letting us come early."

Val stepped aside and welcomed her guests. "It'll give us all an opportunity to get acquainted." Val got each a drink and served them in the living room. She stayed and chatted for a short time. "Please, relax while I finish up with dinner. I won't be long."

"I'll help." Jamie followed Val past the dining area into the kitchen.

"I only have to put things in serving dishes."

The dining room table was set with four white place settings. The plates contrasted against the deep burgundy table cover. Candles were in holders, ready to be lit. A small arrangement of flowers decorated the middle of the table as a centerpiece. "Everything looks beautiful, Val, and the chicken smells fabulous. I'm starved. We didn't have time to stop for lunch."

"Thanks. I made Parmesan Chicken, an old family recipe. Don't confuse it with Chicken Parmesan. This has no sauce and it's baked, not fried." Val removed the baking tray. She set the chicken on top of the counter and closed the oven door.

Jamie's breath caught at the sight of her. The sound drew Val's attention, and for a moment, their eyes locked. Neither seemed able or willing to look away. In the end, Jamie sighed and moved behind the counter. She rested both hands on the cool surface to help her resist a strong urge to put her arms around Val and pull her close. It seemed an eternity, but it was really only a few brief seconds. She broke the daydream with a quick shake of her head and a hard swallow.

"Can I do anything to help you, toss the salad or carry anything in?"

Val turned away and busied herself at the stove. "Yes, help me carry the salad and the chicken in. I'll get the rest." Calling the others to come to the table, they all sat and admired the beautiful meal.

Laughter filled the pleasant evening. Time flew, and much too soon, they'd consumed dinner and dessert. Everyone was lingering over the second cup of coffee or tea. Katherine and Bly sat and chatted. Val and Jamie, who had declined offers to help, cleared the table and washed the dishes. They exchanged farewells, thanking Val for a wonderful evening as they left. Jamie dawdled for a brief moment after the others started for the car.

"Thanks again, Val. I so appreciate what you did. Dinner was wonderful." Jamie winked. "Best of all, no Swiss steak." They both laughed. "I'll call you tomorrow at work." She reached for Val's hand and gave it a quick a squeeze. Before she got into the car, Jamie glanced back for one more look at Val who still leaned against her doorframe.

At home, Katherine said, "I'm tired. I hope you don't mind if I turn in."

Jamie locked up the house and said good night to her mother. Bly was already in one of the two single beds in the guest room. Jamie entered the room, leaving the door ajar so the boys could join her later. Bly rolled up to lean on one arm and smirked. "One thing I'll say for you, Jamie, is that you have fine taste in women."

Jamie's brows arched, as she sat across from Bly on the other single bed. "What's that mean?"

A smile spread across Bly's face. "Lighten up, Jamie, I'm teasing you. What I'm saying is that I think Val is a wonderful person. I can clearly see why you're attracted to her. She is a warm, witty, and intelligent woman. Then, of course, there's the added benefit that she is very attractive, and she has the hots for you. She hardly took her eyes off you tonight, and she hung on your every word. You're crazy if you don't confess that you're in love with her. Stop being so cautious. Speak up. You two need to get on with the wonderful life you can have together."

"Yes, I know I should. You know me, though. If there's something to be concerned about, I do three things. First, I worry about things that are probable to happen. Then I worry about all the improbable things. For good measure, I worry about the things that have no potential at all of happening."

Bly shook her head and laughed. "Sad and so true."

"Anyway, I'm glad that you approve of her and like her. It pleases me that you do." Jamie turned out the light, and they were soon sound asleep.

The next morning, Jamie slipped out of bed, trying not to disturb Bly. Gathering her clothes, she went into the bathroom to shower, grabbed a quick breakfast, and left for work.

At school, she sat at her desk and called Val. "Thanks again for last night. Tonight Mom, Bly, and I are going to see a play at a local community theater. They asked me to invite you to join us."

"I'd love to come. It's a great idea." They worked out all the arrangements before hanging up.

Arriving home, she found her mother waiting for her with scissors in hand. Bly was in the pool, so she enjoyed the time alone to chat with her mom while she cut her hair. When finished, Katherine went to shower and dress for the show. They ate a quick dinner before going to pick up Val. The play was a lighthearted, romantic comedy that everyone enjoyed.

At home, after Katherine retired, Bly told Jamie that she'd called their friend Sandy. "I asked her to drive me to the train on Tuesday morning.

"Oh, that's terrific." Jamie smiled.

"Don't get too excited, she can't do it. Can you drop me before work? I'm sorry, it'll have to be at the crack of dawn."

"Sure. I'll either come back here to see if Mom is up or I'll go in to work early."

"Liz and Sandy have been friends for years. During my discussion with Sandy, she told me that she and Liz have started dating. How about that? She says that it was strange for them to make the transition to dating after all the years as friends."

"Sounds familiar."

"I know." Bly's eyes twinkled. "I find it interesting. In a way, their dating has some similarities to the situation you're in with Val. Like you, they were afraid that if they became lovers, they could lose their friendship."

"Maybe the transition from friends to lovers and back relationships are much more common in the lesbian world than we even know about."

Bly nodded. "True. I mean look at us. Our friendship has certainly survived. It's possible that we're even closer friends due to our involvement as lovers."

The conversation ended when they heard Katherine coming down the hall. She entered the kitchen and joined the other two women at the table. "I just talked to your brother. You know I usually split my two weeks between you. This visit, your brother wants me to come spend a few extra days with him, and I agreed. I thought that Joanie was graduating from the eighth grade next week. Unfortunately, I got it wrong. Her big day is this Friday, not next. I'm going to leave a couple of days early, so I can see my granddaughter graduate."

Jamie smiled a big, knowing grin.

"I know, I planned to stay with you through the weekend. I hope you won't mind if I leave on Thursday. We just have to get me to the train, sometime on Thursday morning."

The confusion about the dates was so typical of her mother. Jamie and her brother often joked about their mother's visits. If they told Katherine specific periods of time that it would be better for her not to visit, their mother always chose those dates they were busy as the exact time she would choose to show up.

"Sure, Mom, no problem. I think there's a train that leaves daily, around one, for his place. I'll check it to be sure. I can drop you off, no problem."

Bly excused herself. "I'm going to go make some calls." She headed to the living room allowing Jamie and her mother some time to talk in private.

Everyone retired after watching the news and weather together. Bly and Jamie continued their discussion from earlier in the evening. Jamie rolled onto her side in her bed. "Why don't you give Sandy and Liz a call and invite them over to the pool on Friday."

"Okay, I can do that. Leave me their number."

Bly grinned. "I have one more request."

"Phew. Only one more?"

Bly laughed, as she raised her middle finger in Jamie's direction making them both laugh. "If I get back in time on Thursday evening, can we go see the band so I can catch up with some other friends there?"

"I'm not sure about Thursday. If I decide not to go, you can use my car. Friday sounds like fun though. I haven't spent time with them in a while, and it'll be good to catch up."

The next morning, they were up before first light. Jamie dropped Bly at the train so she could travel into the city for her workshop, and then returned home.

Katherine was in the kitchen having breakfast when Jamie joined her. "I'm sorry, Mom, that this has been such a hectic visit. With me finishing up at work, Bly being here, and you leaving early, we won't have much time to be alone." Jamie touched her mom's arm.

"We'll have other visits." The smile returned to Katherine's face. "I've had a good time meeting and spending time with your friends."

They chatted until it was time for Jamie to leave for work. Katherine was eager to spend the day with her old friend, Margie.

Jamie finished her breakfast, rinsed her dish, and then said good-bye to her mom before leaving for school. "I'll see you later."

AJ Adaore

106

Chapter Fifteen

Reflections

ON WEDNESDAY MORNING, JAMIE arrived at work earlier than normal. She went to the main office to sign in. A few of the teachers were in early, as well, to work on cleaning out their classrooms. Some were working in the office, recording the last of their student grades. She finished packing everything that she planned to take with her to the classroom. Using a black magic marker, she labeled the boxes with her name and the room number. She wanted to stop by and see Regina, the retiring teacher she would replace in September. After thirty odd years of teaching, the final few days at school would be difficult for the master teacher. Noting the time, she checked her planner for Regina's schedule. *Oh good. It's Regina's prep time.*

Regina greeted Jamie with a smile and apologized for the pile of boxes Jamie navigated around. "So much stuff after thirty-six years. Everything in those two file cabinets in the back of the room, I'm leaving for you. The units of work should come in handy. I know you'll be creating your own teaching materials, too." Regina put her hand on Jamie's shoulder. "At least, these will give you some ideas and resource material to draw from."

"I can't believe this. You're a wonderful teacher. Thank you for such a generous gift. I promise I'll put all these work materials to good use. Jamie covered Regina's hand with her own and gave it a quick squeeze. "I'm overwhelmed by your generosity. "

"Maybe, it will make coming back to the classroom a little easier for you. I have no doubt you'll put everything I've left for you to good use." Regina snapped the lid closed on the last box. "No sense them growing mold in my basement. I'm sure it is hard enough to lose your position because of all this upheaval in the district. Everyone knows that this reorganization is to protect the paper-pushing higher-ups from getting cut and to appease the board. They're top heavy in upper administration, so what do they do? Cut the people in administration who actually work with the teachers and kids. It's disheartening."

"Thank you. It means a lot that you told me that."

Regina raised an arthritic pointer finger. "Mark my words. After a couple years of the principals having to do their own discipline, I have no doubt that someone will have the brilliant idea to reinstate the vice principal positions. Then everything will return to the way it is now. I've been here a long time, and I've seen it all before. The pendulum always swings back to the norm. The whole thing is senseless. And, don't you think for a minute that everyone doesn't know it. We all agree. You're a very good teacher, and the students are lucky to be getting you back in the classroom."

"My original reason to stop in today was to thank you for all your years of devoted service to the school and the students. Now I have to add my appreciation for your materials and for your compassion."

Regina ushered Jamie to the files where she reviewed the units of work she was leaving and showed her how she had the folders organized. It was a treasure trove of information that would make getting started in the classroom in September much easier. It also meant she wouldn't spend her summer making handouts and worksheets for the following school year. Jamie returned to her office with a lighter step, thanks to Regina's kindness.

On the last day of school for the staff, Jamie stopped at each classroom to exchange wishes with the teachers for an enjoyable summer. She sent a memo for the maintenance staff requesting them to move the boxes in her office. She added for them to wait until Regina finished cleaning out her room. Sometime over the summer, she'd need to come in to organize her new classroom and unpack her belongings. Today, she wanted Regina to have an opportunity to finish up in her classroom at her own pace.

Jamie locked up her office and went in to see her boss. "I've turned in the final projects that were my responsibility. I reviewed all the standardized test scores and made a list of the kids whose results I thought you should take a look at. I met with all the teachers about class grouping concerns and based on that information, made adjustments to class lists for your review. Other than that, you'll find everything else in my year-end report.

"I don't know how I'll manage all this without your help. I'm afraid I'll have to relieve each teacher of some of their prep time to help me with the disciplinary chores. I haven't figured out yet how I'll manage to complete all the other tasks you handled for me." By the time Jamie left, she realized that many other lives were affected by her loss of the vice principal position. Everyone in the program would have to pick up some extra chores during the next school year.

Submitting the office keys to Bill made the change from administrator to teacher official. She'd enjoyed working with him and would miss his sense of humor and collegial work attitude. It had seemed like an eternal day. She entered her house and groaned as she sat in her chair in the kitchen. She called for her mom and discovered that Katherine was not yet home from visiting her friend. With the house to herself, she moved to the back porch to enjoy the quiet and solitude. Soon the cats joined her, and she spent a few peaceful minutes relaxing and playing with them before Katherine whirled in.

"What a fantastic day I had." Katherine plopped down in a chair and gushed out the details of her visit with Margie. "We spent the day gossiping about when we worked together before I remarried and moved."

The ringing of the phone interrupted Jamie's description of her day. *Maybe it's Val.* She hurried to answer it. "Oh, hi, Sandy." Jamie tried not to sound disappointed.

Sandy accepted the invitation to come swimming on Friday. They agreed on a time, exchanged some small talk, and both hung up looking forward to the visit.

On the table next to her porch chair, Jamie found a tall glass of iced tea waiting for her, courtesy of her mother.

"Thanks, Mom." Jamie took a long swallow of the refreshing liquid. "That hits the spot."

"The house seems quiet without Bly here. She's lots of fun and seems like such a lovely young woman. How old is she?"

Wondering where the conversation would lead, Jamie replied. "She's a few years younger than me."

Jamie suspected that her mother would be curious about Bly. Earlier, she'd asked Bly what she should say if Katherine asked *the* question?

"I don't see any reason why she shouldn't know I'm a lesbian. Do you want me to tell her?"

"No, let's see if she asks or expresses curiosity. If she does, I'll tell her."

Bly gave Jamie a thumbs-up sign. Jamie rolled her eyes in return.

Katherine took advantage of her time alone with her daughter. "Has your friend ever been married? She is such an attractive young woman with such a pleasant way about her."

Jamie made a final, preemptive effort to head off the next question. "Well, she's had relationships. Unfortunately, they always ended for one reason or another. She just got out of a relationship before she moved to California." *I think I won't mention that she was involved with me.* "Before that, the most serious relationship she had was with someone separated at the time, who decided to break up with Bly and go back to try to make the marriage work. The marriage still ended, but things never worked out for Bly. Too many hurts made it impossible for Bly to resume their relationship." Jamie could feel her spine straighten in pride. She felt impressed that she'd managed to relate a summary of Bly and Cindy's relationship without using a single revealing pronoun.

"Bly doesn't seem like someone who would get involved with a married man."

Jamie mulled whether to just change the subject, or maybe it could provide an opportunity to test her mother's feelings about homosexuality. Knowing how Bly would respond if Katherine asked the question directly, Jamie took a breath. "Mom, last year, Bly dated a woman named Cindy. They met when Cindy separated from her abusive husband. It was Cindy's first relationship with a woman. The fact that she had difficulties accepting herself as a lesbian didn't excuse the way she treated Bly. She hurt her deeply. I think Bly seems much happier now that she's living in California and working at her new job."

"Oh." There was a long pregnant pause before Katherine continued. "You'd never know that she was that way by looking at her."

"That way? You mean gay? Mom, I don't think you can always tell a person's sexuality just by looking at them. You should come to one of the town's league softball games. If judging by looks, you might suspect some of the straight women of being lesbians. Then there are lesbians that are quite feminine, like Bly."

"Jamie, I don't think I like you hanging around with gay women. First thing you know they'll change you into one of them." Katherine shuddered. "I could never make love to another woman." The conviction of her belief was evident in her tone.

"Well, Mom, I don't think it's an issue you need worry about."

"You either. You were already married, so you're safe too."

"You know, I think that sometimes people know early on if they're gay. For others, it takes them some time to figure it out. I'm convinced that there is no way anyone is converted into being gay if they aren't structured that way. You can't catch being gay like the common cold. I'm sure that if you asked Bly, she would tell you that she's a lesbian. She's comfortable with who she is. I think she might also tell you that it can be difficult and stressful if you try to hide your identity. Many gay people live their lives in fear someone will find out their big secret and disapprove."

Jamie waited for the next question. Instead, Katherine decided to go to the kitchen and get more tea. Upon her return, she changed the subject to things that were happening in Florida.

Thursday morning, Jamie woke her mother at the requested time. They ate breakfast together and spent the morning chatting. While in the car on the way to the train station, they had their standard good-bye conversation. Katherine ended each visit with a mantra. "You know I worry about you being alone. I wish you would find someone who would make you happy."

"Come on, Mom. I'm happy. I have good friends and live a comfortable life, despite not having someone special in my life." Jamie navigated the traffic that was becoming thicker as they neared their destination. "Finding someone compatible isn't an easy task. I know you worry. I wish you wouldn't."

Jamie parked in short-term parking and carried Katherine's suitcase to the check in location. She sat in the lounge with her mom and waited until she was called to board. She waved a cheery good-bye, knowing her mother would call when she arrived at her brother's house.

Chapter Sixteen

Reflections

THE BOYS GREETED JAMIE at the door when she returned from dropping off her mother. All too soon, they abandoned her to curl up in their favorite sunspot on the back porch. She grabbed the roll of film she'd taken during her mother's visit and trotted down the stairs to her darkroom. She hummed *Hey Jude,* as she developed the film and hung the negative roll to dry. Arranging the things she needed on the table, she prepared the developer, stop bath, and fixer. Before she could pour them into the color-coded trays, the phone interrupted. She navigated the black painted, u-shaped hallway of her darkroom to answer the ringing phone extension.

"Val." Jamie's grin spread from ear to ear.

"Did your mom get to the train okay?"

"Yes. I'm here alone. I haven't yet heard from Bly, so I'm not sure when she'll show up. Mom left this morning for my brother's. She'll call later to let me know she arrived in one piece. What are you doing?"

"I was just about to have some dinner. Unfortunately, I don't feel like cooking." She encouraged Jamie to make a suggestion that might entice her.

"Hmm...dinner options. I could probably be in the mood for a cheese steak sandwich from Two Brothers, if you're asking for company. I'm working in the darkroom, developing some negatives that I took of my mother while she was here. I'll have to take a break to eat something, I guess. I have to wait for the negatives to dry before I can work with them. There's one special picture I took of my mother that I want to print."

"If I picked something up for us and brought it over to your house, maybe you could make a salad to go with the sandwiches? When we've finished eating, could I join you in the darkroom? Watching you develop pictures sounds interesting. I've never seen it done."

Leaving things in the darkroom as they were, Jamie turned off the light and checked that the fan stayed on. She ran up the steps to the kitchen, where she prepared a quick tossed salad. By the time she tuned the stereo in the living room to a compromise station they could both live with, Val was already knocking at the door. Val's smile was something Jamie would remember the rest of her life. It probably matched her own.

They made small talk while they ate. Jamie stood to clean up the plates. "I think the negatives should be dry enough to work with by now." She rubbed her hands together. "Ready?"

"I can't wait. Let's go." Val followed Jamie to her basement darkroom. She asked a raft of questions on their way. "How did you learn to develop your own films? Have you been doing your own developing for a long time? How'd you get started?" Before Jamie could answer, Val interrupted with, "Oh, look at the entrance. Why is the doorway built in a U shape and painted black?"

"I read some books and experimented. As to the door, many darkrooms have a double entryway. I thought that was inconvenient, so I built my entry to the darkroom in a U shape and painted everything black as an alternative. This way, I can always have an open entryway to the darkroom, no doors necessary. This design allows for better ventilation of the room. If I have to go out to answer the phone or something, I can just leave everything as is. There's no door to open, and no light can travel around the corners with the walls painted black like this."

"Clever."

Jamie blushed at Val's look of approval and praise. "Come on in. Let's check the negatives." Jamie unclipped the negative strip from the line where it was hanging. She inserted it into the carrier of the enlarger. Reaching overhead, she flipped the switch for the safe light and then turned off the overhead light. The room became bathed in a soft, orange glow.

Val looked around. "How can you see to do anything in this light?"

"Give yourself a minute, and your eyes will adjust. You'll be surprised what you're able to see." Jamie started the process. First, she poured the chemicals into the trays, then focused the image on a piece of plain, white paper she'd placed on the tray of the enlarger. She turned the knob on the enlarger to focus the image. "We could make a test exposure." Jamie shrugged. "I'm pretty confident of my guess as to the appropriate amount of time we'll need for the proper exposure.

Let's give it a shot." She dialed the number in on the timer, retrieved a piece of photo paper, and switched it with the plain sheet on the table of the enlarger. She set the timer and pushed the button on the enlarger, explaining each step as she did it to Val. The bulb burst to life, projecting the image from the negative onto the photographic film. After a few seconds, the light went out. "Okay, now the real fun begins. We get to see how good my guess was." Jamie smiled at Val as she slid the paper face down into the developer. Once it was completely wet, Jamie turned the print face up, keeping it submerged with the plastic tongs. "The print is fragile at this point. You have to be careful not to scratch it with the tongs. So the best practice is to grab it by the edge and swish the solution over it. You need to keep the whole surface wet, so it develops evenly." She demonstrated what she meant. "No matter how many times I do this, it never ceases to amaze me when the image begins to appear."

Almost immediately, the image of Jamie's mother began to appear on the paper. "Oh look," Val exclaimed, surprise evident in her voice. "How do you know when it's ready?"

"Usually, I print a test sheet with different exposures. Because I'm just fooling around today, I made an educated guess. I was eager to see this shot I took of my mom." While she was explaining what she was doing, Jamie moved the picture into the stop bath to complete the development process. Using different tongs, she placed the photo into the fixer. "You have to be careful with the tongs. You can go from left to right, but not the reverse. It will contaminate the chemicals. Well, that's all there is to it." Jamie flipped on the lights and held the print up, so Val could examine their results. Then, Jamie placed the picture into the sink to rinse off.

"Fascinating," exclaimed Val. "Do you think I could try one?"

"Sure. It's kind of addictive, isn't it?" The two women developed several more shots from the strip of negatives. They heard a noise upstairs, and Jamie stopped to listen. "I think Bly came home."

"Maybe we should quit for tonight. Can we do this again sometime?"

"I'd love that. Let me clean up here." Jamie quickly stored the chemicals. She finished washing the prints and hung them to dry.

Upstairs, Bly was waiting for Jamie in the kitchen. The three exchanged some small talk, before Bly excused herself to go to bed. "I'm exhausted."

Bly hugged Val. "It was a real pleasure meeting you. Take good care of my friend."

Val leaned back and smiled at Bly. "I will. Have a good flight home.

"It's getting late. Maybe I should go home too." Val gathered her belongings. "I had a wonderful time. I look forward to developing photos again with you."

Jamie walked Val to her car before returning to the house. She and Bly spent a few minutes talking about their plans for Friday with Sandy and Liz.

"I need some rest, I'm tired out." Bly begged off from providing details of her seminar. "I had a wonderful few days, and I'll share the details tomorrow."

Chapter Seventeen

Reflections

FRIDAY MORNING DAWNED WITH the temperature already rising and the air damp with humidity. Spring weather, that had so far been decent, appeared to be planning to throw a monkey wrench in their plans. The sun had yet to burn off the gloomy haze. Jamie sat at the table with a refreshed Bly, drinking tea and rehashing the events of the past few days.

Jamie studied Bly. "For someone who is not what I would call a morning person, you seem pretty cheerful. It seems you had an enjoyable time at the seminar."

"I had a great time." Words flooded from Bly as she described the workshops. "I can't wait to bring some of the state-of-the-art counseling techniques back to the institute. I'd love to investigate and further research their effectiveness. I'm particularly interested in one theory. I won't bore you with the details until I'm sure my boss will approve it as a technique at our facility." Bly tapped her finger on the table. "You've yet to hear the best part of my week." Bly wiggled her eyebrows. "It seems that when I arrived at the hotel, there was no room reserved for me. Well, not exactly. The reservation clerk looked up my name and was unable to locate a room reserved for me. Wait, let me start over."

"Now there's a good idea." Jamie goaded Bly a little. "Maybe then, you'll make some sense."

"Don't be mean. Okay, when I arrived, I went up to the reservation desk and asked for my room number. The clerk looked up my name and was unable to locate a room registered either to me or to my company. Some degree of confusion ensued. I had to wait at the desk, while the clerk went to talk to, I assume, the manager in the back room. While I was waiting there at the desk, guess who showed up?"

"I surrender. Who?"

"Remember Scotty, one of the women we met in P-town last year?

Well, she was attending the conference too. I stood and talked with her while they figured out why I didn't have a room. They determined that when the other guy from work canceled his reservation, the hotel failed to reserve the room in my name. I was stuck, because the hotel had no vacancies. So, while they were trying to figure out what to do with me, I chatted with Scotty while they registered her. She solved the problem by kindly offering to share her room with me."

"Oh?"

Bly waved the innuendo away. "No, nothing like that. It seems that Scotty and Melissa finally moved in together, and they're very happy. Melissa was somewhat reticent about living together. Now that they are, she's sorry they didn't move in together long ago."

"That's nice, a happy ending. I like those."

Bly tipped her head in agreement. "Me too. Wait though, I haven't told you the best part yet. That night at dinner, Scotty introduced me to the most fantastic looking woman I've ever seen. Of course, I fell immediately in lust."

Smiling, Jamie shook her head and rolled her eyes heavenward. "Of course."

"I'm serious. Her name is Dana Corbeaux, and she's fantastic. She has shiny, black hair, pale-brown eyes set off by her olive complexion, and the most beautiful smile I've ever seen in my entire life."

"Wow! You're smitten."

"You bet." Bly held up both hands. "Wait. I haven't told you the best part yet. She's from California. She lives on the other side of the city from me." Bly stopped her machine-gun monologue long enough to take a sip of her tea. "I have to confess, I was immediately attracted to her looks. As I got to know her a little, I found that I was even more attracted by her mind, by what she says and what she feels."

"So, judging by your excitement level, I would have to guess that you have plans to see her in California?"

"It would take an army to stop me. Actually, I'm meeting her at the airport, and we're taking the same flight home. She's a good person, Jamie. We live about forty-five minutes from each other if there's no traffic. I'm excited that we plan to get together when we get back to California. She might come to my place next weekend, and we'll spend next Saturday together. I'm looking forward to getting to know her better."

"I'm thrilled for you, Bly. I hope things work out."

"Me too." Bly stood up to put her cup in the sink. "I think I should write up my report about the conference while things are still fresh in my mind." She excused herself and started to gather the information she'd need for the report.

"I have laundry to do." Jamie headed for the bedroom to gather and sort the dirty clothes and linens into piles.

The two friends completed their chores around the same time. Jamie pointed to the sky. "Look at the rain clouds forming." Within a half hour, the rain was coming down in buckets. "I don't think today will be a good day for the pool with Liz and Sandy. We can still visit and either watch a video or play some games."

Now that she was no longer working at school during the summer, Jamie wanted to avoid calling Val at the office. However, Jamie knew that once her guests arrived she'd be unable to speak to Val. So she broke her self-imposed rule and called Val's school number, dialing the numbers by heart.

They talked for a short time about the prior evening. "I hope we'll be spending more time in the darkroom soon. I had a great time. I always have a good time with you, Jamie."

"I had fun, too." Working in the close quarters in the near darkness was an experience she hoped to repeat soon.

"Do you have big plans with Bly tonight?"

"No, the rain quashed our pool plans. I think we'll just play some board games after dinner. Want to come over?"

"Umm. I have plans for dinner with Marie. I'm not sure how late that'll run. Can I play it by ear?"

"Sure. Not a problem. If you can't make it, call me later tonight?" The evening no longer seemed complete without them chatting at bedtime, even if they'd spent the day together. They always ended up talking until they were ready for sleep.

Chapter Eighteen

Reflections

LIZ AND SANDY ARRIVED about fifteen minutes later than the agreed upon time. Apologizing her way through the door, Liz confessed, "It's my fault we're late. Don't blame Sandy. I got tied up, and we got started a little later than I thought we would."

Jamie accepted the apology and stayed Liz's concern with a friendly hand on her shoulder. "No problem, no harm done," Jamie showed the women into the living room. Once everyone settled, Bly told her friends about her new job and new apartment.

Jamie related the details of her demotion and explained that she'd be returning to the classroom in September. After taking drink orders, Jamie soon returned with the refreshments. She got back just in time to hear the end of Sandy's comment about friendship. Jamie served the drinks before she sat down. In case Jamie hadn't heard their entire conversation while she was in the kitchen, Sandy explained that she and Liz were now dating.

"We can't figure out why, after all these years of knowing each other, we've become aware that there's a different level to our friendship. After a few false starts, we were finally honest with each other about our feelings and have been dating. Sometimes, it's strange having a romantic relationship with each other. We're taking our time, in the hopes we'll end up with each other forever. Other times, the transition from friends to lovers feels very natural. Some aspects are a little disconcerting. We're still very aware of the fact that I live more openly than Liz.

Liz leaned forward. "Both of us worry that we could lose our friendship if things don't work out for us as lovers."

Jamie saw the questioning look Bly was sending her. She shrugged and nodded a go ahead to Bly. She wiped her sweaty palm on her pants and sat waiting to hear what Bly would reveal.

"Ladies," Bly began, "you know that Jamie and I are friends. What you don't know is that we were also lovers for a brief time last year. It ended several months before I left for California. How open we could be was an issue for us as well. I'm able to be out, even at work, and I keep no secrets about being a lesbian. Jamie, on the other hand, being in education, feels she needs to be more circumspect. Although that was a struggle for us, too, it wasn't our only issue. We're only telling you this, because there is no reason you won't remain friends if you're honest with each other."

Liz spoke first. "Thanks for telling us. It's helpful." As a teacher, she understood the trust Jamie was placing in them not to violate her confidence. "People who don't work as teachers don't understand the fear we have of being outed. Still, I know some of Sandy's friends who are lawyers, nurses, or office workers. All of them go to the gay bars. I'm not brave enough to do that."

"Don't be so hard on yourself. I know exactly how you feel." Jamie's kind eyes sought Liz's.

Liz smiled her appreciation. "In the last five years, we've had two superintendents in our district. The first never made any issues about the subject either way. Our current superintendent never makes any secret of his disapproval of gay people." Her expression sad, she shook her head at her reality. "He watches the health teacher like a hawk to be sure the issue is never discussed in health class. If by chance one of the students raises it, he watches to be sure that the tenor of the response is in no way supportive. There's no doubt in my mind that if someone gay were up for promotion, he or she would never get the job if it was known they were gay or lesbian. Nothing would ever be able to be proven. There's just a feeling, an atmosphere if you will, leading to a sense of discomfort and unease."

Sandy smiled and reached over to touch Liz's hand. "I think one of the advantages of becoming more mature is that I'm trying to learn how to accept and love Liz. I'm trying to be respectful of her feelings regarding the privacy issue. Granted, this one is a high hurdle for us. I think I'm willing to try to compromise by being more circumspect near home. If I do that, maybe I can persuade her to be willing to socialize more openly when we're on vacation. Or, maybe we can make a few trusted friendships, locally, where we can be ourselves. That might be a start anyway."

There was a lull in the conversation, and Jamie broke the silence by posing a question. "I hope you won't think me too nosy for asking this question. After being friends for so long, how did you come to realize that you wanted more from your relationship?"

Sandy and Liz glanced at each other and laughed. "It wasn't easy," they said, nearly in unison. "Go ahead, Sandy, you first," said Liz.

Sandy looked over at Liz, her eyes sparkling. "I think it took us about six months before we finally said anything to each other. We found ourselves spending more and more time together. There were times when we would get on the phone with nothing really to say. We simply wanted to hear the other person's voice or sometimes just her breathing on the other end of the phone. We'd tune in the same TV program in each of our homes and watch it together over the phone."

They giggled, again in unison. "I think I recognized it first." Liz squeezed Sandy's hand. "I was afraid to say anything for fear of harming our friendship."

The couple looked at each other and smiled. Sandy picked up the story again. "Finally, someone asked me out, and I accepted the date. I spent the day with Liz and had plans to meet my date around seven. As the time grew nearer for me to leave Liz, I realized that I had no desire to go out with this other woman. What I wanted was to stay with Liz." Pausing for dramatic emphasis, Sandy continued in a more facetious fashion. "So, in a moment of crazed weakness, I confessed to Liz that I didn't want to go on my date, because I was in love with her. Lucky for me, she was feeling the same thing. I called my date to cancel and, as they say, the rest is history."

"I love hearing stories about how couples get together." Jamie stood up. "I'm sorry. I hate to leave this conversation. Unfortunately, I have to attend to dinner if we want to eat sometime before we all keel over from hunger."

The others volunteered to help.

"I'm good. I just have to throw a salad together and take the meat out of the oven." The three friends continued chatting, while Jamie finished up the meal preparation. She called them for help when everything was ready, and they helped carry the food to the table then sat to enjoy the meal Jamie served.

Jamie looked around the table, as everyone ate and told stories over dinner. She studied Liz first, noting that she was pert and petite with dark, serious eyes and short, dark, curly hair. Of Italian descent, her olive complexion made her appear perpetually tanned. Sandy was a contrast in coloring and personality. Bubbly and personable, she had light-blue eyes and short, reddish hair. *They make a good couple. One's strengths augment the other's, as they take turns to shine and bathe in the limelight. Liz, being more serious, balances Sandy's spontaneity with a bit of stability. Sandy's effervescence lightens Liz. They make a good match and are lucky they found each other.* "I'm so glad the two of you came over. Thanks for sharing your story with us."

Lamenting the lousy weather that had ruined their pool plans, the women debated about what to do with the rest of the evening. After some discussion of options, they unanimously settled on a game of Trivial Pursuit. Jamie headed to the hall closet to retrieve the game. After she dropped it on the table, she hastened to answer the doorbell. "Val. This is a pleasant surprise."

"I hope you don't mind," Val stepped back a small step. "You said to drop by." She looked past Jamie and saw the women at the table. "I'm sorry, I didn't realize you had company besides Bly."

"No, I'm always glad when you come to visit. Bly has some friends here visiting, and we're just about to play a trivia game." She stepped aside so Val could come into the house. "Come and join us."

Introductions were made all around. Jamie introduced Val as a friend from school. Immediately, Val apologized for interrupting the game.

Bly spoke up right away. "No, we're just getting started and looking for someone to join who's smart enough to win the game. Jamie and I have often played for hours with nobody able to get enough pieces to finish up. Either we're not too bright or we're too evenly matched. Jamie mentioned that the two of you play often and that you're a good player. Come on, sit down and join us."

The request was met by encouragement from both Liz and Sandy. Jamie added a final, "Please stay."

"Thank you for making me feel so welcome." Val took a seat at the table, picked a colored piece, and the game began. The competition stretched on until, two hours later, Val won. With good nature, she accepted the congratulations and the teasing heaped upon her by the group. Val stood and thanked everyone for including her in the game. "I very much enjoyed the evening." She said good night, and Jamie walked her to her car.

"Your friends are all very fun people, Jamie. Thank you for including me, I had a wonderful time."

Jamie opened the car door for Val. "It made me happy that you came by. It was a nice surprise to see you. Have a good time at the cabin this weekend. If you call me when you arrive home and it's not too late, maybe we can get together to do something." As Val settled into her car, Jamie closed the door. She waited for her to lower the window so they could continue their conversation.

"The weather at the cabin should be good this weekend, and I'm looking forward to some time there. It won't be the same without you to share it with me." Val's eyes twinkled. "Come up after Bly leaves."

Jamie bent down a little so she could look at Val. "Sorry. I can't, not this weekend. I promised to take Bly to the airport. I think by the time I get home and drive to the cabin, it would only give me a few hours there, and I'd have to drive back. We couldn't even drive home together, because we'd have two cars. I can definitely come next weekend."

"I know. It didn't make sense to ask, I thought...never mind. Next time."

"Call me when you get home, okay?"

"Will do. See you then." Jamie watched Val drive away. As she turned to go inside, she found that Liz and Sandy were ready to leave too. Sandy turned to Jamie. "Thank you for an enjoyable day. We had a wonderful time."

"Me too. I'm sorry we couldn't use the pool." Jamie promised them a rain check, and they all laughed at the emphasis she placed on the word rain.

Jamie and Bly awoke Saturday morning to a beautiful day. Bly packed, and the two friends relaxed over breakfast. Before they knew it, it was time for Bly to leave. Jamie drove her friend to the airport and pulled into a spot in the drop-off zone. She popped the trunk lid to retrieve Bly's suitcase. Both had tears in their eyes, as they embraced and bid each other good-bye. Jamie handed Bly her bag. "It was good to see you."

"You too. I'll call you next week sometime." With a final hug and a jaunty wave, Bly entered the building, and Jamie headed for home.

At four o'clock, Jamie flopped into her favorite chair. In a flurry of activity, after she got home from the airport, the laundry had been washed and folded, and the beds changed. She'd vacuumed the pool and adjusted the chemicals, and used the darkroom to finish printing the remaining negatives from her mother's visit. While working in the darkroom, she lost track of time. Before she knew it, a print for each of the negatives on the roll was drying on the line. After cleaning up the chemicals, she made some phone calls to friends and arranged to get together with a couple of them.

The house was strangely quiet after so much activity the previous week. She checked the time and glanced at the phone, willing it to ring. She missed the ritual of the phone call she shared with Val every night. It was a long time before she finally drifted to sleep.

Chapter Nineteen

Reflections

ONCE SCHOOL ENDED, LIFE took on a new routine. Val would speed over to Jamie's house after work and spend the evening. More and more inseparable, they no longer asked if the other was available. They both assumed they would spend the evenings and weekends together. Without saying a word, it seemed they'd become a de facto couple in all ways except for one. Jamie was satisfied with the arrangement, until she looked at Val. *That mouth, oh how I want to feel those fabulous lips pressed to mine.* She couldn't keep her eyes off the woman. It seemed Val caught her looking at least several times a day. There was a perceptible sexual tension in the air that Jamie felt to her core.

Evenings were spent together in comfortable companionship, sometimes with friends, sometimes alone. Weeknights, weather permitting, they enjoyed the pool. They passed time playing games, watching TV or videos, or going to the movies. They enjoyed playing racquetball and tried to get in a couple of games a week. Sometimes, they sat together reading or talking. Jamie usually prepared dinner for them because, being on vacation, she had the time. Val would go to her apartment when she'd finished at the office, for a quick change of clothes. In a few minutes, she'd head to Jamie's for dinner and whatever activity followed that. They spent time with Liz and Sandy, getting together to enjoy an activity or simply share dinner. If Val suspected the true nature of their relationship, she never mentioned it. Weekends for Jamie and Val meant time spent either at the pool or at Val's cabin, if it wasn't rented. Jamie loved her time with Val. Always, just below the surface, was an increasing desire for more, but she still hadn't marshaled the courage to confess her feelings to Val.

It was already late in July when they had to spend a weekend apart, the first in over a month. Robbie was on vacation, and Jamie had volunteered to take care of his dog while he was away. Val went alone to the cabin to retrieve the keys and clean after her tenant for the week had vacated the place. Val planned to spend Saturday, Sunday, and Monday at the cabin alone. That meant three days apart without even a phone call for the now nearly inseparable duo.

Jamie went from one activity to another. She must have glanced at her watch five times an hour. It wasn't as if she had nothing to do. Three times, she'd stopped herself from reaching for the phone to tell Val something. She drew her hand back when she remembered there was no phone at the cabin. Saturday night, she turned down an invitation from Liz and Sandy to go to a movie. "I'm sorry, I'm just not in the mood." By Sunday at noon, she was looking for something to do. She thought she might play in her darkroom after she checked the pool and pulled some weeds. Still in the back yard when the phone rang, she raced up the back steps, two at a time, to answer on the fifth ring.

A familiar and welcome voice said, "Oh, good, you're there. I thought you weren't home." A rush of warmth spread through Jamie when she pictured Val on the other end of the line. In her mind, she could see her smiling. She had the sexiest lips. A quick vision of that mouth joined with her own only served to increase her initial response. *I'm in sad shape when all it takes is the unexpected sound of Val's voice on the other end of the phone to make me wet.*

"Guess where I am?" Val said mysteriously.

Jamie paused to think. "Well, the cabin doesn't have a phone. Hmm, Belle's, I think?"

"Nope, you are off by about two hours."

"What?" Jamie leaped to her feet. "Are you home? Is everything okay? I thought you weren't coming home until tomorrow evening." Jamie's tone changed. "I hope nothing is wrong."

Val's warm laughter served to calm Jamie. "Everything is fine. I just felt like coming home. I thought if you don't have any plans tomorrow, maybe we could do some shopping."

Choosing her words with care, Jamie found it hard to suppress her smile and her heartbeat. "That's a date. Maybe, if we get an early start, we can spend some time in the pool also. It is all nice and clean. By the way, I'm glad you're home."

Val's soft reply, "I missed you, too."

Jamie swallowed the lump in her throat.

"Ah. Well, I guess I'd better figure out something for dinner."

Jamie considered available dinner options. "I could be in the mood for a meatball sandwich from Frank's. If you picked up the food for us and brought it over here, I could make a salad to go with the sandwiches."

"You drive a hard bargain. What else do you want to do?"

"I taped a movie with Lynn Redgrave, Mariette Hartley, and Sada Thompson a couple of months ago. It's called *My Two Loves*. I love all those actresses. I think Rita Mae Brown was one of the writers. I'd love for you to stay and watch it with me. Have you heard of it?"

"No. I'd love to watch it with you, though." Val affirmed that she, too, liked all three of the actresses, and they agreed that the movie should be good. "Okay, I'll be there as fast as I can."

Food and drinks in hand, they walked down the hall to the TV room, where Jamie set up the tape. She sat down next to Val on the love seat and waited for the program to begin. The movie was about Gail, portrayed by Mariette Hartley, and Lynn Redgrave's character, Marjorie. The two women become close friends, and after some time, a romance ensues. The climax pivots on the choice that Gail must make. Gail's mother wants her to pursue a relationship with Barry Newman's character. Marjorie wants her to stay with her.

As the movie ended, Jamie stood up and pushed the rewind button on the machine. She turned to Val and looked her in the eyes. "Which one do you think she should have chosen?"

"From the way the program was presented, there was no real choice." Val rolled her eyes. "Barry Newman portrayed such a jerk, that I can't imagine any woman wanting him. Lynn Redgrave and Mariette Hartley's characters seemed to have a wonderful relationship. It brought happiness to both of them. The only thing keeping them apart was societal pressure and family disapproval. I'm sure it would have been a difficult choice for Gail's character to stay with Marjorie. Both her mother and daughter so vehemently disapproved. And yet, that was where she herself seemed to be the happiest." Val hesitated. She licked her lips and took a long breath. "Uh, Jamie, could you ever love a woman, in the same way those two women loved each other?"

This was the opportunity Jamie had been waiting for. *Why can't I just tell her that I could, or that I already do? All I have to say is 'I do love a woman, an amazing and special woman. I'm looking her in the eyes right now.' It would resolve all the wondering on both our parts.*

Jamie choked. She heard herself say, "I'm not sure. I believe love is love, and you should embrace it whenever you find it if it makes you happy." She steered the conversation back to the movie. "As for Gail, she faced a difficult problem. Her mother and daughter, and the others, created such a stink. I think she and Marjorie made each other happy when no one knew about them. The minute anyone knew the nature of the relationship was when the battle began. Surrounded by so much disapproval, Gail would have to be a strong person to follow her heart. What about you? Could you have a relationship with a woman?"

Val paused as if deciding what to answer. "Yes, I think I could given—" At that exact moment, the doorbell rang and cut off the rest of Val's sentence.

"Hold that thought. I'll be right back. Let me get the door." Jamie hurried toward the front door.

Val followed Jamie to the living room to discover Robbie standing in the hall. After exchanging greetings, he thanked Jamie for taking care of his dog over the weekend, exchanged pleasantries with Val, and climbed the stairs to his apartment.

Jamie turned to find Val standing there ready to leave. "I think it's time for me to go too. It's late."

Jamie opened the door to the hallway for Val. "As always, I had a wonderful time with you." There was a moment when they both stood frozen in the hallway. Neither was ready to end the evening or say the final good night. "Threshold paralysis." Jamie smiled in response to Val's puzzled expression. "You know, when neither person can make the break to say good-bye or good night. Both people stand there frozen to the threshold."

Val threw her head back and laughed.

"I love to make you laugh. I take it you've never heard of the malady."

"Nope. That's a good expression for it, though." Val reached for the knob to the outer door. "Okay, I'll be the brave one then. Good night, Jamie, it was fun." With a final smile, she opened the outer door and hurried down the walk to her car. Before she reached the car, she chuckled and retraced her steps. "False alarm. Since I didn't even make it to the car, my prior claim of bravery doesn't count." She gave Jamie a hug good-bye before turning to hurry down the sidewalk to her car.

As Jamie prepared for bed, her mind drifted back over the evening. She realized that she and Val had never finished their conversation. Val's admission that she was capable of loving another woman made Jamie wonder. *What would the rest of her sentence have been? Good Lord. I hope it wasn't something like, 'I could love another woman, if all the men dropped off the face of the earth and we were the two sole survivors.'* Val seemed to have an open-minded view of the relationship between Gail and Marjorie. Twice, Jamie reached for the phone to call Val, and twice, she pulled her hand back. *I'll be seeing Val in a few short hours. I guess it can wait.*

Chapter Twenty

Reflections

ANXIOUS FOR HER DAY with Val to begin, Jamie awoke early, showered, and took extra care with her hair. To go with her jeans and boat shoes, she picked her favorite blouse, the one that brought out the green of her eyes. She retrieved the paper from the front porch and read it while she ate her breakfast. With nothing left to do other than wait for Val, she paced the length of the house several times. The sight of Val's car pulling up in front of her house caused her heart to leap. She bounded down the front porch steps to greet a smiling Val. "I thought you'd never get here. It seems like I've been ready for hours, even though I know that's not true. I'm so looking forward to spending the day together. How are you this morning?"

Neither brought up their unfinished conversation from the night before as Jamie joined Val in her car, and they started for their destination. After exchanging the normal small talk and discussing their plans for the day, Val shifted into drive.

"Oh, I forgot to tell you last night that this weekend I went to the bookstore and found a book that told me all about you. Now I know all your secrets."

Not understanding what Val was talking about, Jamie felt her stomach turn over at least once. She felt her face flush and her brow furrow in question. She forced her voice to remain even. "Really? What do you mean?"

Careful to keep her eyes on the road, Val reached into her purse and produced a copy of Linda Goodman's *Sun Signs*. "Here, this is for you." She handed it to Jamie. "I spent most of Saturday night reading and underlining everything I found to be true about you. Look under your sign.

Heaving what Jamie hoped was a silent sigh of relief, she took the book from Val. For the rest of the drive, Jamie and Val teased about the things that Val had underlined. Jamie felt flattered and embarrassed by all the positive things Val highlighted. They laughed together about all the quirky characteristics she'd circled. In some places, Val had made additional notes in the margin. For a while, Jamie continued to read silently and chuckled when she read one of the chosen passages about how Leos dealt with food, wine, music, and beautiful women.

Jamie smiled when she noticed that the underline included wines, food, and music but ignored the part about beautiful women. "Thank you. I can't believe how much time and effort you must have taken to do this over the weekend."

Val glanced over at Jamie and back to the road. "It was the closest way to have you with me without you actually being there."

Neither found anything they wanted to buy. They agreed it was not a good day for them to shop and decided to return to the pool. While floating on their rafts, they talked about Val's most recent trip to the cabin. "Yesterday morning, before coming home, I met with Jake, a local carpenter/handyman. We discussed some changes I want to make to the cabin. For some time now, I've been saving money to reopen the loft. Years ago, when my father was using the cabin as a hunting retreat, he closed in the loft area above the living room. He wanted to make the place easier to heat in the winter." Val smiled in recollection. "We never used the upper area and our tiny, old, potbellied stove couldn't heat the whole cabin. So he closed in the loft and put in the slightly larger stove that's there now."

"Does the stove heat the place sufficiently now in the cold weather?" Jamie twisted to face Val so she could see her expressions.

"It does an okay job. I'm replacing it this week with a bigger one that allows me to see the flames. It also has a blower on it, which should distribute the heated air better. Oh, don't let me forget, I have a favor to ask you later." The rest of her plans tumbled out. "I wanted to make the first-floor bedroom into more of a library and office. I want to keep it as a place where guests could stay as well. Maybe I'll add a comfortable chair, some bookshelves, and a small corner desk. I can either add a sofa bed or make up the single bed that's already there into a day bed with a cover and some throw pillows."

"That sounds good."

"I mentioned to you, once before, that I'd love to live at the lake full time someday. I know it won't happen until I retire though."

"It's a wonderful plan. It's good to have dreams. I've always wanted a craftsman cottage." Jamie chuckled. "Maybe someday."

"It is good to have dreams. So, any changes I undertake now are designed to make living in the cabin full time more functional. I asked the carpenter to give me an estimate for what it would cost to reopen the loft and remove the shutters from the window up there. I also want to build a safety rail along the edge of the platform and reinstall the stairs. I plan to put the double bed up in the loft and position it so that I can see the fire. I think the loft bedroom would also be warmer than the first-floor bedroom, since heat rises."

Jamie closed her eyes to better envision the changes Val described. She murmured a sensual, "Mm, sounds romantic."

"Jake made some rough measurements and sketches of what would be required before he left. He told me that he didn't want to tear off any paneling yet, until I decided to definitely go ahead with the changes. So, the estimate he promised me was what he called the worst-case scenario. He called me this morning with the figures. I was shocked at how much it would cost for everything. The money I've saved will barely pay for the materials, and his labor is more than twice that amount." She seemed to deflate. "I guess I'll have to keep saving until I can afford to make the renovations, or I'll have to try to do a little at a time. I have money invested that I could cash in to use. Once I save it, I hate to cash out savings for a luxury, and I don't want to take a loan. I'd rather save toward my goal. I try to not touch my investments once I've made them. The renovations are definitely a luxury, not a necessity, just something I've always wanted to do. I should get a small raise when I become Principal. I'll save all of that, so I hope I won't have to wait too long to save up."

"The renovations sound impressive, Val. I think it would add even more appeal to an already charming place." Jamie pulled her mat a little closer to Val's. "If you have the sketches the carpenter made with you, I'd love to see them."

"Sure, when we go inside." Reaching for Jamie's hand, Val said, "Jamie, I have a favor to ask you. It's a big one."

Raising her eyes to meet Val's, Jamie nodded to indicate she was listening. If she were honest, she would admit her attention was distracted by Val's grip on her hand. She was able to focus better when Val released it.

"I almost forgot to ask you. A few weeks ago, when I scheduled the appointments for this week, I made a mistake about the dates. I thought that this was the week I would be there. I made an appointment for tomorrow, after three, to get a phone installed in the cabin. I don't like being out of reach when I'm there. I compounded it when I agreed to let Jake install the new stove this Thursday. He told me he was going away and this would be his only availability this month. The neighbor who has my extra key is elderly, and I don't want to impose on her to stay with the workers for an extended time. I need someone to be there in case there are any questions."

"Would you like me to do it?"

"Would you?" Val exhaled. "I hate to impose. I know I can't take off from work, so I was hoping you'd be willing to go up there to meet the installers for me?" She shifted on her mat. "I'll give you the key, and you can stay the week and enjoy yourself. If you stay for the week, maybe you'd like to bring the boys up there with you. Even though Robbie attends to their needs, I know you worry about leaving them alone when you're gone for more than a few days."

"I can definitely go meet the installers." Jamie watched Val's body relax. "Staying the week seems most reasonable rather than driving back and forth several times. I'm not doing anything anyway. It pleases me to be able to do you a favor. I promise the boys will be well behaved." She grinned. "I promise to be well behaved, too."

Val's laughter caused warmth in Jamie that spread from her core to the top of her head.

At the end of the day, they locked up the pool, and each showered and changed. They made sandwiches and ate them while reviewing the information Jake had given Val. After discussing the renovations, they retreated to the TV room to see if anything good was on. Deciding nothing was worth watching, Jamie said, "Want to play a game?"

Val tipped her head. "Sure. What do you have in mind?"

"Um...Scrabble?"

Val sighed. "That's good. Get the game out."

Jamie retrieved the now-familiar box from the closet. Spreading pillows on the floor, the pair stretched out next to each other shoulder to shoulder in front of the board, so each could have a view. While Val laid the tiles for her final winning word, she used the top of her bare foot and began to play with Jamie's lower leg. The slow movement of Val's foot against Jamie's skin caused a ticklish sensation that sent spears of heat to Jamie's center. Afraid that she would not be able to control her reaction to Val's touch much longer, Jamie popped up and reached for the game box. "I'll put this away."

Val got the key to the cabin from her purse and gave it to Jamie. At the door, they exchanged a hug. *Is it my imagination that Val just held on to me a little longer than usual?* As Jamie prepared for bed, her mind drifted back over the evening. She still felt aroused, as she had been for most of the evening, if not most of the day. After tonight, she was as sure as she would ever be that Val was attracted to her. She decided that it was time to have the terrifying conversation about their feelings. She was sorry that she hadn't done it before Val left, so she could see Val's expressions and better judge her reactions. She sat on the edge of her chair and waited. Jamie grabbed the phone on the first ring, knowing it would be Val calling to tell her she was home.

Jamie swallowed hard when Val opened with, "Jamie, I'm sorry, did I upset you?"

"No, Val, you didn't upset me." Pausing to bolster her courage, she decided that it was time to tell Val what she was feeling. "I do need to talk to you about something...do you remember when we watched the video, *My Two Loves*?"

"Yes," Val replied, her voice tentative.

"That night, after the program ended, we discussed the show. Remember, I asked you if you could ever love another woman? You surprised me when you replied that you could. You never finished the sentence. You gave me an honest answer. I told you that I wasn't sure. Remember?"

"Yes, vividly. I remember being puzzled by your answer. You're such an accepting person, so loving and giving. Your reply especially surprised me because you have gay friends."

Jamie paused for a moment to take a deep breath before she continued. "Well, I wasn't as honest with you as you were with me, and that's bothered me ever since. You, of all people, deserve better than that from me. I should have responded that I not only could love another woman emotionally and physically, but that I already have. I hope that what I'm telling you will be kept between us and that it won't change your feelings for me. Your opinion of me is important, and I don't know what I would do if you no longer wanted to be my friend."

"Oh, Jamie. I care for you, and what you just told me could never change what I feel for you. I suspect the woman you are speaking of is Bly?"

Jamie blinked. "Yes, it was Bly."

"Um, do you mind if I ask if you're still involved?"

"No, I don't mind." Jamie sensed that Val felt embarrassed asking the question. "You can ask me anything." She decided to explain further without making her ask. "We were involved for a matter of months, and it ended long before she left for California. It was a strange affair, right from the beginning. We knew after a short time together that we would never be able to maintain a love relationship long-term. We had too many differences."

"Were you friends first?"

Jamie sighed in recollection. "Yes. We had a good, strong friendship before the physical attraction happened. For me, it was my first acknowledged sexual attraction and involvement with a woman. I struggled with accepting the new sexual feelings I had for her." Jamie took a deep breath, again wishing she could see Val's face to judge her reaction. "I questioned if I was a lesbian or only attracted to Bly. I entered counseling to help with that, to help resolve feelings about Josh, and a few other issues."

"And were you able to resolve your feelings?"

Jamie cleared her throat. "I don't know. Things happened. She was in need of support and love. I was lonely. I already loved her as a friend and then realized that I was attracted to her physically. We literally negotiated a relationship based on our mutual needs, I guess. I think that if either of us had been at a different place in our lives, the affair would have never happened. When we agreed it was time to let go of the physical part of our relationship, we worked at keeping our friendship. It took us some time, but we ended up with a great friendship." Jamie stopped and held her breath.

"I'm glad you told me, Jamie. I think I understand some things you've said before better now. This is what you were talking about the times you told me you wished you could live your life more honestly, isn't it?"

"Yes, I figured that didn't make sense to you at the time." Jamie paused to give Val time to process everything she'd just revealed. "You haven't interrupted, despite the fact that you must have a million questions racing through your mind."

"Was Bly the only woman you were attracted to?"

"No. She's the only attraction I've ever acted on."

Both women were quiet for a moment. Jamie filled the silence that hung between them. "Okay, Val there's more." Jamie mustered her courage, took a deep breath, and said, "Tonight, a little while ago, during the game, you were playing with my leg. I have to admit to you that the lightest brush or touch of your skin on mine creates such a sexual response in me that I have a hard time being near you sometimes. You see...I've fallen in love with you, and I want more than a friendship with you…much, much more."

Val exhaled the breath she'd been holding for at least a minute. "I love you too, Jamie."

Jamie jumped up from her chair. "You do?"

"Yes, I do. I've loved you for months."

"For months?"

"Yes." Val giggled. "Are you ever going to speak in whole sentences again?"

Jamie stammered, "Um, I'm…I'm working on it. You have to give me a minute to believe that you feel the same way that way I do. No. I can't believe it. You love me? You're sure? I love you."

"Yes, I'm sure. In fact, I've never felt this sure about anything else in my life. So you have to believe me."

There was a moment of quiet. "I feel like I want to laugh and cry at the same time." Jamie gushed. "Not cry, like a sad cry. Maybe a happy cry because I'm so relieved that you feel the same way about me as I feel about you."

"Me too."

Simultaneously, their desire to be together spilled out. "I wish you were here." Their shared laughter was evidence of a joyous sense of freedom to speak their minds.

"You are so lucky I'm not there." Val seemed almost giddy now that the truth was out.

"No, I'd say that I'm unlucky that you are not here. If you were here, I could finally kiss you and hmmm, how should I say this politely?" Jamie paused for emphasis, "I could have my way with you…yup, I'd have my way with you, without a doubt."

"What makes you think I'm that kind of girl?" Val asked, sounding coy.

"Wishful thinking?"

They both laughed so hard their sides hurt.

Val's laughter finally ended with a small groan. "It's all your fault you missed your chance. If you hadn't waited so long to tell me how you feel, you could have found out earlier tonight or, for that matter, long ago. I've been throwing myself at you for weeks."

"Have you? I hadn't noticed," Jamie chuckled. It was such a pleasure to be able to drop her guard and not watch every word.

"What made you wait so long to tell me how you felt? Weren't you sure?"

Growing more serious, Jamie attempted to answer. "I guess, I was afraid of rejection, afraid I would lose your friendship. I had concerns about professional ramifications if you weren't having the same feelings. I'd guess you had to deal with similar feelings."

"I understand exactly what you're saying. I've been worrying about some of the same things too. I've wondered how we can be together without anyone knowing about our relationship." Val fell silent.

"We'll figure it out together. It'll be easier now that we can focus on that one thing." Jamie sat down again. The cats jumped up, one on her lap, the other onto the arm of the chair.

Val changed the course of the conversation. "Remember when I told you about the guy I was pinned to?"

"Yes, I do. What about him?" Jamie scratched the ear of the closest cat.

"Well, he told me, when we broke up, that he thought I was cold. I believe frigid was the word he used. Truth is, I guess he was right, as I was never that attracted to him or either of the other two guys I dated. When my dad became disabled, and my mom as well, I focused my energy on them rather than myself. I haven't dated anyone since my mother became ill. It seemed easier that way."

"Then we started hanging out together," Jamie encouraged.

"Yes, yes we did, and for the first time in my life, I knew a feeling of attraction, of lust, for another person. I'm not even sure what loving another woman entails. I just know I want to be able to hold you and touch you, and to know that you want to be with me the same way." She laughed self-consciously. "Can I say again that I wish you were here?"

Glancing up at the clock to check the time, Jamie considered before rejecting the idea of a quick run over to Val's house. "I know, me too. Look at the time. You have to get up in a few hours. I didn't realize how long we've been talking."

"I know how you feel. I don't want to hang up and let you go. What are we going to do, Jamie? I want to be with you. I hate having to leave you at the end of the day and can't wait to see you after work. I want to have a full relationship with you. If we begin spending overnights with each other, people will talk. Yet, I don't want to live without you."

"I don't know." Jamie wiped her hand across her eyes. "Let's talk more about it next weekend. I don't want you to rush into anything you might regret later. I need you to be sure that you're willing to risk all that we have involved here. The last thing I want is for you to be hurt in any way by loving me."

"I told you that I have no doubts, Jamie. I love and want you. To me, the facts are plain and simple. I love you and I want to be with you. I've waited too long for you. Now that I've found you, how could I pass you by?"

The emotional strain of their revelations, as well as the lateness of the hour, forced them to end the phone call. Each must have said "I love you" three times before they brought themselves to hang up.

Before she slept, Jamie thought about Val's cabin plans. Although she wanted to be with Val, she'd made the promise to her that she'd go to the cabin to meet the phone installer and see to the stove installation. She formulated a plan in her mind and couldn't wait to get started bringing it to fruition.

Chapter Twenty-one

Present Day

THE APPEARANCE OF VAL'S nurse interrupted Jamie's story. "Jamie, Val is awake if you'd like to see her."

Jamie sprang to her feet and hurried to Val's hospital room. Kelly waited by the door, as Jamie tiptoed over to Val's bed.

Val's eyes fluttered open when Jamie placed a soft kiss on her forehead.

"Hey you." Val's voice sounded husky.

"Hi, sweetheart. How are you feeling?"

"Some better." Val cleared her throat. "My foot hurts though."

"I'll go get the nurse to see if she can give you something more for pain."

"You stay with her, Jamie," Kelly called from the door. "I'll get her."

Val squeezed Jamie's hand. "Who's your friend?"

"Your ambulance driver, Kelly. Remember? She's been wonderful to me. She's had me blabbing for hours about how we got together. It's kept me from losing my mind with worry about you. I don't have a car here, so she hung around to give me a ride home."

"We'll have to do something nice for her when I get out of here."

Kelly returned with a nurse they hadn't seen before. She pulled the chain on the fixture above Val's bed, and the light that had glared downward now illuminated the ceiling. "That should be easier on your eyes. What's happening?"

"My foot hurts."

The nurse checked the orders and looked at her watch. "I can give you something to help with that. I'll be right back." She disappeared through the doorway. They could hear her rubber-soled shoes squeaking on the tile floor, as she retreated down the hallway toward the nurses' station.

Waving her hand at Kelly, Jamie said, "Come in and meet my gal."

Kelly approached the bed and treated Val to a sighting of her double dimples.

"Sweetheart, this is Kelly. She's been amazing." Jamie swiveled to face the taller woman. "I don't know how I'll ever thank her."

Val looked in the direction of the woman standing behind her lover. "Thank you for taking care of my honey for me. I hear you kept her from torturing the nurses and doctors."

"It's been my extreme pleasure. I hope you'll feel better soon."

The nurse interrupted their conversation and handed Val two pills in a small, white cup. She helped her wash them down with a sip of water. "These will give you some pain relief and should help you get some more rest." The nurse patted Val's arm. "I'll be back to check on you in a little while." She faced Jamie. "She'll sleep soon. When she drifts off, I suggest you go home and get some rest yourself. You've had a long day. Rounds are tomorrow around eight. If you're here then, you can get an update from the doctor." The nurse made a note on Val's chart. "Please. Go home and get a good night's sleep."

"Yeah, Jamie. What she said. Please." Val's eyes were half closed already.

"Okay, Val. I'll go, if it's what you want. I don't like it."

"I know. Humor me, though. I won't worry about you if I know you're home."

"Okay, sweetheart." Jamie gave Val's lips a quick kiss. "Don't forget."

"Ditto."

Jamie glanced in Kelly's direction. "Ride home?"

"Sure. Follow me." Kelly looked over toward Val. "Hope you feel better soon." Kelly led the way to the doorway.

Jamie stopped to look back at Val, and her eyes filled.

"She's in good hands." Kelly put a warm hand on the smaller woman's shoulder. "Try not to worry. Come on, Jamie."

Jamie brushed her palm over her eyes. "Okay. I don't want to go. For some reason, everyone thinks I'm going to sleep tonight."

"You will. Come on, I'll give you a ride home." Kelly stepped out the door and started for the elevators.

Jamie darted back into the room for a quick kiss. "I'll be back soon, sweetheart," she said to an already sleeping Val. She scurried out the door to catch up with Kelly. "Would you mind swinging through Burger Buddies? I'm hungry."

Kelly glanced at her watch. "Can you eat that stuff this late at night?"

"Sure, can't you?"

"I'll make an exception." Kelly was still trying not to laugh, as she opened the door to her truck and helped Jamie navigate the high step into her vehicle.

"Maybe you'd better do the drive through. That way I only have to get out of this thing once."

Unable to control it any longer, Kelly grinned as she climbed into the driver's side of her truck. "It sounds like you don't like my mode of transportation?"

"I didn't say that. I'm sure if my legs were three times longer, like yours, and my age was thirty years younger, I'd love it."

A laugh burst from deep inside Kelly's chest. "Let's go get you some junk food."

They ordered and received their meals at Burger Buddies. Jamie insisted on paying, and Kelly handed the bag over to her. Jamie set it between her feet so she could handle the drinks. "This smells heavenly. Hurry so the fries aren't cold by the time we get home."

"I will."

They settled in Jamie's kitchen to eat their meals. Kelly asked, "Do you think you have enough steam left in your tank to finish your story? You kind of left me hanging at the good part."

"I've got the steam." Jamie chuckled. "Lord knows after eating this late, I'll be up at least another couple of hours." Jamie took the last bite of her sandwich. "You're not getting details of the hot parts, you know. What I will tell you is how they came to pass."

Kelly almost spit out her soda. "I understand completely. So, tell me what happened. You left off with just having both confessed your love for each other."

A faraway look came into Jamie's eyes. "Well, it was a short night of sleep that night. It was such a relief, to be able to say I love you to her after having to hide my feelings for so long."

Chapter Twenty-two

Reflections

WAKING EARLY, DESPITE A lack of sleep, Jamie got up, showered, and dressed. "Come on boys, let's get you fed. I can't wait to get started. There was a spring to her step, as she gathered the necessary supplies for the cats for the week. She could always get anything she forgot up at the store near the cabin. While the cats ate, she gathered her toolbox, saws, and hammers. She put them into a large bucket and carried everything in the pile to the car and locked it in the trunk.

Back inside the house, she retrieved the carriers for her cats from the basement. The minute she set the carriers on the sofa, the cats disappeared. Jamie began her search for the two wily creatures. They knew something different from normal was afoot. The carrier usually meant vet, and they wanted no part of that. Below the front window was the entertainment center, a favorite hiding spot for them. She leaned over to peer behind the furniture. "Are you guys back here?"

Motion from outside the window caught her attention. Jamie's forehead creased when she saw Val's car wheel to a stop in the driveway. She swiveled to look at the schoolhouse clock. *Hmm. What's up? Val is due at work in a half hour.* Concerned, Jamie opened the door even before Val could knock.

Val flew into Jamie's arms and hugged her close. Val pressed Jamie back against the door, as their lips met in a searing kiss that set them both on fire. I love yous interrupted the passionate kisses which were followed by more passionate kisses. "Wait, wait." Jamie pulled away from Val long enough to ask, "Why are you here? Don't you have to be at work?"

Breathless, Val gasped out, "Yes, I have a meeting in about half an hour that I can't be late for." Val's eyes sparkled. "I couldn't bring myself to let you leave for the cabin without seeing you and at least kissing you."

Tugging Val into her apartment and kicking the door closed. Jamie pulled Val close. Taking her time, she gave Val a slow, deep kiss. As Val relaxed into her, Jamie explored Val's mouth with her tongue. *I'm glad I didn't underestimate the power of those lips.* As they kissed, Jamie slid her thigh between Val's, allowing them to bring pressure to the areas of their bodies aching to be touched. She slid Val's blouse out of her waistband. A mutual groan escaped their lips, as she slid her hands up Val's back to the clasp of her bra. Still kissing, Jamie succeeded in unhooking Val's bra. She slipped her fingers under the garment's band and slid them toward the front of Val's body.

Leaning back, Jamie gave the band a gentle tug. Val's full breasts slid into her eager hands. One ample breast in each palm, Jamie massaged the nipples into erection with her thumbs. They both moaned and stumbled backwards to fall onto the sofa. Jamie broke the kiss long enough to push Val's blouse and bra up, allowing her to access to Val's breasts. She fastened her mouth on one and tugged at the nipple with her mouth and tongue. The aroma of Val's perfume filled her nose, as she enjoyed the sound of Val's obvious pleasure. The throbbing between her own legs was becoming almost painful with need. When the clock chimed, Jamie raised her head and looked into Val's eyes. Curbing her own passion, she exhaled a ragged breath. "Oh God. Are you sure you have to go to your meeting?" Her voice was husky.

Val's eyes snapped open. "My God! My meeting." She took a deep breath and pulled Jamie's head down to her lips for a soft kiss. Val smiled, as she gave Jamie's shoulder a gentle push so she could sit up. "You must promise me to never again start something you cannot finish."

"Agreed." Jamie pulled Val to her feet and helped her hook her bra. "It was more fun unhooking you."

"Umm. True." Val tucked in her wrinkled blouse. "I would never have wanted to miss this visit for any reason." She looked down and brushed her hands over the front of her body in an attempt to smooth out the wrinkles. "Look at me. You'd think I just picked this blouse up off the floor." Val finished straightening her clothing as best she could and leaned into Jamie. She pulled away from their lingering kiss and inhaled a long breath. "We're pretty good at this kissing thing, aren't we?"

"Yes, we are." Jamie brushed her lips against Val's. "I can't believe I'm going to say this." She shook her head and stepped back. "You'd better go if you want to be on time. I'll call you when the phone is working at the cabin to tell you again that I love you."

Val stopped at the door. "I don't want to go."

"I know. I don't want you to leave more." Soft eyes reinforced Jamie's message. "Don't forget that I love you."

"Ditto."

Jamie laughed. "I pour my heart out and say I love you, and that's all I get? Ditto?" She started toward Val.

"Stop." Val placed her palm on Jamie's chest. "Don't come one step closer. It's all I can do to force myself to leave you as it is." Before Val turned to leave, she slid her hand down Jamie's chest and tweaked her nipple. "I'll never forget. I love you, too."

As Val got in her car, Jamie watched from the door, her heart so full she feared it would burst. After the taillights disappeared, she went into her bedroom to put on dry underwear. Everything was ready for her trip. She collected the now visible cats and placed them in their carriers.

"Okay boys. How would you like a trip to the country?" The boys gave her a noncommittal glare from behind the bars of the carrier doors.

Last-minute details were the only thing remaining. Jamie left a short note for Robbie, reminding him to keep an eye on the pool in her absence. She added a reminder that the cats were with her and not to worry when he found them missing.

In their carriers, the cats howled their disapproval of the journey. For about the first five miles of the trip, Jamie thought she might need to reconsider her decision to bring them. It was their good fortune that they settled down and went to sleep before she reversed direction and returned them to home.

Twenty minutes later, Jamie looked over at the now-sleeping cats. "You big fakers." She cast them a disapproving look. "I think you'd better get used to this trip. And when you wake up, we're going to have a chat about your best behavior."

Being alone made the trip seem longer than usual, even though it took the standard amount of time. She arrived at the cabin just before ten. The boys were awake and curious, so she unloaded them first and secured them in the bathroom until she'd finished unloading the car.

By the time the car was empty, she could hear the boys were protesting their confinement and meowing their displeasure with being isolated. She opened the door to allow her feline companions freedom to explore their new environment. While they sniffed their way around the house, she looked for the best place for their litter pan. The now-filled litter pan found a home in the large walk-in closet where the washer and dryer were. The cats came when she called them. In turn, she placed each in the pan so they would know where to find the proper place for their personal business. She would place them in there several more times in the next hour to be sure they knew where it was. While they checked things out, she did some investigation of her own.

She found the ladder under the back porch of the house and carried it inside and propped it against the loft wall. She climbed up and examined the paneling that covered the loft. It was obvious to her that Val's father had planned for the loft closure to be temporary. Jamie retrieved her hammer and pry bar from the collection of tools near the door. After repositioning the ladder, she gently pried off the molding and the first piece of paneling. The fact that the board was only tacked in place supported Jamie's theory that Val's father had intended to reopen the loft someday. By removing three more boards, she opened a space wide enough to fit through. The area was too dark for her to be able to see much. She carried the ladder back outside and propped it against the house. With slow and careful steps, she climbed to investigate the shuttered loft window. With a little effort, the shutters groaned and swung back on rusty hinges. She pressed her nose against the large window covered with many years of accumulated dust and peered in. No good...too dirty.

Jamie traveled back down the ladder and searched the kitchen. Armed with the bucket, sponges, and spray window cleaner that she found there, she made short work of washing the accumulated grime from the glass. Cupping her hands to her eyes, she again pressed her nose to the window glass. Inside she could see what looked like piles of lumber in the dim light.

Retracing her steps, she returned to the place where she'd removed the loft's paneling. She carried the bucket with her as she squeezed through the opening she'd made and entered the loft. Thanks to the light from the recently washed window, she was better able to see the contents. *Oh boy, sweetheart. Your dad saved you a ton of money.* Her smile widened, as she examined the space.

Val's father had stored the safety railing, stairs, and banister for use again at a future date. She rubbed her hands together at her discovery. *Pocket change should be enough to buy anything else I need to open this loft.* Jamie did a little happy dance. She washed the inside of the window to let in more light and did a further inspection of the neatly stacked items. Everything seemed to still be sound. *All this stuff needs is a good cleaning. Then I can paint or varnish.* Now that she was able to stand on the floor of the loft, removing the remaining paneling was an easy task. Jamie worked with care. She wanted to save the paneling for another project she had in mind, so she piled the boards along the wall of the loft.

Around three fifteen, Frank, the phone installer arrived to connect and install the phones. Jamie imposed on him to help her slide the stairs from the loft to the living room floor. There was a notch on the side rails of the steps, designed to rest against the floor of the loft. It would be an easy job to screw them in place. She imposed further and asked him to help her with the paneling. Standing in the loft, she handed the boards down to the phone installer who stacked them for her in the living room. When he refused her offer to pay him, she thanked the friendly man with an ice-cold soft drink. While they drank their sodas, they admired their handiwork.

After Frank left, Jamie tested the phone by calling Val at work. "Is this my wrinkled princess?"

"Hush. Tell me the number and I'll call you when I get home." It was obvious that Val wasn't free to talk. Following a short pause, she did say, "Don't forget."

"Forget what?" Jamie's smile spread wider, as she tried not to laugh.

"You know what."

"Oh that what." Jamie put her hand on her heart. "Yes, I know that, and I definitely won't forget. Call me later tonight, after dinner. I love you."

"Ditto," Val was chuckling, as she disconnected.

Jamie ate a quick sandwich and returned to her project. Now that the stairway and paneling were out of the way, she could better explore the second level. In one corner, she found a coffee can filled with the lag bolts and screws needed to refasten the stairway. *I hope the screws for the railing and banister are in here too.* Still using the ladder, she descended to retrieve her toolbox. Thanks to her power screwdriver, reattaching the stairs was a short job. With the stairs now screwed in place, work would go faster.

Piece by piece, she carried the paneling out and stacked it against the house. Tomorrow, she would buy a tarp to keep the weather off.

Cooling temperatures were forecast for the next couple of days. Judging from the feel of the air, rain would come as well, sooner rather than later.

Tired from her day's exertion, Jamie quit work a little after seven. She leaned against the wall in the living room and admired her achievements of the day. Val's plan was to center the new wood stove between the two bookcases. Jamie stood near the bookcases and peered up into the loft. Despite the addition of the narrow stairway against the opposite wall, she thought that the living room appeared larger. The open loft added height and light to the room it overlooked. Jamie gave a satisfied nod. *I can't wait to see how pleased Val will be with the results.*

By now, the cats were comfortable with, maybe even enjoying, their new environment. She checked to be sure they'd found the litter, scooped, and then went to the kitchen to feed them. She showered and then sat on the sofa enjoying some time playing with the cats and their new toys she'd brought with them.

The ringing phone made everyone jump. Jamie hurried to answer, knowing it would be Val. They talked until bedtime, finally exhausting their supply of news. Jamie didn't mention her labors. Instead, she described the boys' adjustment to their new digs. "They've taken over already and act like they've lived here forever." She looked at the cats curled up next to her. "And they've been on their best behavior."

Val's voice lowered. "Have you been on your best behavior, too?"

"I sure have. Frank wasn't my type at all. He had thin lips."

"What do you mean?"

"I guess I never told you how much I love your mouth. I remember forcing myself not to stare at it, wondering how it would feel to have your luscious lips against mine." Jamie licked her lips, as she recalled their morning kisses. "So, you see, Frank wasn't my type, because he lacked a mouth like yours." Val's laughter made Jamie's heart sing.

"Well, if all it takes is a plush pair of lips, I may have to reconsider this..."

"No! There's nothing to worry about. You're stuck with me now. I can't wait for Friday. I wish you could get out of work right now."

"Me too. You know how it is. End of the school year, last-minute hustle."

"I do. It doesn't stop me from wishing though." One of the cats got up and curled in Jamie's lap. She petted his soft fur. "I'm going to focus on the positives. You can travel light. You won't need clothes for the full two weeks of vacation. I have no plans of ever letting you out of bed."

"Won't you grow weak from hunger?"

"Nope. I'll be feasting on you. We'll live on love."

The two women talked away the evening. "It's so hard to let you go." Val yawned. "I have to get to sleep, or I'll be good for nothing tomorrow. Don't forget, I love you."

"I won't. I think of you every minute, because I love you, too." Jamie paused. "Now, see how it's supposed to be done?"

A melodic burst of laughter from Val warmed Jamie from her head to her toes. "I do. Sometimes we can't speak freely, so the other way works, too." Val yawned again. "Okay let's try it again. I love you."

"Ditto."

They were both laughing when they hung up. The next morning, the light coming through the window awakened Jamie. She got up and hurried to complete her morning rituals, feed the cats, and scoop. The boys were already ensconced on the porch, waiting for the sunspot to appear. Following a quick breakfast of juice and a stale roll that was fresh when she'd brought them with her, she headed for the store to buy food for the next few days. Handing over her money, she asked the clerk for directions to the hardware store. Although small, it was well equipped. Before long, she had found the pulley, rope, gloves, and other supplies she needed.

After making two trips from the car to the cabin, she stored the food in the kitchen. At last, she was ready to begin the tasks for the day. Her first job was the most difficult. She had to secure the pulley and rope to the ceiling. Using them, she lowered the banister and railing to the floor of the living room. After she cleaned up the stairs, she took the banister and railing out to the back yard. Following a thorough cleaning and a light sanding, she gave a coat of varnish to the soft patina of the old oak. She left them to dry, gleaming in the sun, and returned to the house for lunch. She called Val and chatted for a few minutes. Each was counting the minutes until Friday.

Construction was at a standstill until the railing and banister were dry, so Jamie set about cleaning the loft. By the end of the day, she had everything glistening. She carried in the banister and railing, and leaned them against the wall. Leaning over backwards, she stretched out her back muscles and looked up at the loft. *Nah. I think I'll wait until tomorrow to install them.*

With a cold beer in hand, she went out on the porch to enjoy the sunset while she waited for Val's call. She grabbed the phone before the end of the first ring. "Hey there. How was your day?"

Val explained that she was keeping busy at work and was hoping to finish up everything before vacation. "I wish I could be there with you."

"I wish it more."

"That's impossible. You have no way of knowing how much I'm wishing it." Val's voice thickened. "I've waited for you all my life. It's not fair that now that I found you, I can't be with you."

"You tempt me to jump in the car and come home to you."

"Um...that sounds so good. It's not sensible though. Tomorrow, the stove comes and you'll be busy with that. I'm almost finished here at school. Then we'll have two glorious weeks together."

"You're making me ache. I love you so much." Jamie sighed.

They lingered, talking sweet nothings for another hour before hanging up.

Thursday morning, Jamie got up early and worked to install the glistening banister. She took a moment to admire the workmanship in the old wood and run her hand over the smooth, polished surface. She gave a satisfied nod of approval.

Using the rope and pulley, she struggled to get the railing up the stairs. It was heavy and awkward. With patience, one step at a time, she finally managed to get it to the loft just as Jake arrived to install the stove. "Holy crap, woman! Look at what you've done. I thought I was at the wrong house.

"You must be Jake. I'm Jamie, a friend of Val's."

"Yep. Jake." He tipped his hat. "I think the old wood gives the place a better feel than new construction would have."

"I think Val will like it. It looks like it was always here." Jamie risked asking a favor.

Jake willingly agreed to hold the railing steady while Jamie anchored it in a couple of places.

Jamie firmed up two bolts fully and finger tightened the others. "That should hold it until I can get the others cranked down."

While Jake installed the new stove, Jamie worked in the loft to finish the railing. Jake impressed Jamie with how complimentary he'd been of the work she was doing. He seemed not the least bit upset by the missed opportunity to do the job himself.

"I'm about finished down here." Jake yelled to Jamie. "You need anything else done that I can help you with?"

"Now that you offer, there is one thing. It'll be a lot easier if you help me with the bed."

Together they carried the double bed from the bedroom up the steps to the loft. She offered Jake something to drink. "Can't. Gotta run. Next time. Hope you like the stove. Let me know if you need anything else. I left the directions there. You shouldn't have any trouble, though. It works pretty much the same as the old one. It's just bigger and allows you to see the flames." He touched the brim of his hat, before he hurried out the front door.

Tired, Jamie sat down on the top step to admire her handiwork. The new stove was beautiful, dark charcoal in color with brass accents and double-glass doors. *Lovely.*

She grabbed a quick bite, found the vacuum, and set about removing the dust that covered her work area. While she was at it, she gave a quick once over to the rest of the house and restored order to the living room. Despite the fact that she hated to dust, she made quick work of it, whistling her favorite Beatles tune as she completed her task.

She set about looking for furnishings for the upstairs bedroom. A small table not in use in the corner of the porch found a new location next to the bed as a night table. A borrowed lamp from the downstairs bedroom provided the perfect amount of light in the loft. She tucked in the sheets and smoothed the spread into place. Her hand lingered, as her mind's eye pictured Val waiting for her there. The thought alone made her wet.

The boys left the porch and joined her in the living room once she was done working for the day. Shrugging her shoulders against the chill in the air, she wrapped her arms in front of her as she checked the thermometer. "Brr, boys. The temperature is at least eight or nine degrees lower than it was at noontime." The falling temperature and cool breeze blowing over the surface of the lake brought a damp chill to the house. Jamie shivered again and closed the windows to the cool rain just starting to fall. She spoke to her feline companions. "It's getting a bit chilly. Maybe later, we'll try the new stove. Come on, time for dinner." She fed the cats and grabbed a bite of food for herself.

Around seven thirty, Jamie tried to call Val and still got no answer. Following her nice hot shower, she tried the phone again. Her brows furrowed, as she glanced at the clock. *Where is she? Maybe she stayed late at work to finish up a few things.* Jamie turned on the TV to help pass the time. The rain was coming down in earnest now. She rubbed her arms trying to warm up and went to the bedroom to get a cozy fleece sweatshirt. Reconsidering, she said, "What do you think, boys...shall we try out a small load of wood in the new stove to see how it works?"

With tinder from the tinderbox, matches, and some paper, she made short work of bringing a small blaze to life in the new stove. The door closed with a solid clang, as Jamie turned the handle and sealed the fire inside. Using the vent below the door, she fiddled with it to adjust the flame until she eventually got the fire picture perfect. "There you go, boys. Good job, even if I do say so myself." She settled on the sofa, a cat on each side, and they watched the flames dance in the stove. The blower kicked in as the stove heated up, spreading the stove's warmth throughout the cabin.

Glancing over her shoulder, she looked up into the loft. The stove was in the perfect location. Val would have her wish of being able to lie in bed and watch the fire through the glass of the stove's doors. The cats jumped down and cautiously approached the fire. They hunkered down at a safe distance and tucked their feet under their chests, as their eyes closed in appreciation of the radiating heat. She reached for the phone and rang Val again with no response. *Where could she be?* Jamie stretched out on the sofa to enjoy the fire and think about how much she wished Val was there with her.

Chapter Twenty-three

Reflections

JAMIE ENJOYED WATCHING THE cats inch closer, as they became more comfortable with the stove. She chuckled that a newly found confidence wavered only once when a log popped. Jamie was glad they had a healthy respect for the hot metal of the device. She stacked two more logs on the bed of glowing embers and closed the door on the flames.

During the last hour, the tempo of the rain had steadily increased. At first, because of the noise the rain made on the roof, she wasn't sure that the sound she heard was someone knocking at the door. The pounding became louder. *Who would be visiting at this hour?* As she approached the door, Jamie flipped on the light and peered out into the downpour. There stood a drenched Val impatiently waiting for Jamie to open up. Anxious fingers fumbled with the lock and eventually met with success. A soaking wet Val literally threw herself into Jamie's welcoming arms, and their lips met in a long, wet kiss.

"You're soaked." Jamie pulled the shivering woman tight and buried her nose in Val's neck, inhaling her scent. "I can't believe you're really here. Thought you were coming up on Saturday. I was missing you so much just now and was worried after calling so many times with no answer." Closing the door, she led the not-quite-dripping Val to stand in front of the stove to warm herself in front of the fire. They stood there holding each other as they talked.

"Oh, Jamie, I couldn't wait another day to see you." Val looked up into Jamie's eyes and placed a soft kiss on her lips. "I worked late every night this week to finish up. I got permission to take one of my Personal Leave days and left after work today. The drive was worth every miserable minute now that I'm here with you. I'm sure..."

Val stopped in midsentence when she noticed the stairs. Then she raised her eyes to the peak of the roof, taking in all the changes Jamie had made to the loft. For a few seconds she just stood there, unable to speak until the words tumbled out all at once. "Jamie, how? What...how did you do this all by yourself?" Approaching the stairs, she put her hand on the banister and ran her hands over the smooth, polished surface. "Is it okay to go up?"

Nodding to Val that it was safe, Jamie followed her up the stairs to the loft. Val stood in the middle of the room looking around. Her jaw hung open as she took in the changes. She crossed to the safety rail and peered down into the living room. "I can't believe it. It looks just like it did when I was a little girl. How, Jamie? Where did you get all of this?"

Jamie took a seat on the bed and watched the woman she loved. Her smile grew, as she observed Val caress the room with her eyes. "I found the stairs and railings behind the paneling. I'm so glad you approve of the changes."

"Approve? That has to be the understatement of a lifetime." Val twirled around one more time to be sure she hadn't missed anything.

Jamie sat on the bed and enjoyed watching Val as she checked out the newly opened space in her cabin. "Your friend Jake didn't know all this stuff was up here, so the entire cost was less than thirty bucks for supplies, instead of the enormous bill for materials he gave you." She grinned. "The work was free, a labor of love."

Val approached Jamie. Still standing, she straddled Jamie's legs and leaned over to place a soft kiss on each of Jamie's cheeks, before she kissed her on the lips. "Thank you." Val's eyes were bright and slightly moist.

Jamie encircled Val's waist with her arms. She fell back onto the bed and pulled Val forward on top of her. They simultaneously exhaled a long slow breath at the pleasure of finally being together without the need to hold back their feelings. Their mouths sought each other, and their kisses grew deeper and more demanding. As much as Jamie wanted to strip them both naked and find release for her arousal, she wanted to be sure that she savored every minute of this first joining. They kissed, taking time to explore each other's mouths with their tongues. As their need for each other built, Jamie rolled them so that they were next to each other, pushed her leg between Val's, and felt her strain against her thigh.

One by one, she released each button on Val's blouse, stopping to kiss the newly exposed skin as each button opened to her touch. The sweet torture ended, as she encircled Val's naval with her tongue then plunged it into the sensitive area, drawing a groan of pleasure from her partner. The damp blouse stuck to Val's shoulder, as Jamie helped release her arm from the sleeve and shrug the garment free. Val made eye contact with Jamie. "I love you more than you will ever know."

Jamie looked deeply into Val's eyes before she replied, "I love you too."

Val slipped Jamie's sweatshirt over her head. "No bra?"

"I took my shower already."

Val touched her finger to Jamie's lips. She traced it down over her chin to her breastbone. Inch by inch, she slid her finger across Jamie's breast, her destination the peak. As she approached the nipple, it contracted, becoming erect and sensitive.

Jamie failed to breathe as she watched, anticipating contact from Val's mouth. Jamie's breath hitched as their eyes met. Val extended her tongue, barely making contact with the wanting nipple. Jamie arched her back, pushing up in an effort to increase the contact. Her moan brought Val's eager mouth down in full contact with the sensitive nipple. Val suckled Jamie's breast, teasing it with her tongue.

While Val made love to Jamie's breast, Jamie circled an arm around her lover and unhooked Val's bra. "Off," Jamie whispered. Once Val shrugged free of the restricting covering, Jamie pulled her closer and used her own breast to stimulate Val's. Nipple brushing erect nipple caused Val to sigh. "Mm. You feel so good."

Jamie took control. As she continued to stimulate Val's breasts, she felt Val begin to move her hips as she strained against Jamie's leg. Leaning back slightly, Jamie brushed her fingers up Val's arm and journeyed up her body to stroke Val's forehead. She gently kissed each brow and eyelid then returned to Val's lips. She knew they were both eager for more, but she wanted to prolong Val's pleasure for as long as possible. Millimeter by millimeter, Jamie trailed her fingers over Val's chest teasing each nipple in turn. She pushed Val's breasts together so that she could tongue them simultaneously.

"Jamie, I want you so much," murmured Val as she reached for the button on her jeans.

"No." She pushed Val's hand away. "That's my job." Jamie reached around Val and ran her fingernails slowly from her shoulder to her waist several times, before slipping a finger beneath the waistband of the jeans. Her thumb slid playfully toward the snap then withdrew to focus on another part of Val's responsive body. Replacing her thumb with her tongue to stimulate the swollen nipple, Jamie trailed down Val's stomach to, at last, release the button on her jeans. Grasping the zipper, she lowered it a tooth at a time until Val, eager to be free of the jeans, pushed Jamie's hand aside and slid the jeans over her hips and onto the floor. She grasped the waistband of Jamie's sweatpants and stripped them from her.

Naked, after months of waiting, the two finally touched body-to-body and skin-to-skin for the first time. Val whispered, "Oh, Jamie." Her eyes closed, as she shivered against her lover. "This is heaven. I've never felt like this before."

"I know. Me either." They remained unmoving, pressed together, savoring the sensations coursing through their bodies. Jamie slid her thigh between Val's legs and could feel her silky moisture as Val pressed down and began to move against her.

"I never imagined being with you this way would feel like this," breathed Val, as she tried to press harder against Jamie's leg.

Jamie was equally breathless. "The best is yet to come, my love." Not wanting Val to come just yet, Jamie withdrew her thigh and began to trace small, light circles down the length of Val's torso, using just one finger. As she reached Val's waist, she slid a palm over Val's hip and reached as far down her leg as she could before retracing the path up to Val's breast, using the light touch of her nails to stimulate Val's skin. Her touch raised goose bumps as well as a sigh of pleasure. She rolled Val on her back and used her tongue, her hands, and her lips to tease Val to an increasingly higher level of excitement. Starting with her palm on Val's stomach, she slowly stroked her way downward and across the sensitive area of Val's inner thigh. She let her finger brush over Val's sensitive clitoris, as she stroked her way down and then ever so slowly retraced her journey upward again.

Nearly frenzied, Val grabbed Jamie's wrist, trying to increase the pressure as Jamie's hand touched her center. She clutched her thighs together to trap it in place. "Oh God, please," she begged. "Touch me."

Jamie kissed Val deeply, as she began to honor Val's request. Using her knee, she gently spread her lover's legs to gain better access to the area Val was begging for her to touch. As Val opened for her, she teased again before slowly spreading the slippery opening to enter Val with one finger. The sensation nearly sent both of them over the edge.

Wanting to please Jamie too, Val slid her hand under Jamie, between her legs, to cup Jamie's sex with her fingers. Not wanting to come yet, Jamie closed her thighs together so Val couldn't move. "Not yet," she whispered. Jamie continued to slowly stroke in and out, fanning their mutual excitement with each stroke. With Val completely aroused and begging, she withdrew and spread some of the moisture on her fingers over Val's clit to make the stimulation there softer. She moved downward and slipped in first one finger, then added a second. As she stroked in and out, she brushed Val's clit with her thumb.

"Faster," Val gasped. The scent of their mutual arousal filled the air around them.

Judging by Val's breathing and hip movement meeting Jamie's thrusts, Jamie figured Val was close. She relaxed her own thighs to free the grip she had on Val's hand, thus allowing Val access to stimulate her. "Now," she gasped, as she pressed down on Val's hand. It only took a few strokes. Neither able to hold on any longer, they climaxed together with loud moans, as pleasure washed over them.

Val pulled Jamie over on top of her and circled her with her arms. Together they rested until their breathing returned to normal. "I never knew it could feel like this," sighed Val. She began to explore Jamie's body, gaining confidence as Jamie responded to her touch. Touching, kissing, and teasing Jamie into arousal again, Val entered Jamie, bringing her to an intense climax. Val pressed her core against Jamie's thigh until she, too, moaned in release.

Both spent, they cuddled together, limbs entwined. "This is where I belong. You feel like coming home," whispered Jamie, as she kissed Val softly.

"I know what you mean. How can something that feels so right to us be…"

"Shh. Let's not worry about what others think right now." She pulled Val close. Soon, lying naked in each other's arms, they drifted off to sleep.

Jamie awoke a few hours later and slipped from bed. She quietly went downstairs to lock the door, turn off the lights, and check the stove. The fire was nearly out and the blower had automatically turned off. Jamie stirred the embers and positioned two smaller logs and a larger one on the coals and then blew. She grinned when the flames shot through the dry wood and started them on fire. With a final poke to the wood, she gave a satisfied smile, hung the fire iron from its hook on the wall, and returned to bed. As she slipped beneath the covers and snuggled against her toasty-warm lover, Val pulled her close.

"You're cold." Val wrapped a leg around Jamie.

"Yes, and you're toasty warm. I guess we finally figured how to warm you up."

Now fully awake, Val laughed. "I guess so. Have I told you yet today that I love you?"

"I think you've been quite remiss," Jamie teased.

Val snuggled closer and rested her head on Jamie's shoulder. She rested her hand on Jamie's hip, and then slid up over increasingly familiar territory to rest it on Jamie's breast. "In all the times I've thought about loving you, I never imagined it would be this good."

Jamie placed a soft kiss on Val's lips. "By the way, whoever that clod was who told you that you were frigid obviously didn't know what he was talking about."

Val giggled and nuzzled her face into the crook of Jamie's neck. "I guess we have completely proven him wrong."

"Actually, he has been wrong several times now." They both laughed with the sheer happiness of the light conversation and the comfort of being together. Only half serious, Jamie rolled on top of Val, "Want to prove him wrong again?"

"Mm. You feel so good." Val ran her fingernails lightly over Jamie's back. "I used to wonder what it would be like to be close to you this way. I couldn't imagine how two women's bodies would fit together, but they do. It's as if our bodies were designed to be held against each other. I think this is my favorite position with you, just lying here fitting together."

They took their time making love again. They explored, learning the secret places that brought the most excitement and satisfaction to the other, enjoying equal pleasure in touching and being touched, giving and receiving.

The next morning, Val awoke slowly. Jamie watched her growing awareness that she was being studied. Val blushed. "Did we really make love most of the night?"

"We did. Sorry?"

"Never. I love you."

"Ditto," Jamie said with a smile.

Now fully awake, Val giggled. "You're bad. You know, I thought you'd never get the idea that I was attracted to you. You were so dense."

Propping herself up on one elbow, Jamie looked down at Val. "I beg your pardon?"

Val traced her finger down Jamie's forearm. "Well, you were. Every time I would say something you'd either walk away or make a joke out of it."

"Give me one example," challenged Jamie.

Val faked a pensive look. "Let me see, where to begin."

"See, I knew you couldn't think of one." Jamie laughed with delight.

"Don't be too sure of yourself. What about the time I told you to make me an offer I couldn't refuse?" Val raised her eyebrow and smirked. "You said you weren't feeling very creative. Ha."

"Okay, so you can name one. Big deal. Bet you can't think of another."

"What about the time I said I wouldn't be able to keep warm without you?"

"Yeah, I remember that. It was on the school phone. You totally freaked me out until I assumed you were referring to my superior fire making abilities, not to my natural climate control." By now both women were grinning. "I have an idea," said Jamie.

"I'm sure you do. But if I don't get to the bathroom, I might explode. Anyway, you need to get me some sustenance. Or are you planning to keep me a prisoner up here all day?"

"Oh no, the honeymoon is over already." Jamie tossed the covers off of them.

"Not on your life. I think you'll enjoy what I have in mind later."

"Okay, let's go." Jamie jumped up. Together they made the bed after joking it might be worth just leaving it unmade, because it might not be too long before they found themselves back in it.

Chapter Twenty-four

Reflections

THE TWO WOMEN DESCENDED the stairs then took turns in the bathroom. Over breakfast, they continued their discussion about what each had been thinking and feeling while their relationship developed.

Jamie stood up and stretched. "Time for my shower, I think. I need to prepare for the activity you promised me upstairs."

"I have something in mind you'll like. Meet me out back."

The air, scrubbed clean by the night's rain, was starting to warm, and the lake glistened beneath the bright sun. Jamie stood behind the cabin, waiting for Val who soon emerged carrying a bar of soap and two towels. Behind the house was an enclosure Jamie had never paid any attention to. "What's in here?"

Val reached out and tugged on the door to reveal an outdoor shower.

"I thought this was some sort of storage area."

Grabbing Jamie's arm, Val stepped inside pulling Jamie in with her. The enclosure was roomy enough for both women. They stripped quickly. Val adjusted the water, and soon they were soaping each other's bodies. Warm water, cool air, and soapy bodies added up to an erotic morning shower for the new couple. "Honeymoon still going okay for you?" Val whispered, as she reached between Jamie's legs and made her come.

Her knees still weak, a quick kiss was all Jamie managed before dropping her head to Val's shoulder. "You don't hear me complaining."

Refreshed by their showers, the two went inside to dress and discuss what they wanted to do with their day. Jamie suggested they build some bookshelves for the first-floor bedroom, now known as the office. "We have two whole weeks to work and play. We could get started building what you want in there this morning then later, when it's warmer, we could spend some time at the lake."

"I hate to see you work so hard." Val took Jamie's hand in her own and brought it to her lips. "If it's what you want to do though, that sounds fine. It could be fun. Let's do that." Val ran her fingers from Jamie's wrist to her fingertip. "Before, I used to watch your hands when you talked. You have such expressive hands. They're very feminine and yet capable of such heavy and skilled work. I used to marvel that you could do carpentry work and still not have dirty or broken nails. Your hands are strong, then so gentle. They can excite me with just the simplest touch."

"You're embarrassing me." Jamie gave Val's hand a gentle squeeze.

"You'd better get used to it, I'm a hopeless romantic."

The weather warmed up. Over the next several days, work on the bookcases progressed, despite the interruptions for kisses, caresses, and love making. Following a trip to the store for paint and other supplies, they transformed the pile of old paneling into bookshelves. They added a small desk between the two sets of shelves they built. Two butterfly chairs, placed on either side of the window, created a wonderful place to read and work. Converting the single bed into a day bed was as simple as a trip to the store. They added a bright cover and some throw pillows in a contrasting color. While there, Val made a quick run to a used bookstore to buy a good supply of paperbacks neither had read to begin filling up the shelves. As they spent time at the lake, they began to collect little mementos of their walks. Their special little objects soon found a home on one of the newly built shelves.

One night, after dinner, they were sitting on the deck enjoying the sunset over the mountains. The cats were curled up on the sofa next to them.

"Happy?" asked Jamie.

"Never been happier."

"It's warm. If we were home now, we could go skinny dipping in my pool." Jamie wriggled her eyebrows.

A devilish glint appeared in Val's eyes. "Why not do it here? There aren't many people around. The people closest to us aren't here this week. It's dark, and this part of the lake is relatively private anyway. It's a little riskier than at the pool." Her gaze drifted toward the lake, paused, and then returned to Jamie. "I'm game if you are."

"You are the number one risk taker," laughed Jamie. "You're on." Once in the water, she teased her partner. "I can see the headlines now, *School Principal Caught Naked with Fellow Teacher*."

Sliding her fingers between Jamie's legs, Val grinned. "Um...from what I can feel, you're no fellow."

The two laughed. It didn't take long before they became serious about what they were doing, and they sank lower beneath the surface. The cool water against their heated bodies created new sensations for the lovers. Huddled closer into Jamie's arms, Val shivered.

"Although I'd like to take credit for that, I don't think I was responsible."

Val kissed Jamie on the nose. "Afraid not. I'm freezing." Her teeth chattered together to prove her point.

"Come on. Let's take a hot shower and get in bed. I'll warm you up, and we can have an early night." They returned to the cabin, again showered together in the outdoor shower, and fell asleep in each other's arms.

The vacation days passed all too soon. One night, while lying in bed, they began to discuss the fact that their idyllic retreat would be ending in a couple of days.

Val groaned. "I can't believe our vacation is almost over. I feel so sad. It wouldn't take much to make me cry."

"I know, we'll have other weekends..."

"Not like this past couple of weeks, though. Soon we'll both be returning to work." Val rested her head on Jamie's shoulder. "This is my second favorite position. I hate to think this is our last night sleeping together. I've never been able to sleep with anyone else in the same room, and now I don't know how I'll sleep without you next to me."

"What about me? I thought I had nothing left to give to a relationship. Now I awaken everyday filled with such happiness that I want to spend the rest of my life just loving you. Each day we spend together makes us seem so right." Jamie nuzzled into Val's hair, enjoying the scent of her lover. "How did you come to realize that you loved me?"

Val exhaled with a chuckle. "I don't know, it just came to me one day. I realized that I couldn't wait to get home from school, take my shower, and either call you or have you call me. I could barely contain myself until we got together. When did you first know?"

Jamie tried to think back to the first time she got a rush from touching Val, or when she first recognized the attraction. "I can't pinpoint an exact time. I remember telling Bly that it was too bad you were straight. I know there was a time in the car when our arms touched and you didn't move away. That night, I considered the possibility that you might be attracted to me. I always managed to convince myself that it was only wishful thinking on my part. I've always had a difficult time dealing with the fact that I'm attracted to women. Was it hard for you to reconcile your feelings for me?"

"No. I guess it's a little surprising that it wasn't." Val switched positions, and propped her head on her hand. With her left hand, she traced circles across Jamie's naked belly and breasts. "I've been unmoved by anyone for so long that it didn't take long for me to recognize that I felt attracted to you. I think the day you gave the curriculum report for your building is when I first recognized my feelings as love. I remember that I wasn't able to look at you while you spoke. I feared that everyone in the room would know what was in my heart. I thought it had to be imprinted on my forehead or something. I was more concerned that you'd be horrified and that I would lose your friendship if you knew what I was feeling about you. I think I worried less than you did about school or society and what it perceives to be right or wrong. I guess, because I had to wait so long to find the person for me, when you finally came along, I didn't care that you happened to be a woman. Like you said, love is love." She leaned over and kissed Jamie's lips. "I didn't know what to expect from the relationship at all. In the beginning, I didn't even give much thought to where it would lead or what we would do in bed. I just knew I wanted to be with you, to be close to you, physically. Most of the time, I was busy wondering how I was going to get you to indicate what, if anything, you were feeling for me."

"I worried about everything. The thing with Coach being accused scared the spit out of me. I was afraid it would end in a witch hunt for anyone else who might be gay." Jamie pulled Val closer. "I'm usually more of an optimist than you are. I'd say you're much more of a pragmatist than I am. And less of a worrier."

Val shook her head. "No. I don't think it's that I worry less than you do. I think we worry about different things. While you were worrying about what society would think of our love, I worried about whether you would love me back."

Jamie fell quiet for a moment. "Now that you know I love you, do you think things will change when we go back home? Will you start to worry more about what people will think of us if they find out? Will you stop wanting to be my lover because of the pressure and fear about someone discovering our relationship?"

"My biggest concern is that when we go back tomorrow, we won't be able to be together like this until next weekend. Now that we've become lovers, I do wonder if others will suspect. If we continue to spend every weekend alone together, will we attract attention?" Val rubbed her ear. "I can't think of a way that we can stay together without people noticing either your car at my house or vice versa. At least, coming here is less obvious. At home, there's no reason for us to be staying over. Know what I mean?" A deep ridge appeared between Val's eyebrows as she sighed.

Jamie smoothed the frown from Val's brow with her fingertips. "I know, I've been thinking about that, too. Well, let's not worry about it right now and waste the last night we have together. I have better things in mind for us to do." Jamie began kissing her way down Val's body.

"Mmm," sighed Val. "I do like the way you think."

Chapter Twenty-five

Reflections

PACKING ON SUNDAY AFTERNOON depressed both women. Soon, they had everything loaded into the cars except the boys who seemed more reluctant than anyone to leave. The lovers stood in the cabin, arms wrapped around each other. Val looked up at the loft. "I can't believe how much work you did here. It's so wonderful, I hate to leave."

Jamie exhaled a long sigh. "Me too." She wrapped her arms around her lover and snuggled her nose into her neck. They remained unmoving for a long time.

Jamie put her head up and swallowed hard. "I guess we have to do this."

They added the cat carriers filled with the protesting felines to Jamie's car. Responding to the cats, Jamie said, "I don't blame you one bit for crying. You won't get any arguments from us."

Val and Jamie returned to the cabin to make a final check of the doors and windows, and to be sure they hadn't forgotten anything. They knew there were decisions to be made. Most of the day, they'd tried to come up with possible solutions to their problem. How could they be together without attracting the attention of their school community? They even made a written list of plausible solutions as well as implausible ones.

"Hey do you remember that TV show about two police officers, one male and one female?" Jamie scratched her head. "It was called *MacGruder and Loud*. Precinct rules prohibited work partners from being romantically involved. For sure, they couldn't live together. Their solution was two apartments, one next to the other. They opened a hole between the two apartments and built a bookcase on each side that covered the opening. With the bookcases open, they could go between the apartments without anyone seeing them. Closed, nobody suspected anything. Despite the fact that it didn't last as a series, I did think their solution was pretty ingenious."

Although Val giggled about that solution, it didn't stop them from giving the idea careful consideration.

Jamie walked Val to her car. "Have you been able to think of any way we can be together tonight?"

"I think so. My car is due in the shop tomorrow. Instead of dropping it in the morning, let's just drop it when we get home. We'll stay together tonight. You'd be picking me up at the dealer's tomorrow morning and driving me to work anyway. I don't see any problem with that, do you?" Val brushed a piece of fuzz from Jamie's shoulder.

"No, then I can pick you up after work and we'll grab some dinner."

Val led the way toward home with Jamie following. The boys voiced their protest loud and long. From her experience on the ride up, Jamie knew that she'd have to listen to their complaints for the first few miles. Once they realized they were not going to the vet, she was confident that they'd settle down.

The two women followed each other down the highways till they arrived at Jamie's home. Jamie unloaded the cats first and carried them into the house. Once freed from their carriers, the boys immediately set about sniffing every square inch of the place as if they'd never been there before. "Wow, you guys are too funny. It's your house and that's you that you smell."

With Jamie's car emptied, they drove both cars to Val's apartment to unload her bags. Val's apartment was a co-op in what was once a massive Victorian home. At some point, the owner divided the mansion up into several one-bedroom apartments. Each person living there owned a portion of the house. They shared expenses for upkeep and maintenance through a monthly fee. Val's apartment, although smaller than Jamie's living quarters, had tons of charm. There were tall ceilings, many period details, and a beautiful fireplace in the living room. It was tastefully decorated, and although comfortable for one person, it might be cramped for two. Privacy was not one of its advantages, because the apartments shared a common entryway.

Val stowed her belongings in their proper places. It only took a minute or two for her to pack the clothes she would need for work the next day. They drove their separate cars to drop Val's car off for service.

Val placed her keys in the envelope and dropped it through the slot in the shop door. The keys clattered as they hit the floor. "Mission accomplished," Val said with a grin. "Onward to the Chinese restaurant to pick up dinner."

Val rested her hand on Jamie's thigh as they drove. Jamie covered Val's hand, entwining their fingers. Jamie kept a watchful eye on the mirrors so Val could move her hand if another car came near to them.

As they drove, Jamie sighed. "Well, dropping your car allows us to be together tonight." She tossed a wink in Val's direction.

"Yes, unfortunately, this is only one night out of the rest of our lives. Too bad my car doesn't need an oil change every night."

Jamie changed lanes and passed a slower moving vehicle. "We can either take the attitude that we'll be brave, or foolish, depending on your viewpoint. We can live our lives until someone takes note. Because my place is larger and I have the cats, it would be easier if you stay with me. If someone notices and says anything, we'll have to figure out what we're going to tell them. It will have to be either the truth or some plausible story. I still haven't been able to figure out a reason we would be staying with each other every night except for the obvious one. Have you?"

"I've been thinking about it too," Val glanced over at her lover. "Another option is that we can continue sort of as we have been most of this summer. We hang out together till late evening. Except, of course, the time we're together will be better, because now we can have sex." Val's lascivious grin made them both laugh. "The bad thing is that we won't be able to sleep together overnight. It'll be like having a curfew. All illicit activity must take place before eleven."

Jamie bobbed her head in agreement and smiled. "Umm. There is another upside, because we have your cabin for weekends. We can leave here as early as possible on Friday afternoon. We can stay till Sunday night, maybe even Monday morning, if we're willing to get up early enough to make it back here for work. We'd only be able to do that until the bad weather hits, though." Jamie shrugged. "That's not optimal, for sure. On the up side, at least we'll get to be together overnight for two, or sometimes three, nights a week. What do you think?"

"I don't like it any more than you do." Val sighed. "I guess it is better than the first option. I'm not sure I'm ready for that. I'm just starting my new job as Principal. The one advantage of you going back to the classroom is that, as a teacher, you have tenure again. Unfortunately, I serve at the pleasure of the board. Because I have tenure as a teacher from the years I spent in the classroom, they might have a hard time firing me. Still, it could get ugly."

"Mm. At least we've got some ideas. Let's think about it and talk about it some more this week." Jamie pulled in and parked at the Chinese restaurant. "I wish we'd called ahead. The takeout line is almost out the door."

"Let's go in and eat here instead of bringing the food home."

They didn't continue their conversation from before, as it was depressing both of them. Instead, they reminisced about the wonderful two weeks they'd spent together, the changes in the cabin, and how much the cats enjoyed being at the lake.

Finished with dinner, the two drove back to Jamie's house. Val went into the kitchen to get them something cold to drink, while Jamie threw in a load of laundry. On her way back toward the kitchen, she picked up her mail. She sat on the sofa to sort the few bills and a pile of junk mail. She saw there was a letter from Bly.

Carrying a cold glass of ice water into the living room and handing it to Jamie, Val asked, "What are you doing?"

"Just looking over my mail. I got a letter from Bly and some bills." Jamie placed the letter on the pile with the rest of the mail and crossed the room to Val. "I'm too tired to read Bly's letter right now. We can look at it tomorrow. I think if I don't pay the bills soon, they will come to repossess me. Then we won't have to worry about how we can be together. I'll be too busy being some other prisoner's sex slave in debtors' prison." She crossed the room and took Val in her arms for a soft kiss.

Val leaned back and sought Jamie's eyes. "Was that a wishful tone I heard in your voice?"

"Never! I only want to be *your* sex slave."

They retreated to Jamie's cozy TV room to relax. For the time being, they let the 'elephant in the room' topic rest and pretended they didn't have to make any decisions. Jamie received a couple of phone calls that night from people wondering where she'd been. Liz and Sandy called wondering if Jamie would like to come and join them for dinner. Jamie asked them to hold a minute. She covered the mouthpiece of the phone with her hand to ask Val if she wanted to go. Getting Val's enthusiastic agreement, Jamie accepted the invitation.

"Do you mind if I bring Val along for the evening?"

"That would be wonderful. She beat us up last time. It'll be fun to see if we can beat her."

They made tentative plans for a date the following week and

agreed to be in touch to confirm as the time grew closer. The twosome watched some mindless TV, then retired to bed early. Tired from the stress of dealing with their future together, they cuddled and exchanged back scratches. They made gentle love and agreed that this was the way they wanted to be forever.

Chapter Twenty-six

Reflections

JAMIE AWOKE BEFORE THE alarm went off. Val was sleeping on her shoulder, and Jamie cradled her closer. The movement awoke Val who mumbled, "I love you," into Jamie's neck.

"I love you, too. How'd you sleep?"

"Fine. I don't want to leave you and go to work though. Maybe I'm sick?" Val grinned, mischief dancing in her eyes. "I'm sure you'll have more fun today than I will."

"You may be quite correct." Jamie stretched. "There's nothing I would rather do than entertain you all day. Unfortunately, someone has to bring home the bacon."

Reason prevailed, and Val yawned and stretched before she sat up. "You didn't know that you'd be a kept woman, did you?" They both grinned. "I wish I could stay with you. I'm sure, after two weeks away, I'll have work piled up and covering the top of my desk. It'll take me a week to organize it and figure out what there is to do. Also, I have things to learn from the boss before she retires. I have to go."

Jamie pulled Val back next to her. They cuddled for a while, enjoying being close to each other. Val sighed. "This is the way I want to spend the rest of my life, waking up next to you. I don't want it to be on a part-time basis. The thought of waking up alone tomorrow morning depresses me. Isn't that strange? After waking up alone for nearly forty years, two weeks with you and I don't want to wake up alone anymore."

"No, I don't find it strange, I feel the same way." Jamie adjusted her position, fluffed her pillow, and rolled on her side so that she could look into Val's eyes as they talked. "Before we got involved, I was afraid of starting another relationship. Afraid of being vulnerable, afraid of being able to live up to what a new lover might expect or deserve from me.

Now that we're involved, I can't imagine what I was afraid of. You're so easy to please, and so easy to love."

Val smiled and placed her palm against her lover's cheek.

Jamie finished her thoughts. "Everything I do for you stems from this abundance of love I feel. It seems to flow forth with no effort. The simplest thing pleases you, be it a touch, a kiss, a flower. No matter what it is, you appreciate it. That makes it a pleasure to think of what might be the next thing I can do that will make you smile. Somehow this feels so right." Jamie rolled over to embrace Val, and they ended in their favorite position with Jamie on top so that their bodies touched full-length.

Val smiled and ran her fingernails down Jamie's back eliciting sounds of pleasure. "We fit, don't we?

"Yes, finally, I feel that I've found the place where I belong...right here with you."

They held each other until Val groaned and pulled away. "We've got to get up."

They got ready and ate a quick breakfast before Jamie drove Val to school and dropped her off. Back at her house, the day seemed to drag by, as Jamie did chores around the house. She laundered the sheets, changed the bed, cut the grass, and vacuumed the pool. She looked at her watch...only two p.m. She had another two hours before she could pick up Val.

Bills and catching up on the mail occupied the next hour. She paid the bills then decided to tackle Bly's flowery and almost impossible to understand handwriting. Every time Jamie tried to read one of her letters, she had to call and have Bly translate several words. Even a short letter would take time to—what was the proper term—to read? No, to decipher was more accurate. With a big sigh, she opened the letter. Hallelujah! Bly had decided to print. "Well, thank you. That makes things easier," Jamie muttered to herself with a chuckle.

Dear Jamie:

I hope this note finds you well. I've been trying to reach you by phone to no avail. I guess you're away. At the cabin, I hope. So I'm resorting to pen and paper. Please, call when you get home. If I don't hear from you this week, I plan to give Robbie a call just to be sure you're still alive. Just kidding...I know you would have called if you had trouble.

Dana and I have been dating since we got back to CA. We are spending most weekends together. We're doing what we call long-term dating. We have one long date from Friday night to Sunday night followed by four nights of long telephone calls.

I live in one suburb east of the city, and she lives on the other side, directly opposite. The drive is a killer, straight across through the city. Of course, to make it worse, it's prime traffic time when we want to get together after work. The drive home is usually easier. Still, it gets harder and harder to leave after a date. I tried coming home in the morning once. Although I couldn't fathom it, the morning commute is ridiculously worse. We do sometimes meet during the week in the city. She has obligations at home. I don't want to get into it here...will fill you in when we talk in person.

The sex is fabulous. It's passionate and sweet at the same time. This is her first real relationship with another woman. We're getting along well, and she's wonderful fun to be with. She's bright, funny, and has the patience of a saint, which is a necessary and admirable quality for someone involved with me. If I were younger, I would have hired the U-Haul already. Unfortunately, there are issues, as I mentioned...more to follow.

I've enclosed some pictures of her alone and of the two of us together. You have to admit she is 'hot.'

How are things between you and Val? I hope you finally mustered up enough courage to tell her what you were feeling. It was painful to watch you struggle so. She is fabulous and would make a perfect match for you. I know you have obvious differences in tastes. When you come down to it, for the most part, they are for things that are unimportant. You and she mesh on so many of the important core values. I think you'd make a wonderful couple. If it happens, I wish you all the happiness in the world. You deserve it.

Love ya,
Bly

Checking the time, Jamie figured she might be able to catch her friend during her lunch hour. She got out her address book and looked up Bly's work number. She answered with her formal work greeting, "You're speaking with Bly Marshall, how may I help you?"

"Can you talk?" Jamie knew she wouldn't have to identify herself.

"Jamie. Thank God. I was about to send a search and rescue team out for you. Where the hell have you been? You had me worried."

"I told you I was going away in August." Jamie smirked. "Clearly, you don't listen."

"Yeah, but you were gone three weeks."

"Almost. I left early to do some work on Val's cabin. The first week, I worked on Val's loft and made some renovations for her." Jamie explained the changes to the cabin in more detail.

"Is there anything you can't do?" Bly said, "Why don't you come out here and visit me? I need a library too. So what happened the next two weeks? Was Val pleased with everything you accomplished?"

"Yes, more than pleased."

"And?" Bly's voice rose at the end.

"So, I finally managed to express how I felt about her. I still can't believe it. She loves me back. We spent two wonderful weeks together. It feels so right to me, Bly."

"Congratulations. I'm happy for you both. Give her my love and tell her that I wish you both well."

Jamie thanked Bly for the sentiment. "So, you and Dana look happy. She is beautiful, by the way. You didn't exaggerate."

"So you got my letter?"

"Yes, thanks for printing."

Bly laughed. "Yes, Dana's great, we're great. That pretty much tells it all. Well, that's not true. There are a couple of issues. Literally. She has two kids. They're young, eight and ten, a girl and a boy. Her husband has custody on weekends, so they're easy for us. We don't often get to see each other during the weekdays, like I said, due to the commute and the kids. She doesn't want them to know about her, because she's afraid her husband will find out and try to take them away."

"Oh, that must be difficult for you."

"Yes, I'm having a hard time. She's afraid of her children finding out and, of course, her husband too. He's the jealous type. She's afraid of his reaction to her involvement in a lesbian relationship. He's not all that interested in the children, and he often cancels his weekend visits with them. As much as I care for her, I don't see it working out for us in the end. Ten years would be a long time for us to wait until her youngest is eighteen. By then, who knows? Old habits are hard to break. If she stays in the closet that long, I'm afraid she won't ever want to come out." Bly heaved a sigh.

"Think counseling would help her? Maybe if you went together. Liz and Sandy, it seems, are trying to work things out so they can be together. Maybe you could too."

"Well, we'll see. The threat of her losing her children has made even me cautious. I don't want her or the children hurt."

"That must be disheartening."

"Yeah. You know from experience how I feel about keeping that secret." Bly exhaled a long breath. "As much as I can't see this working out for us, I can't break it off. The kids are adorable and she's amazing. When is the world going to wake up and realize we all want what they have?

"Does she know how hard this is for you?"

"Umm. She knows. I'll keep you posted. I want my next live-in relationship to be my last. I need to find a woman who isn't worried or cautious about our being a couple."

"So, you're already saying this won't end well with Dana?"

"I don't know. This could have a painful ending, for more than just Dana and me. I don't want the kids affected if we can't work things out. Then there's her maniac husband. Nobody knows what he'll do."

"I hope you can figure it out. Nothing is ever simple is it?" Jamie switched the phone to her other ear. "Val and I have decided we want to live with each other, and we both feel we can be together forever. The only thing stopping us is that we're afraid people will notice overnights. So now, we're dealing with how we go about having a relationship while keeping it a secret at work. Isn't it odd that we're all in the same boat?"

"Yes. I can't believe I'm still dealing with this same issue. I'm sick of being alone, and I like this woman so much. We're not rushing into anything. Neither of us is ready to jump until we're sure I can live the life she needs me to live."

After some more general chat, they hung up. Jamie missed Val and couldn't wait for the time to pass until the end of the workday. She prepared a salad and grilled some chicken. A cold supper would be nice for a summer night. She put the dinner in the fridge and called Val. "Ready to come home?

"Yes," she chuckled. "I was ready about six hours ago. Can you come get me?"

"Sure, I'll pick you up as soon as I can get there. Then we'll get your car and come home for dinner."

"Sounds perfect. Can't wait."

"Ditto."

AJ Adaore

Chapter Twenty-seven

Reflections

JAMIE PICKED UP VAL, and they drove over to the car dealer to pick up the car. They followed each other back to Jamie's house. After dinner, Jamie showed Val the letter from Bly and told her the details of the conversation they'd had that afternoon.

Val wondered how Bly would ever be able to resolve the issues about secrecy that stood between her and Dana. "I can sympathize with Dana. Her first duty as a mother is to protect her children from harm. If their father decided to make an issue of her dating another woman, she could run the risk of losing them."

"True, even though California is a bit more liberal than some other states. Unfortunately, you still read about people losing custody because of their sexual identity." Jamie smiled. "I'm glad I don't have to worry about anyone trying to take my boys."

Val shook her head. "At least we can be thankful for some small blessings."

"I did tell Bly we're involved. I should have discussed it with you before confirming, but when she asked about us, I didn't want to lie to her. Also, I felt safe telling her because she's so far away. She thinks you're great, by the way, and wished us all the best."

"Maybe we should talk about who we want to tell and what benefit it would be to our relationship for them to know."

Jamie nodded. "I'm sorry."

"No, it was a good decision. I'm thinking of the future."

"I think you're right. Next time, we decide together."

"I'm not sure about who we should tell. How do you feel about it? I don't have the need for the world to know about us. In fact, I think it's better that we try to keep us as secret as we can," Val said.

"I hear what you're saying. I do think that we, as a couple, need a support group." Jamie tilted her head, as she tried to express her thoughts. "You know what I mean? A group of friends who love us and will help validate our existence as a couple. Do you agree?"

Val looked away, considering her response. "I guess, in theory, that's a healthy way to live. In reality, it scares me to death."

"It's ironic that I'm the one saying we need to tell some others when, in the past, I've always been the one on the side of secrecy. I know that, like you, I'm not ready to leap out of the closet." Jamie looked at Val.

"We share the concern about people from work knowing. I guess we can deal with the rest of the world on a case-by-case basis. I agree with you that living in isolation isn't healthy."

"We need friends. Friends we can confide in and share our joys and sorrows with...friends who can provide approval of our being together. We'll meet with too many people who won't approve of us. I think we need to have a source of, I guess for want of a better term, confirmation, or encouragement. I've no desire to be a flag-carrying lesbian, nor do I want to live in isolation."

Val pressed both hands to her face and dragged them down each side. She sighed from her soul. "I don't know. I haven't given it much thought. At the cabin, we didn't think about other people and how to handle them. I was too busy falling in love to worry about what would happen next. Who would you want to tell about us?"

Jamie smiled then leaned over and kissed Val. "I don't know. When I was younger, and to my mind straight, I never thought about telling people that I was a heterosexual. I just lived my life. I mentioned that Josh and I went here or there. My conversation was peppered with Josh and I..." Jamie gestured with open hands. "Now that I realize I'm a homosexual, I can't see why I need to announce myself as such either. Let people assume what they will. They'll do that anyway. I'd like to just live like I always have. If there is someone that either of us wants to confirm our relationship for, we discuss it. If we agree, we can figure out how to let him, her, or them know."

Val listened, her expression intent and her head tipped slightly, as Jamie spoke. Sometimes, she nodded her agreement. Sometimes, her eyebrow arched in question, as she considered a point Jamie was making.

Jamie continued. "I think that coming out to people is a continual process. I was always under the impression that 'coming out' was something you did one time. You know, once I let the cat out of the bag I would never have to struggle with whether to tell someone again. That proved to be untrue. I didn't want everyone from work to know. Still, I felt that I needed some people to know, or I would have shriveled up and wasted away from loneliness. Each time, I would think about whether I should tell someone. Did they need to know? How would they handle that information? Would they respect my confidence? It came down to how important that person was to me and whether, in the end, I would be happier if they knew. There are less than a handful of people who know about me. There's Bly, of course, Robbie, Sandy and Liz, and maybe two or three others. Other than Robbie, they are all segregated from where I live and work. The fact that you and I work at the same school district does complicate things."

"Robbie knows about you? Can I assume he's gay?" Val seemed genuinely surprised.

"I shouldn't say anything. You should ask him yourself." Jamie rolled her eyes. "Yes, he is, although few people know about him either. Bly never hid that she's a lesbian, nor did most of her friends."

"Doesn't Liz teach?"

"Yup. Sandy has always been more open than Liz who's more careful because she's a teacher. Of all the gay women I know, I think we probably have most in common with them. It might be nice if Liz and Sandy knew about us. We've had fun with them this summer. If they knew, I think it would make social interaction with them easier and more relaxed. It's hard work keeping a secret as huge as the fact that we love each other. If we don't come out to them, we'll always need to be on guard."

"Have you told Robbie about us?" Val wondered.

"No, the only person I've told is Bly. If you're comfortable, I'd like to confirm for Robbie. Actually, Robbie already suspects. He told me the day we spent with him at the pool that you were attracted to me."

"Noooo. How did he know before we did?"

Holding up a hand with a raised index finger, in a gesture designed to give pause, Jamie said, "Wait. Remember that you're dealing with someone who has sensitivity to other people who are gay. It's called gaydar, or having a trained eye. Don't forget that he spent the whole day observing us interact in the pool. We were already in lust by then, I think, though we probably hadn't admitted it even to ourselves."

"I don't know, Jamie. If we tell Robbie, having him know could put my career at risk."

"I'll respect your wishes about him, even though it'll be nearly impossible for me not to tell him. He knows me so well...I'd bet he'd almost know how I feel about you by looking at me. I'd trust him with my life."

"Then we'll trust him with mine too." Val smiled and shook her head. "Too bad it's not just as simple as 'I love you.' Instead, we have to deal with all this intrigue. It sort of puts a damper on the joy of falling in love. At least we spent two carefree weeks at the cabin."

"I do have one other person I want to tell." When Jamie hesitated, Val sought out Jamie's eyes with her own and waited for Jamie to finish. "It won't be easy…I want to tell my mom. She's always so concerned about me living my life alone. I know that it will ease her mind on one hand, that I have someone who loves me. I'm not sure how she'll take the news that it's another woman. One advantage is that she likes and respects you."

"Oh, Jamie, I'm not sure I could look her in the eye after you tell her." Val reached for the comfort of Jamie's hand. "If it's something that you feel you need to do, I'm sure I'll adjust to the idea."

"I hope so. She wants to see me happy. So I think she'll accept it, even though it might take some time."

Val slumped in her seat. "Most of my friends are people from work. At least they're not ones we need to discuss, since neither of us wants any of them to know."

"Don't worry. We'll work all this out. In my heart I know that there is nothing the two of us can't achieve together."

"I just have one thing to ask." Val ran her fingers through her hair. "I'm not upset that you told Bly. I understand why you did. From now on, promise that we'll try to decide together if we tell someone. It would be optimal if we make the decision together." Val shrugged. "If someone asks one of us, and we decide that we need to confirm, we must tell each other that we've done so. I don't want to be in a position of thinking someone doesn't know when they do."

"Okay, agreed. Now, there's one final issue. How can we be together without everyone noticing?"

"I think we have no option right now, other than to do as we discussed yesterday. Lots of people manage to date. Although it's not what we want, for now, it will have to be enough until we can figure out what else to do. We'll manage somehow. During the week, we'll live our lives visiting each other till bedtime. Then we have to go to our respective homes. We can use the cabin on weekends until the weather prohibits it. Let's see how intolerable that is, and we can see what happens. Maybe we'll come up with a solution." Val put her head in her hand.

"The *MacGruder and Loud* solution is looking better and better."

"And we do have experience building bookcases." Val brightened and grinned. Seconds passed and she continued. "Two things. We both have teachers we work with living in our neighborhoods. The fact that my car is here every night or your car is at my place every night may become noticed. It could be an issue that shows up in the future. Also, now that I'll be the principal, I'll be getting the calls Marie used to get for teachers who'll be out sick. I'll have to get an answering service or something."

"No problem, we can get an answering machine tomorrow. I know it's not what either of us wants." Jamie took Val's hand in hers. "On one hand, it will slow us down. We think we're sure about wanting to be together forever. Let's say that for the next six months we have hot, passionate, lusty sex. Then, after you've had your way with me, what happens if you decide that you no longer want to be my honey?" Jamie smiled at Val.

"Not a chance." Standing up, she pulled Jamie to her. Val leaned back and looked at Jamie. "Now, what were you saying about hot, passionate, lusty sex? Let's try some of that and see if we're tired of it."

They weren't. At eleven o'clock, Jamie shook Val awake.

Val looked at the clock and groaned. "It's the bewitching hour. I need to get dressed and go home." Val got up, dressed, and left. At her home, she undressed, got into bed and called Jamie. They talked for a while before they said good night and went to sleep in their separate houses.

The next night, they repeated the routine. Only this time Jamie stayed at Val's place and it was Jamie's turn to dress and drive home. Each night, they'd linger on the phone. They'd wake up early each morning and call so they could talk to each other while they drank their tea and coffee. They always hung up by six forty-five, so Val could take her sub calls.

Thursday evening, Val had been at Jamie's place. They walked to the door and kissed good night. Together, they stepped into the landing between the inner and outer door. Jamie flipped the two switches that turned off the lights for the outside steps, the inside landing, and stairway. Pulling close, the two held each other, not wanting to let go of the last kiss good night. They didn't hear Robbie approach the door. It was hard to say who was more surprised when he opened it, catching them in their loving embrace.

"Sorry, sorry, sorry, excuse me." He squeezed past the two lovers and ran up the stairs.

"Well that takes care of telling Robbie." Smiling, Jamie looked at Val for her reaction.

Red faced, Val was already beginning to giggle, "I would guess so. Actually, I think in some ways it's less embarrassing this way. I still have a hard time imagining how it will be to sit down and tell someone out of the blue. 'Hey guess what?' Honest. It doesn't bother me that he knows. I know that you trust him and that's good enough for me. Maybe now I'll get to know him better, and we'll all be friends."

With a final hug and kiss good-bye, Val left for home. The door had hardly closed when Robbie came tearing down the stairs. His impersonation of Lily Tomlin as Ernestine the operator was near perfect. "Oh Jamie, I've never been so embarrassed." Dropping the character accent, he continued. "I'm sorry. With all the lights off, I didn't see you until it was too late. If I knew you were there groping each other in the dark, I would have struggled with the lock or jiggled the handle." He grinned then hugged his friend. "I'm happy for you. It looks like things are going well. I guess you finally got past the I-don't-want-to-lose-her-friendship and how-can-I-tell-her-what-I-feel-we-work-together stage. Way past it."

"Don't be crass. Okay, you might as well come in. I know you want to hear all the dirt." Jamie and Robbie got comfortable in the living room.

Once settled, Robbie listened to Jamie's story about how she and Val finally came to share their feelings. "Now, our only problem is that she lives there, and I live here, and we don't like it."

"So, move in together." Robbie's shrug indicated the solution was obvious to him.

"No, it's kind of soon for that. Besides, if and when we decide to do that, what would we tell people? What plausible reason would there be? Val has a new position, and neither of us is comfortable with people from work knowing about us. Moving in together could be professionally risky."

"I'm sure you two smart women can come up with something creative. You've said yourself that the cut in pay would be a financial hardship for you. Val supports two homes. She'd have to welcome a decrease in expenses. Rent out one of your places and tell people you're moving in together to cut expenses."

The conversation with Robbie planted seeds in Jamie's mind.

Neither knew that it would end up leading to a solution for her and Val. As she thought about it, hope grew that there was a light at the end of their tunnel that wasn't the train. Changing the subject away from her and Val, she asked Robbie what was new with him and his boyfriend.

"We broke up while you were gone. We agreed that there was no use in prolonging the agony. It's been coming at least six months. He's attracted to someone else. He hopes we can be friends. At this point, I don't want to be his friend. He's broken my trust, and I just can't stand to be with him now in any capacity."

"Oh, Robbie, I'm so sorry."

"I know. I wished you were here last week. I could have used your shoulder to cry on. In some ways maybe it was better that you weren't here. I managed to get through it by myself, and I feel good about that. It's still painful, although, if I were honest about it, I was as ready as he was to let go. So that's about it for me. I get to start all over again," Robbie said with a sad smile and a shrug of one shoulder.

The two friends talked for a while longer, until Robbie finally went upstairs. Knowing it was too late to call Val, Jamie went to bed missing her. How could she want to be with her so much? Even more puzzling was how she could be thinking of a forever, so soon after they'd become a couple. Val seemed to feel the same way about forever, but she was a more patient person, willing to try the turning-into-a-pumpkin routine for a while. Before Jamie closed her eyes, she started thinking about Robbie's idea. With their relationship still so new, it might be too early to broach the subject with Val. The solution would demand dramatic changes for both of them. Changes she herself had concerns about undertaking so early in the relationship. She decided not to say anything and to wait and see how the next few weeks went. In the meantime, she'd investigate some possibilities. Val would let her know if or when she was ready for the next step, and Jamie would be ready.

Chapter Twenty-eight

Reflections

JAMIE CALLED VAL AT home before she left for school the next morning. They talked a bit about the night before and then turned their attention to their weekend plans. After she fed the cats and played with them a spell, Jamie packed for the Labor Day weekend. It was tradition that on the last day before a long weekend, the administrative staff was able to leave a couple hours early. It was a benefit for the two women heading to the mountains. The long drive gave Jamie an opportunity to discuss their situation with Val on the way up. Jamie opened with the fact that she had told Robbie that their goal was to someday live together. She shared his suggestion that they could use the financial angle as a reason for the move.

"You know I love you, right?" Val smiled at Jamie. "Maybe not being together as we want to be is extra difficult because we're so new as a couple. I don't know, though. I hate to be apart from you, and I can't in my wildest imagination see that changing. We have the cabin at least until the winter hits, and then what do we do to be alone for more than a few hours?"

"I know," responded Jamie. "I want more time with you, too. I don't understand how people can have long-distance relationships. Maybe it'll be easier once I go back to work and have less free time. I miss you so much when you're at work."

"We've only been together a few weeks. Even though I know it's irrational, I feel like I waited so long to find you, and I don't want to waste any more time. My heart wants us to be together full time. My head says we should give ourselves a chance to be sure we both want this."

"Do you have doubts?" Jamie studied Val's face for an indication of what she was thinking.

"Not a one. I'm sure I won't change my mind about wanting to be with you." She studied Jamie's eyes. "Do you have doubts about us?"

"About us, no. At first, I used to have doubts about me. Sometimes. I used to worry about if I'd be a good enough partner for you. I've had a failed marriage already, and an unsuccessful relationship with Bly. That scares me, and I don't want to have that happen to us. So, I have to agree with you. I want us to be sure. Because we're doing this once, and then you're stuck with me for a lifetime."

"Perfect. I can't think of a better ending than a lifetime with you," Val squeezed Jamie's hand.

"I wonder. Is it possible that we're being overly paranoid, thinking that people care about what we do? Do you suppose anyone is actually wasting their time watching our comings and goings? I mean, think about it? Who is going to know what we're doing? What if we just stayed overnight when we wanted to? Who would know?"

"Sure, anything is possible." Val shrugged. "Maybe we are being too cautious. As the expression goes, time will tell."

The cats had complained about the length of the trip to the cabin for the past forty-five minutes. "Phew!" Jamie made a show of wiping her brow. "Thank God that's over. They were plucking my last nerve. Come on, let's get unpacked and get them into the cabin so they'll shut up."

The two women completed the task of unloading the supplies and the cats. They had it down to a science. While at the cabin, they felt life was normal. They cleaned, cooked, ate, read, and made love. Falling asleep together and waking up together the next morning was such a treat for them. It was the way they wanted it to always be.

Val had some work to do. She needed to organize an emergency/snow chain for the staff. While Val organized the contact information, Jamie worked on her handouts and lesson plans for her first week back in the classroom.

The last morning at the cabin before school opened, they lamented that their summer was over. Soon, Jamie would be closing her pool, and they would both be busier at work. They dragged their feet until the last minute. Jamie dropped Val at home. After helping her carry everything into her house, she went home to prepare for work the next day.

Later that evening, Jamie called Liz and Sandy to firm up a get-together for Friday. Afterward, she called Val. They talked only a short time, both wanting to get a good night's sleep. There were no students on the first day of school, because it was a scheduled workshop day for the teaching staff. First thing in the morning, the elementary school staff met in the auditorium, where Val's introduction as the new principal was well received.

Jamie's day went equally well. Several teachers stopped in to welcome her back to the ranks. The teacher across the hall offered to share units with her if she needed any materials. Jamie finished decorating her bulletin boards and organized her classroom. Sitting at her desk, she double-checked the names of the students in her roster for changes. After reading through her lesson plans for the next day, she gathered her handouts and homework assignment list and went to the office to make copies. She looked around and smiled, feeling prepared for her first week back in the classroom. Only one more day and the kids would be back.

With Jamie back in the classroom, there would be no opportunity for her to see Val during the day. Her half-hour break was too little time for them to meet for lunch, and they'd agreed it wasn't a good idea anyway.

At the end of the week, Jamie and Val got together with Liz and Sandy. Coming out to them was as simple as holding hands when they met them at the door. Liz and Sandy greeted them with hugs and congratulations. The conversation that followed was relaxed and unguarded. With three of them being in education, they had a common fear of exposure, something that was hard for Sandy to understand and accept. Although Liz and Sandy were still living separately, they were talking about getting a bigger place for the two of them. When the time came, it would be easier for them, because they wouldn't be changing their address within the same HR department. No one would know with whom Liz was living, only that she had moved. Jamie and Val would be registering a common address at the same HR office.

The four played Trivial Pursuit and laughter rang out often. "This has been fun." Liz looked at Sandy who nodded her head. "Let's do this again next week." With everyone agreed, they made plans to get together again the following week.

Val and Jamie continued meeting after work at one house or the other. Most often, Val came to Jamie's place. Jamie finished work earlier and could get dinner started. They also felt that Jamie's house was more private.

One uneventful month led to another, with the new couple ever more confident in their relationship. No doubts existed that they wanted to spend the rest of their lives together. Yet the solution of how to do that still eluded them. One night, in early December, they were watching TV at Jamie's house. The phone rang at a little after nine. Jamie answered and, after a few seconds of conversation, she handed the phone to Val. "It is one of your teachers, Madeline." Jamie raised her eyebrows and shrugged her shoulders at Val's questioning look. Madeline lived at the other end of the block from Jamie and, unfortunately, worked in the elementary department that Val supervised.

Taking the phone, Val answered, "Hello, Madeline, how can I help you?" When Val hung up she approached Jamie. "Remember the conversation we had about how no one would notice us?"

"Yes." Jamie experienced the same feeling she would get if she were driving and a policeman turned on his flashing red and blue lights to pull her over. Her stomach rolled, her face grew hot, and her pulse rate increased.

"We were wrong. Madeline called me here, because she wanted to explain why she would be absent from school tomorrow. She also wanted to give me an opportunity to reach a sub."

"There's a procedure in place for that. She's supposed to call in the morning."

Val nodded. "I know. She told me that if she left the message on the tape, I wouldn't get the call in time to get the sub she wanted. Madeline already called the sub. She told her not to accept any other assignment and to expect a call from me."

"Oh no."

Val waved her arms. Her speech came in bursts, her voice raised. "That impertinent little twit has the balls of life. Can you believe what she said? I could picture her posture from her snotty little voice. I'd bet my house she had that hip cocked and her hand resting on it."

"Calm down." Jamie had never seen Val this angry.

"Calm down my ass." Val pulled at her collar as if to release some steam. "Wait till you hear this. She told me that she knew I was always at your place, so she thought it would be more convenient to just call me here instead of at my home. The nerve." Val blew out an angry breath and said with a shrug, "So much for nobody noticing us."

Jamie circled her arms around her lover.

Val rested her head on Jamie's shoulder. "I don't want to go."

Jamie pulled Val to her as they stood at the door. "I know. I need you tonight, too."

Val lifted her head. "We have to face it. Our close friendship, if not the true nature of our relationship, is no longer a secret."

"I know. I have an idea. I'll tell you about it soon." Jamie kissed Val good night and watched her walk to the car with slumped shoulders. She longed to run after Val and wrap her in a protective bubble.

Jamie resolved to begin researching a solution. She'd been toying with an idea ever since her conversation with Robbie.

Chapter Twenty-nine

Reflections

VAL ADDED TO HER list the last thing she wanted Jamie to pack for her. "Eleven whole nights together, Jamie. I can't wait."

Jamie hugged Val close. "Me too."

Somehow, they'd managed to make it till the last day of school before their Christmas vacation. The students ran toward the buses at lunchtime. The teachers were able to leave an hour after the students. Val had to stay until normal time that day and had to attend a meeting on Thursday. The early dismissal gave Jamie a free afternoon and a full business day free. She volunteered to pack for their trip up to the cabin. This vacation would be their longest time together since August.

Wednesday night, Jamie told Val she had an idea. "It will require some thought and investigation."

Jamie held Val off when she begged to know more about her idea. "Let me get some facts and figures together before we talk about it. I promise, we can discuss it while we're on vacation."

Thursday morning, after Jamie fed the cats and played with them a bit, she got out her calculator and began to figure expenses. She made a quick call to a friend of hers who was a realtor. By half past eleven, Jamie had already been to the realtor's office to pick up the information he'd copied for her. Her little gray cells were in overdrive. Before long, Jamie called Val's office to see how things were going at work.

Val answered on the first ring. Once she ascertained the call was from Jamie, her demeanor and the tenor of her voice changed. She morphed from the formal tones of a professional to the soft tones of a woman in love. "Guess what? At the meeting, they told us we're allowed to leave at one. It's like Death Valley here. Only a few of us are here working. Quite a few folks took the afternoon off to get a jump on the holiday. Why didn't I think of that?" Not waiting for an answer, she rushed to ask. "Can you be ready to go early?"

"Sure. Packing was easy. Most everything we need is already there."

"Okay, let's take my car. It'll give us more room for the boys. I'll pick you up as soon as I can. I hope we can beat some of the traffic."

By one-thirty, the protesting cats and the two women were pulling out of the driveway. The protests waned by the time they pulled onto the freeway. Traffic was much lighter than expected, and they arrived at their destination a few minutes before four. Released from their confinement in the carriers, the cats seemed happy to stretch their legs and inspect the cabin. Val and Jamie were happy to do the same.

Settled in front of the fire, sipping some cream sherry, Jamie brought out the folder she'd put together earlier that day. On top of the folder were the copied pages of information the realtor gave her on income properties. "Let me show you what I did this morning." She reviewed the figures with Val, tallying her own financial responsibilities. "I made a best guess for your expenses."

Val reviewed the numbers and supplied corrections and some extra information about her finances. Jamie added all the figures twice before Val tallied them. At last, the pair was sure their totals were an accurate representation of their income and expenses for a monthly, as well as a yearly basis.

"Jamie, what are you driving at with all these figures?"

"Okay, bear with me for just another minute." Jamie pushed the completed tally toward Val. "There. Look."

"Okay, I see. Between us, we spend a lot of money to live. We already knew that. Where are you going with this?"

"Look, I know that we've only been a couple for about four months. Even before that, we were pretty much inseparable for months. I've known you for what?" Jamie stopped to make a quick mental calculation. "Seventeen years? Although the couple thing and the sex thing are new, we've had a friendship and a solid professional relationship for years."

Val cocked her head. "Does time matter?"

"Not to me. I want to be able to share my life with you for twenty-four hours a day, not only until eleven every night."

"Yes. I couldn't agree with you more. How?"

Jamie ran her fingers through her hair and took a deep breath. "Maybe what I'm about to propose will seem rash. Still, I hope you'll consider it with an open mind. I was thinking that part of the problem with us living together full time is where we're living. One of the teachers you supervise lives on my block."

"Yes, and almost everyone at school drives past my condo on their way to work."

"What if we moved up river to Watertown or the outskirts of that area? We would definitely have more privacy. It's not that far from school and it would put us at least a half hour closer to the cabin for the weekends."

Val's pursed her lips as she calculated time. "That might even make extending some weekends a possibility."

"Umm. True. I hadn't thought about that. Wait though...the best part is that it's financially a good move for both of us." Jamie pulled the stack of papers from the realtor out of the folder. "Here, let me show you. It'll cost me some money up front. I'd have to put in a heater for the second floor, so I can let each tenant pay for their own utilities. If I rent my apartment, the income from it and the one upstairs will pay all of my expenses for the house and I'll come away with around four hundred to four hundred fifty dollars a month in profit. Everything depends on the rent I get.

"From the figures we have for your place, you can realize almost the same. If we pool our resources, we could buy a little apartment building, maybe with two apartments. One big enough for us to live in, and the other could give us extra income. Financially it's a great move. We'd be building equity in the properties and would be able to live together. It's a financially sound business venture. It also provides a plausible explanation for anyone from work who's nosy enough to ask. You know there'll be at least one."

"Helen." They laughed in unison.

"Yes, Helen." Jamie rolled her eyes. "You know, once she has the information, she'll spread it among the other busybodies who have inquiring minds."

Holding up her hand, Val halted Jamie. "One problem with this. I'm not sure the bylaws allow me to rent my co-op."

"Oh well, it was a thought." Jamie sank her face into her palms. "We'll get other ideas, I'm sure." She smiled at Val and stood up to go poke the fire.

"If I can't rent it, why can't I sell it?"

Jamie tightened the latch on the stove door and turned, raising her eyes to meet Val's. "Are you sure you're ready to do that?

Val leaned forward. "If it means we can be together, I'd do almost anything short of selling my body on Canal Street. My co-op is a nice place to live. The downside is that there are a lot of rules. We're required to register guests with the co-op board if they're staying longer than three days. There's no noise allowed after eleven, no parties…we have a two page list of prohibited things. Before we make any definitive decisions, let's get the facts, and we can go from there."

"You amaze me." Jamie gave Val a weak smile. "I think I'm feeling a little frightened by the enormity of such a move. It surprises me that you're willing to make such a drastic change. I kind of just sprung this on you. I've been worrying about this for months. What if we rent our places and, God forbid, something happens between us? What if our relationship is discovered? What if we do all this and then decide that we can't stand the pressure of being in a lesbian relationship? Selling might be pretty tough to undo."

Val laughed. "Jamie, stop. Listen to yourself. Don't you have more faith in us than that?

Jamie's eyes filled. "I love you so much. I wouldn't want anything we decide to hurt you, ever."

"I think I loved you before you loved me. I had a lot of time to think over what I was getting myself involved in. You're someone who nitpicks and analyzes things to death."

Val's assessment caused Jamie to flinch.

"That's not a criticism," Val rushed to add. "It's just that you are so much more cautious and analytical than I am. It's good for me to have someone like you who is more deliberate and cautious and who doesn't act in a hasty way. I tend to be a bit more rash in my decisions, and rarely, if ever, change my mind afterward. I bought my co-op after one visit. It was the only place I looked at. The minute I laid eyes on it, I knew that I wanted it.

Jamie's eyes twinkled. "Now you tell me. Should I be upset it took you seventeen years to fall in love with me then? You took your time taking me off the market. Maybe you're not that sure."

"I've never been surer of anything in my life." Val stuck her hands out and wiggled her fingers, beckoning Jamie to come to her. "I waited almost forty years for you, and I don't want to waste any more time. I don't care if we have to move mountains. I would do it with a spoon if it meant we could be together. I have no doubts about us. I am one hundred percent sure I want to be with you for the rest of my life. Are you ready?"

Jamie stood and approached Val who was still sitting. Wiggling her knees between Val's thighs Jamie put her arms on Val's shoulders and leaned over to kiss her. "Yes. I'm ready. No doubts at all."

"All this will take months to execute, and now that we've decided we want to do this, I want it to happen tomorrow." Val sighed. "We didn't know how bad living apart would be until we did it. Otherwise, we could have started earlier to make plans to be together."

The pair looked at each other. Shaking their heads, they rolled their eyes upward in unison.

"Who are you kidding, Val? We knew after the first few nights."

"I know." Val put her hands on Jamie's hips and gave a gentle push. "Let me see the places that are available now, anyway. Even if none of those work, it'll be good if we become familiar with the market and the area, so we can recognize a good deal when we find one."

Together, Val and Jamie looked over the available properties. Jamie pushed the last one away. "None of these fit our needs."

"We'll have to keep looking. If we are meant to find something, it'll happen."

The prospect of living together became a goal for them, and their holiday time together passed before they knew it. Because they'd invited Liz and Sandy up to spend part of the vacation with them, they decided to replace the single bed in the guest room with a sofa bed. They managed to arrange delivery for the day before Liz and Sandy arrived.

The four enjoyed the day. During dinner, Jamie and Val revealed their plans to move in together. Sandy and Liz exchanged a look then began to laugh. "You won't believe it. We've been looking for a new place to live. We're giving up our apartments to rent a bigger place that will accommodate both of us. Our goal is to try to save for a down payment and buy a house within the next year or so."

As their vacation ended, the group worked to winterize the cabin. Jamie and Val drained the plumbing, knowing that would be the end of their refuge at the lake for the season. It was too involved a process for just a weekend visit. They stood at the car, looking back at the cozy little cabin. Val sighed. "It's sad to think we won't return until spring break."

"I know. What makes it even sadder is that there won't be any more overnights unless we go away somewhere for a weekend."

Chapter Thirty

Reflections

RETURNING TO THEIR SCHOOL routine and forced nights apart was painful after their extended time together. The following Saturday, Jamie made an appointment with the realtor to begin their search for a new home. Val reviewed the co-op rules and learned that she could rent her place as long as the other owners approved of the tenant. It was similar to the process required if she decided to sell.

They explained what they were looking for to the realtor. He made appointments for them to tour a small, three-unit apartment building and a two-family house. Unfortunately, none matched what they wanted. They agreed to broaden their search to include areas a little further from where they worked. The perfect place, proved to be elusive.

On a Saturday, two weekends later, they went for a drive to familiarize themselves with a couple of new towns within their search area. The next town up from Watertown was a lovely little river town. Millville was the site of a huge, old paper mill that had been converted to apartments. The town itself was quaint, with many Victorian buildings, colorful awnings and multi-colored paint jobs. Neither woman had found an occasion to stop and visit the town for at least fifteen years. They'd paid no attention the many times they drove over the bridge into the larger city across the river.

They stopped and had lunch in a little café, where they found the townspeople to be friendly and welcoming. The community itself was famous for its art galleries and antique stores. Nestled between the larger stores were little shops selling handmade crafts of leather, pottery, or silver. As they settled at a table in front of the café window, they watched the people pass by. They picked out several same-sex pairs whom they identified as potentially gay or lesbian couples, strolling by on the street.

Val observed, "This seems like a much more liberal town than where we live."

Examining the café, Jamie spied a bulletin board on the wall. On the windowsill nearby, there were stacks of two free newspapers. One was the *News For Women*, and the other was a gay newspaper from the larger city across the river. As they were leaving the café, they picked up a copy of each and stopped to look at the fliers and business cards on the board. One notice, in particular, caught their eye.

Jamie pointed to the *For Sale by Owner* posting that had a color picture stapled to it. They read the description of a lovely, craftsman cottage. "Let's take a drive past."

Val copied the address and phone number down, and the waitress was kind enough to give them directions to the property in the ad. They left the café and followed the directions to the cottage. From the outside, it was perfect. The picture of the house, taken in a warmer month, showed that the landscaping would sprout into colorful blooms when spring arrived. Now, lush evergreens and small, winter-hardy shrubs protected the cozy looking home. Bird feeders hung from tree branches in the side yard. While parked in front of the cottage, they noticed an elderly gentleman standing on the glassed-in porch. He waved at them to come in. So, the two women pulled into the driveway. They climbed the stairs and greeted the older gentleman standing in the open doorway.

"Welcome. I'm Joe Fisher."

" I am Jamie and this is Val. We saw your ad posted in the café and fell in love with the picture of this cozy looking home with the beautiful landscaping."

Joe smiled and stood up straighter. "Yes, it is beautiful, especially in the spring. Too bad you can't see it looking its best. I still like it this time of year, especially in the snow. The pines look so lovely when they're dusted in white." Joe stepped aside. "Come in. Let me give you a tour."

The main floor of the house included a master bedroom and bath, a kitchen, dining room, and a living room with a beautiful fireplace. Jamie ran her hand over the elaborate carvings on the fireplace mantle and commented on each detail specific to the craftsman style of construction.

"I'm sorry you won't meet my wife today. She's down visiting our son. We're moving into a mother-in-law suite in his home, so we can be nearer to our children and grandchildren." Joe glanced around his cherished home. "It's not our idea to sell. My son thinks we're getting too old to care for it properly."

Jamie put her hand on the older man's shoulder. "I'm sure it's sad to leave a home you love."

"We built it ourselves. That's why we wanted to sell it privately. We wanted to be sure that the people buying it would love our home as much as we have." With that, he took them upstairs to show them two decent sized bedrooms, a small sitting room, large storage closets, and another bath.

They returned to the first floor. Joe stopped to show them the porch on the front of the house. Furnishings on the small, windowed porch included two cozy chairs with a table and reading light between them. "Oh look, Jamie." Val pointed to the bookshelves beneath each window. "You won't have to build them."

"You know how to build bookshelves?" Joe arched an eyebrow, as he swiveled toward Jamie, appraising her with a new interest.

"Yes, I love to work with wood."

"Then, come with me." Joe barely disguised his smile. He led them into the kitchen, and opened a door that led to the basement. They passed a laundry room and another finished room stacked with boxes. Val pointed and said, "Jamie, this room would make a great office."

"Come, girls. This way." Joe opened another door and reached in to switch on the light. His face glowed, as a he stepped back to let Jamie precede him into the room.

"Oh wow! Look, Val." Jamie stepped aside to reveal a fully furnished woodshop, complete with several pieces of woodworking equipment. The room and the equipment gleamed from care born of love.

"If you buy the house, I'll leave the equipment for you, as I have no need for it at my son's place." Joe's eyes glistened.

Jamie looked over at Val who nodded a quick affirmative response. "Joe, assuming the price is within our ability, we'd like to talk about purchasing this house. We hope you and your wife will consider us as potential buyers."

"Let's go back upstairs. I have some information and figures written down for potential buyers. It lists the price for the house and all the expenses associated with owning it."

Jamie and Val looked over the paper. Joe had even included average costs for heat and electricity. The two women exchanged a glance. "Joe, we'll be honest. This price is at the top of our budget. We'll have to do some talking first, before we can make any commitments.

Let us review the information and talk about it, and we'll call you in a few days." Jamie handed the paper to Val who put it into her purse.

"That's fine. Oh, since you're handy, Jamie, maybe I should mention the carriage house in the back. I didn't show you that."

Jamie's eyes snapped open. "Carriage house? Where?"

Joe led them again through the house. They stood on the back porch. "There."

Jamie and Val saw the building he was talking about. It was a small garage that could house two cars. Above it there appeared to be a second floor. The building was painted white and trimmed in a complimentary color to the house.

Val touched Joe on the shoulder. "May we look inside?"

"Sure. Let me get my coat." Joe disappeared inside the house. A few minutes later, he led them to the building. They entered through a side door into the garage area and followed Joe up the steps at the back of the building to a large room above the garage. The kitchen and bath were located near the front of the open space. There was no doubt they would need to do some modernizing. Although there was dust accumulated through years of disuse, the place appeared to have all the basics. The rest of the apartment was one large room with a tiny bedroom taking up one corner.

Jamie gestured to the kitchen. "We could put a half wall there to make a counter. With some elbow grease and a little money, this has the potential to be a cute little apartment."

Val asked Joe if it would be legal to rent the apartment.

"Yes. It was functional up till a few years ago. It got to be too much work for us. I can give you the documentation certifying it if you're interested in buying."

"Well, Joe, this apartment might make it possible for us to afford to buy your house because of the added income. We'll have to review our figures first. Can we have some time to talk about it?"

Joe nodded his agreement. "Of course, my wife would have to meet you and agree first anyway. You have my approval." He told them, "Martha will be back on Friday. If you think you want to buy the house, maybe we can meet and talk about it on Saturday?"

Jamie stuck out her hand. "Let us gather our financial data together and figure out if we can meet your asking price. We'll call you by Wednesday, if that's okay."

The two women bid good-bye to Joe and got in the car. They couldn't stop talking about the property and how perfect it was for them. "The house is in perfect condition." Jamie indicated that she had looked over the heat, electric, and plumbing. "Everything seems to be in good working order. The plumbing is all copper, and the electric has been updated to 200 amps. We'll need to make some improvements to the kitchen countertops. That can wait though, because the cabinets seem sturdy. Joe and his wife built them."

"What did you think about the baths?"

"Both baths are functional. The upstairs bath, newer than the first-floor bath, is a bit more modern. The first-floor bath is in keeping with the style of the house and could use some updating. I think if I replaced the vanity, sink, and fixtures it would do wonders. All the tile work is sound. All in all, the house shows pride of ownership. It's move in ready and won't need any effort on our parts except for painting inside."

Val relaxed into the car's seat. "I love it. The big question is, can we afford it?"

***

From the papers spread in front of her on the table, Jamie located the page with all the figures they'd worked on during their vacation at the cabin. They approximated the income from the carriage house apartment and added it to their figures. They counted every penny they could put their hands on. No matter how they tried, they came up short.

"I'll sell my co-op," Val said, no reservation in her voice. "The money I get from that, after I pay off my mortgage, will give us a healthy down payment. Look," she said. Estimating the sale price of her condo, she recalculated the amount that would remain on the cottage. Using the formula given to them by the real estate agent, they computed the amount their mortgage would be for thirty years based upon the current interest rate. They added in the taxes and other expenses, and came up with a total. Being cautious, Jamie added seventy-five dollars a month to the totals. "That's for incidentals we might have missed, or for unexpected repairs."

"We can do it." Val reached for Jamie, and they hugged. "Good thing you're holding on to me. Otherwise I'd be jumping up and down."

It would take most of the money they each had in liquid savings. Val had the cabin that she owned free and clear. Neither wanted to mortgage that. They figured that with the added income from the apartment rentals, they could swing all other expenses, plus they would still realize a good profit. The partners would have just enough savings to make them comfortable. They felt confident that they could pay for any unforeseen problems, and would have no difficulty making payments, even if any of the apartments were empty for a month or two.

"From my experience, here in my house, the first year is the hardest." Jamie ran her fingers through her hair. "I remember thinking, when I bought this, 'How will I ever be able to have any expendable money to do fun things.' The next year, we got our annual raise and it got easier. By the third year I was saving a couple thousand dollars a year. I'm sure we'll be fine."

Val said she would talk to the other property owners in her co-op. "I know, a while ago, there was a waiting list of people interested in buying into my place.

"Let's call Liz and Sandy and tell them about the house."

Liz and Sandy squealed at the news, overjoyed for their friends. After a brief chat, they agreed to drive by the property one night, after work, and to have dinner in town. After they concluded the call, Val and Jamie reviewed their figures again, to be sure they were accurate. While the women were talking about their plans, the phone rang again. Jamie answered it and listened for a couple of minutes before she started relating the figures she had written down regarding the costs associated with the rental of her apartment.

Val arched her brow in question and mouthed the word who.

"Hang on a minute." Jamie covered the mouthpiece of the phone with her hand. "This is Liz and Sandy on the phone. They think they might want to rent this apartment when we move. They're going to call us back in a few minutes."

Jamie answered the phone less than five minutes later. Following a few minutes of conversation she hung up.

"What'd they say?"

Jamie grinned. "They're interested. They might have some questions for us when we meet for dinner later in the week. They're pretty sure they want it, though."

On Sunday, Val contacted the other owners of the co-op. There were two parties who were on a waiting list for an apartment in the house. Val got their contact information and called them on Sunday afternoon. Unfortunately, neither was still interested.

Later, she and Jamie called the realtor and asked if they could meet the next day. Monday after work, they met with him at Val's apartment. She showed him around the place and he left to do some research. He called Val the next day with a suggested asking price for the unit. She reminded him that they were not allowed to place *for-sale* signs on the property. He cautioned that the lack of a sign could be a deterrent to his ability to sell her place. She didn't care, because the lack of a sign worked to their advantage. They didn't want to announce the sale to the world just yet. She told him not to move on a listing until they had spoken with the Fishers and made sure they were buying the property from them.

They called to confirm their appointment with Mr. Fisher. Joe set a tentative date for Saturday. "Do me a favor, though. Call to confirm with my wife, Martha, on Friday, to be sure she'll be home and everything is set."

Before going out to dinner, they picked up Liz and Sandy, and drove past the Fisher's house. Their friends loved the look of the cottage and wished Jamie and Val luck in getting Mrs. Fisher to agree to the sale. Liz and Sandy also confirmed that they wanted to rent Jamie's first floor apartment when she moved. They all agreed on terms. Because they were so busy, the rest of the week flew by.

On Friday, they called the Fishers and, at last, had a confirmed time for the meeting to see the house again and discuss details. Saturday, at two on the dot, they pulled into the Fisher's driveway. A beaming Mrs. Fisher greeted them at the door. "Come in, come in out of the cold, girls," she said, as she ushered them into the cozy living room. A fire was burning in the fireplace, making the house warm and welcoming.

Jamie again expressed her admiration for the focal piece of the room. After introductions, the older couple again showed the two women through the house. Mrs. Fisher pointed out little details of workmanship that Mr. Fisher had been too modest to boast about when he toured them the first time.

Returning to the living room, Mrs. Fisher brought out some cookies and a pot of tea she had steeping. "We can enjoy these while we talk." Mrs. Fisher wanted to know what they did, where they worked, and how they met.

"We met through work over fifteen years ago and have been friends for a long time." Val took a cookie from the plate Mrs. Fisher offered. "Between us, we own three other properties. We want to join forces and make some money off of real estate."

Jamie took a sip of her tea. "We were looking for a home outside of the city. We hadn't found anything we liked until we saw your house. We fell in love with the cottage the minute we saw the picture of it in the café."

Val jumped in. "The carriage house was the icing on the cake. It will provide us with extra income once we make the necessary repairs."

"Okay girls." Mrs. Fisher chuckled and took a cookie from the plate. "You've said the only thing I needed to hear...that you fell in love with the cottage. Let's talk about the details."

Negotiations were amiable. The Fishers agreed to reduce the price a little when they found the girls wanted to make a large down payment on the property. Additionally, they offered to finance the remainder owed at a half point below the rate quoted by the real estate agent. Val and Jamie would have to provide proof they had good credit and were financially responsible.

The Fishers indicated they would have their lawyer draft an agreement for review by Jamie and Val's attorney. They suggested the two attorneys handle the private mortgage agreement as well. Val explained she would need to sell her co-op first. Timeframes were not an issue to the Fishers, as they were moving into their son's place. They gave Val a four-month contingency-of-sale period, but would be willing to move sooner if she sold faster. The Fishers told them they would have their lawyer call when he had the agreement ready, and they would go from there.

Once the verbal agreement was in place, the whole transaction went as planned. The Fishers' efficient attorney had the papers ready for their review in two days. Jamie's attorney made only a minor change to the agreement. While Jamie and Val were there in his office, he called the Fishers' attorney who agreed to the change. The two women signed the agreement and made the deposit in the office of the Fishers' attorney the next day. Once the papers were in hand, Val met with her realtor and signed the contract agreeing to the listing for her property.

Val arrived at Jamie's house after work a few days later, breathless and excited, and greeted Jamie with a kiss. "Guess what?"

"You love me?"

"Always." Val brushed Jamie's response away with a flick of her hand. "I sold my house."

"In three days? Maybe you should have asked more."

Val shook her head. "I don't care. It means we can get moving and be together that much faster. Apparently, the woman who made the offer recently inherited a large sum of money when her mother died. There was no financing required, as she planned to pay for the apartment with cash. The members of the co-op should approve the sale with no difficulty when they hear the woman is paying cash. The papers I received were signed. I faxed my agreement in from work. The transfer of the property will occur in two months."

"I think this calls for a celebration. With the Fishers' financing the house, it gives us a little more cushion. I couldn't be more thrilled."

Jamie opened a special bottle of Beaujolais they'd bought. Following their toast, the enormity of their next undertaking hit home. "I'm feeling a little bit overwhelmed. We both need to pack. We'll have more than enough furniture to fill the new house, plus double sets of dishes, pots and pans, glassware, and silverware."

They agreed Jamie's chestnut table and corner cupboard would go in the dining room, and Val's smaller table and chairs would go into the kitchen. Val took a sip of her wine. "I'm so happy that Mr. and Mrs. Fisher agreed to let us store some things in their carriage house before the move so we won't have to pay for storage."

In preparation for the move, Jamie packed her house and put most of the boxes in her garage. They cleaned out all but the basics so that they had room to paint. Robbie, Val, Liz, and Sandy worked to paint the first floor so it would be ready for Liz and Sandy to move in. Finally, the settlement date arrived and the transfer of properties took place. During that week, and the next weekend, the group tackled the rooms of the Fishers' house that required painting. They rented a large moving van and together moved Val and Jamie's belongings into the new cottage. The next day, they moved Liz and Sandy's belongings into Jamie's apartment.

"I'm dragging and we still have to move the stored items from the carriage house into the new place," Jamie said. The friends groaned as they carried the last of the boxes into Jamie and Val's new house. Sandy struggled to her feet. "Who wants a beer?" Everyone raised his or her hand. "If I ever see another box or moving van again, it'll be too soon."

Nobody disagreed. By the time their friends left, they were too tired to unpack anything that night. Jamie and Val found the boxes labeled *linens* and made up Jamie's bed. Before crawling in, they released the cats from the laundry room where they'd been confined during the move. Each woman carried a cat upstairs and gave them some food. Once the boys finished eating, Simon and Chips were returned to the laundry room and shown their litter pans. This time, the door was left open so they could explore their new home.

Exhausted yet happy, Jamie fell into bed next to Val. "Honey, I'd love to make love to you, but I'm so tired, I don't think I can muster up anything more than a quick kiss good night."

Val's only response was to throw a limp arm across Jamie's tummy. Deep breathing followed, a few seconds later.

Over the course of the next couple of weeks, everyone settled in, including the cats. Jamie and Val unpacked and straightened out the furniture. The felines found a safe vantage point and watched as familiar items appeared in their new house. Jamie got the bigger first-floor bedroom, because she had a king-sized bed. Val's queen bed went to the larger of the two bedrooms upstairs. The two single beds from Jamie's apartment took up residence in their guest room. Decorating involved putting Jamie's things in her bedroom, and Val's in her room on the second floor. Jamie gave her living room furniture to Liz and Sandy. Val's newer furniture they put in the living room of the new house. They used the furniture from Jamie's TV room to make a TV room upstairs in the sitting room.

Once the big pieces were in place, the rest went pretty smoothly. They shopped for special pieces to fit specific areas. Before they'd even moved in, they saw a mirror, inlaid with colorful glass, which they liked and bought for the bedroom.

Val motioned. "A little to the right, hon."

Jamie wielded the hammer and tapped the nail into the wall to hang their first, jointly purchased, item prominently on the bedroom wall. Val smiled at her lover. "It's beautiful and so well hung."

"What an opening line that could be." Their shared laughter ended with a sweet kiss.

All that remained before considering the move a fait accompli was to face the dreaded Helen from HR and change their addresses on their school records. Helen was a notorious busybody. The pair knew she would have a million questions for them when they turned in the new address information and she noticed it was the same address. They agreed to bite the bullet and inform her of the change as soon as they were completely settled.

Chapter Thirty-one

Reflections

VAL AND JAMIE WORKED on the house a little every day. Although not a stated goal they set between them, it seemed that they got into a routine of making love in each room as they finished it. Within a week of buying, and only weeks before spring break, they had finished unpacking. Val set the last item on the mantle.

"There. What do you think?"

"I'm pretty happy with what we've done. I'm sure we'll make changes from time to time. For now, I love it."

It was a new Saturday morning ritual. They'd sit on the porch to drink their respective morning beverages, coffee for Val, tea for Jamie.

"Well, we're done with the house for now and, surprise of all surprises, everything fits." Jamie added two teaspoons of sugar into her large mug of tea and stirred it in.

Val reached out to touch Jamie's hand. "Yes it does. I'm so happy."

Jamie stood and took Val's hands. She kissed her on each cheek. The next kiss was filled with promise and joy. Like a flash fire, it escalated into a passion born of love. Still kissing, they moved to the first-floor bedroom. Clothes flew in all directions as sometimes happens with experienced lovers. Jamie's lips found Val's breast.

Val moaned and allowed her hands to roam over Jamie's body. She touched spots that she now knew by heart, the ones that would bring Jamie to the point of begging Val to come inside.

"Faster," Jamie murmured against Val's neck.

Val rode Jamie's thigh until she felt her lover's hand move between them. They both moaned as Jamie's fingers slipped inside. The lovers kept pace with each other, both peaking at the same time. Val curled against her lover.

Jamie kissed Val's eyebrow. "You make me so happy. I can't imagine my life without you. I'm so glad it's you."

"Ditto," Val mumbled into Jamie's neck, making them both giggle.

"I thought you told me you were a romantic."

"I am. What...you think ditto isn't romantic?"

The pair chuckled and kissed again. Spent, they lay entwined. Jamie looked at the clock radio. "If we don't get up, today will be a day when nothing constructive gets accomplished on the carriage house."

Val began to roll Jamie's nipple between her thumb and first finger, eliciting an "Ummm." She looked at her lover. "I can't get enough of being with you this way." She raised her head and grinned. "Do you have enough energy to do some work today? If you do, then I must be doing something wrong."

"No, you're doing everything right." Jamie pulled Val closer and gave her a quick kiss. "Maybe, after a little nap, we can get in a couple of hours of work this afternoon."

Leaving their bed proved to be a challenge. It was after noon by the time they began work on the carriage house. They both knew that the sooner they finished, the sooner they could begin collecting rent.

Sunday morning found them on the porch again, having breakfast. They began to talk about the dreaded task of changing their address at school. When Robbie showed up to help them paint in the carriage house, he interrupted their discussion about the possibility of one of them getting a post office box.

After hugs, kisses, and greetings, they asked Robbie his opinion about the PO box. "Um...I think it's a waste of time.

Robbie had the rapt attention of both women.

"What do you mean?" Jamie and Val asked in unison.

"Well, because I knew you would be upset, I debated about telling you. It seems that the cat is already out of the bag, so to speak. You two are quite the topic of conversation."

"What do you mean?"

Robbie held up both hands. "Don't shoot the messenger." He poured himself a cup of coffee and sat down. "Well, the woman who bought Val's apartment was the niece of one of the women who works in the high school. Apparently, at the weekly bridge game, speculation about why the two of you might want to move in together was the hot topic."

"We knew that could be an issue." Jamie reached for Val's hand. "How do you know this?"

"On Wednesday, Candy, one of the bridge players, approached me to get the 'dirt.' I gave an Academy-Award-worthy performance. I told them that you'd said it was a good move, financially, for both of you. I explained that Jamie had already rented out her apartment, and that you'll have another apartment to rent here at the new place."

Jamie put her hand to her mouth. "Oh, no. What did she say to that?"

"Nothing. I didn't give her the opportunity. I pivoted with a move that would have left a Buckingham Palace honor guard green with envy and left the room. Big-mouthed Candy had lots of hot gossip to spread."

Val and Jamie both put their heads in their hands.

"I'd hoped that what I told her would give you some way to justify your move together, other than the obvious one, of course." Robbie shrugged. "I know that word was spreading because, by Friday, another teacher asked me if it was true that you two had bought a house together." Robbie patted Jamie's arm. "I'm sorry, Jamie. I guess it proves for sure what a small world it is, doesn't it?"

Val cleared her throat. "Wait a minute. Let's think about this. In my opinion, from what you've said, the gossip is curiosity driven. Let's give them our version of what they want to know."

The expression on Jamie and Robbie's puzzled faces made Val laugh.

As the three friends worked on the carriage house, they discussed a plan to extinguish some of the speculation. Together they developed a list of school friends and colleagues to invite to a small gathering at the house.

Jamie laughed when Val said, "Don't forget the ring leader."

"Ah yes, Helen." Val dipped her paintbrush. "Maybe if she sees the separate bedroom quarters it'll slow her down." She swiped her forehead with her forearm, leaving a trail of paint in its path. "Another thing we have going for us is the fact that everyone knows that you were married before, Jamie. That might create some doubt about our involvement as a couple in the minds of some of them."

"Well, then there's the rumor that you used to be a nun." Jamie struggled to keep a straight face.

"Whaaaat?" Val's voice raised about three octaves and twenty decibels.

Jamie and Robbie doubled over, barely able to breathe.

"Good one, Jamie." Robbie patted his friend on the shoulder, leaving spots of paint behind.

"Very funny, you two." Val couldn't hide her own smile. "It's worth a try. It might be enough to reduce and contain the rumors. It might remove us from being the hottest topic in the rumor mill."

Jamie shrugged. "Maybe. If not, at least we get to have a party in our new place."

On Monday morning, they went together to face the dreaded Helen to submit the changes to their home addresses.

***

The couple finished planning their open house and invited the selected group to visit one evening before the spring break. Everyone who came loved the house. Several commented that they could see how Jamie and Val fell in love with the place. They stressed the income aspect of their purchase. Several of their guests went to visit the carriage house apartment, which was nearing completion.

Their party seemed to be a success, because gossip slowed. A week after their open house, Jamie held up the front of the paper to show Val. "Look. The school librarian made the front page for public nudity and solicitation." It was hard to say if it was their open house or the headline and its associated scandal that slowed the gossip about them. They only knew that the librarian replaced them as the primary topic of the gossip mill. In the end, being out of town was like magic. Nobody could see them coming or going, and as the weeks passed, the gossips moved on to other topics.

With Robbie's help, Jamie and Val worked to finish the carriage house. As they neared the end of construction, they placed an ad on the bulletin board in the café. Two days later, a single, guy responded. The women looked out the porch window as he pulled into the drive and got out of his car.

Jamie turned to Val and whispered. "My God! He's got the body of Adonis. You'd better be good to me, I could jump the fence for him."

Val was still chuckling when the fellow knocked at the door. They spent time talking to the handsome blond before agreeing to rent to him. He filled in the application. "The name on here is Michael. I prefer Mickey.

"The only work remaining is for us is to stain the carriage house floors before anyone can move in." Jamie folded his application in half and stuck it onto the clipboard she was carrying. "We'll have to check your references and finish up out there. The place should be ready by the beginning of next month, although I'll let you know definitely if you're approved as soon as I finish the required credit and background checks."

"I'd love to move in as soon as possible before the end of the month. How would you feel about me helping you finish up?"

"We like folks not afraid of a little work. You have yourself a deal if everything checks out."

"My old landlord is home and expecting a call." Mickey grinned. "At first, I guarantee he'll tell you not to rent to me. He doesn't want me to move. I've never missed a rent payment and help him out around the house. He's planning on selling soon, though, so I started looking."

"Okay, Mickey, let's go make some phone calls."

It took less than an hour for them to get all the paperwork in order after talking to Mickey's current landlord. After signing the lease and taking a deposit from Mickey, they walked him to his car. As he opened the car door, they noticed the rainbow key chain in his hand and a copy of the gay newspaper on the front seat. Jamie and Val exchanged a meaningful glance.

"Thanks for a pleasant afternoon. I'll see you Saturday morning in my work clothes." He gave a jaunty wave as he pulled out of the drive.

They turned toward each other, as they watched Mickey's car disappear. Jamie had a twinkle in her eyes. "What do you think, Val? Maybe Robbie should join us to work on the floor so he can meet and get to know our new tenant."

Chapter Thirty-two

Present Day

KELLY PUSHED BACK FROM the table in Jamie's kitchen. She balled up the paper wrapper and French fry container, and placed them in the bag. She gathered the trash from Jamie's meal as well. "And so, you both lived happily ever after?"

Jamie chuckled. "Well at least until Val decided to do a swan dive down the steps."

"Oh stop. What happened to Robbie and Mickey? Did they hit it off?"

"I guess you could say that. That's why we're packing. We're moving to the cabin on the lake, full time, and they're buying this house." She pushed her cup into the bag. "A few years ago, we did a complete renovation here. While we were at it, we updated the cabin so we'd be comfortable there both in winter and summer. The lake area is much more developed now than it was when we got together."

"What changes did you make here?"

"Over the years, we renovated the kitchen and all the bathrooms. I gave up my woodworking area and had a media room installed instead. It might be our one mistake, because we haven't used it all that much. Sometimes I miss the shop." Her eyes clouded for a brief moment. She shrugged it off. "No sense keeping it. We finished all the big projects I could do years ago." Jamie stifled a yawn.

"I'd better get going and let you get some rest." Kelly pushed up to her full height.

"I don't know how to thank you, Kelly. I'm sure I'd have lost my mind if you hadn't kept me busy today."

"No, Jamie. It's you I want to thank. You told me a wonderful story filled with love. You also gave me some food for thought."

"Will you leave me your address and contact information? I hope, when Val comes home, you'll come visit us at the cabin."

A laugh bubbled out from somewhere deep inside of the kind woman. "You're not getting rid of me that easily. I'm not busy tomorrow. When you get things straightened out at the hospital, give me a call. I'll come over and we'll get those boxes moved downstairs for you, so you can go through them. Then, when you're ready, I'll help you get rid of what you want to toss."

Jamie's eyes brimmed.

Kelly draped an arm over the shoulders of the smaller woman. "Now, get some rest. I'll see you tomorrow." Kelly handed Jamie a card with all her contact information on it. "Use the cell number. The other one is, uh, no longer working."

Jamie wrote her phone numbers on a slip of paper and handed it over. "The first number is the house number here. The second is my cell."

They walked to the door together, and Jamie watched until Kelly's taillights disappeared down the driveway. She made a quick call to Robbie to tell him she was okay. "Don't worry about me. I'll call you and Mickey tomorrow." As soon as she hung up, she got her jacket and headed back to the hospital.

Jamie tiptoed into Val's room. She picked up the chair and carried it to the edge of Val's bed and settled in.

"What took you so long?"

Jamie jumped. "You're awake."

"I figured you'd sneak back in here. Go home. I'm fine."

"I've been home. You're not there. I want to be with you."

Val reached for Jamie's hand.

Pulling Val's hand to her lips, Jamie placed a soft kiss on each finger curled around hers. "I told Kelly our story today. We have so many good memories, sweetheart. So much laughter and so much love." She held Val's hand to her cheek.

"We had it good, for sure. Aren't you tired?"

"A little." Jamie laid her head on the bed, and Val ran her fingers through her partner's hair. The motion slowed and eventually stopped. Val's hand slipped to the bed. Jamie's head popped up. Regular breathing told her that Val had drifted off to sleep, and Jamie sat back in her chair.

Jamie closed her eyes and drifted off herself for a short time. It took a few seconds to realize where she was as she awoke. She sighed and studied her lover. The passage of time had caused her hair to gray, and some wrinkles, born of their shared laughter, to line her face.

Despite that, the person she saw was the same lovely woman she'd fallen for all those years ago. It was all she could do to refrain from leaning over and kissing that mouth of hers. It was the first thing that had attracted Jamie to her lover, and it still had the same effect on her.

"Are you staring at my mouth?"

Jamie blinked. "Thought you were sleeping."

"I'm awake now. I could feel you here with me, and hear your wheels turning."

Jamie laughed. "I was thinking about my day and meeting Kelly. She helped keep me sane today. I was so worried about you."

"So you told her our whole life story?" Val pushed the button to raise her head a bit. The hum of the motor as the bed elevated seemed loud in the quiet.

"Pretty much. I left out a few things."

"Like…"

Jamie's mind drifted back over the parts of their lives she'd shared with Kelly. "I didn't mention that we both wound up with different jobs, different careers, really." Work was important to their early relationship, as it brought them together. Its importance diminished once they'd moved in together. After they bought the house, Jamie had encouraged Val to return to school. She was only six credits and a dissertation away from her doctorate. "I was so proud of you that day we placed the plaque on your desk that read *Valerie DiLeona, Ed.D.*"

"Mmm. It was a proud day for both of us. Getting the teaching position at the college made such a difference in our lives. A much more liberal work environment, and us no longer working in the same place, must have reduced our collective blood pressures by eighty points."

"True." Jamie leaned forward and put her elbows on her knees. "I didn't believe Regina knew what she was talking about when she said the decision to terminate the vice principals would be reversed. She turned out to be right. It only took three years for the pendulum to swing back. By the time the staff, parents, and principals, pressured the board to reestablish the vice principal positions, I'd already had obtained my counseling degree."

Val chuckled. "The minute that Mickey vacated the carriage house to move in with Robbie, you set up your counseling practice there. You worked so many nights and weekends for the first year. Remember how nervous you were when you took an early retirement from teaching to expand your private practice?"

Jamie stretched her back. "Yes, we have so many memories."

Val cleared her throat.

"Want some water?"

"Um...please. Val looked up at the empty bag hanging on the rack above her bed.

Jamie held the water, as Val sipped from the straw. "Are you in pain?"

"No."

Jamie returned to the chair next to Val's bed. Val tugged on Jamie's hand. "Turn so I can see you."

Jamie stood and reversed her chair so they were sitting face to face, hands joined. "Have I told you today that I love you?"

"Maybe. Since I can't remember if you did, maybe you didn't tell me enough times."

"Ah. I see." Jamie pursed her lips to stop from grinning. "Well, I do."

"You do what?"

Jamie shook her head. "You know. I love you."

"Oh good. Ditto." They both chuckled.

"I don't think I ever told you one thing enough though. I don't think I told you enough that I'm so glad it's you. You've given me so much love and laughter these years. You've loved me and forgiven me all my shortcomings."

Val's eyes crinkled. "You have shortcomings? Now you tell me."

Jamie chuckled. "Does your head hurt?"

"Not too much." Val touched the bandage. "Do I have a bruise?"

"Bruise? I wouldn't worry about it. I like the color blue."

"Oh don't make me laugh hard." Val glanced at Jamie. "You look tired. Go home."

"I will. I have to be back here by eight to see the doctor. Then, depending on what he says, I have to call Kelly. She offered to move those boxes to the main floor, so I can sort them out. She's a sweet kid. Lonely, I think. She mentioned her mom recently passed away."

"I'm sure you told Mickey and Robbie."

"Yes. They're taking care of the house and the cats." Jamie's mind flashed back to the cats she'd had when she and Val got together. They were long gone now and another set of felines was enjoying the lap of luxury with Jamie and Val.

"Did you call Bly?"

Jamie shook her head. "I'll let her know as soon as I know what they plan for you." Bly had never been successful in working out the problems with Dana. She remained in California, and went on to have a series of monogamous relationships.

"It's sad that she never settled down permanently with anyone."

Jamie nodded. "Yes, it seems her record was seven years with one person, before becoming disenchanted and moving on to the next. It's exactly what she said she didn't want. Wonder if she'll fly out for Christmas? We haven't seen her in three or four years, now."

"Her life solidified in California."

Jamie nodded. "Mmm, I guess." Val had embraced a friendship with Bly, despite the fact that Jamie and Bly had once been lovers. In her heart of hearts, Jamie suspected that Val was glad that Bly decided to stay on the other coast.

The nurse came in to check on her patient. She arched a brow in Jamie's direction. "What are you doing here? I thought you went home."

"I did. I came back."

Jamie slid back to allow the nurse room to work around the bed.

"She's doing well." The nurse adjusted Val's covers.

Before she had to open her mouth for the thermometer, Val said, "I'm tougher than I look."

The nurse put her hand on Jamie's shoulder. "You need some rest. Please, go home. I promise we'll take good care of her until you come back in the morning."

Jamie stood up. She wiggled her fingers in Val's direction. "Don't forget."

"Ditto."

Chapter Thirty-three

Present Day

BY SEVEN THE NEXT morning Jamie was back in the hospital, sitting next to Val's bed. Val opened her eyes. "Hi, sweetheart. Did you sleep?"

Jamie rolled her eyes. "I missed you."

"I'd like to say I missed you, too, for the few minutes I was awake."

"Hmm. Well, I missed you enough for both of us."

Val scrunched up her face. "I feel swollen."

"For good reason. It's nothing to worry about, the nurse says.

"Maybe next time I'll try to land on my butt instead of my face."

Val's doctor showed up a half hour later. Following his examination, he sat down on the edge of the bed. "You are one very lucky woman. Your head will heal, as will your ankle. I'm sending you upstairs to the PT floor. They'll teach you the proper way to use a walker, how to manage stairs, and all the rest. You can go home once you're comfortable. After that ankle heals, you can continue PT at home, on an outpatient basis. Two or three months, and you'll be square dancing again.

Jamie opened her mouth, tempted to say that was extremely impressive, because not even once in her life had Val ever square danced before. She snapped her mouth closed when she caught the evil eye Val was casting in her direction.

"Thank you, doctor." Val smiled her most beguiling smile.

"The nurse will help you with the arrangements. I'll see you in my office in six weeks. Any questions?"

Both Jamie and Val shook their heads to his already retreating back.

Two hours later, the nurse came in. "Your transport is here. I hope you will feel better soon." They bid the nurse good-bye. Jamie trotted along behind and waited while they got Val settled in her room.

Millie, the nurse, came in and introduced herself to Val. She looked over the chart at the foot of the bed and faced Jamie. And you're her partner?"

Jamie's eyes widened, as she struggled to keep her chin from dropping open. "Uh...yeah. I'm Jamie."

"Very nice." Millie looked over at Val. "Once she goes home, visiting nurses will pick up her nursing care. They'll care for her surgery site. I assume you will be providing her care at home?"

Jamie's head bobbed.

"Before she leaves here, you'll have to spend a session in PT with her to be sure you know how to help her transfer. Don't worry...it's almost second nature. They just like to be cautious." The nurse fussed with Val's bedding. "You've done very well. Are you in any pain?"

Val shook her head. "No."

"I'll get you some ice for that foot, to help with swelling." She was almost out the door by the time she finished her sentence, "I'll be right back."

Val looked over at Jamie. "It still surprises you when someone openly refers to us as partners, doesn't it?"

"It's so, so different than it was when we got together. Yes. Sometimes it still stuns me that people treat us like we're normal."

"Times have changed, for sure." Val smiled. "Our town was pretty accepting. We've made straight and gay friends there. Once we both left the school environment, we never had to hide our relationship. Our life got much easier and less stressful."

"I know. It still feels strange to me, after hiding for so long, to have someone address it straight on. Pardon the pun."

"Don't you have to get back to the house? You said you had to call Kelly. She's pretty hot. Do I need to be jealous?"

The comment made Jamie smile. "No. She's too tall for me. I'd need a ladder just to kiss her. And some sort of rejuvenation drink to make her want to kiss me back." They both laughed.

Jamie stood and approached Val. "I need to get going." She put her hand on Val's swollen face. "Poor baby." She placed a gentle kiss on Val's lips.

"Be careful today. Let her do the lifting."

"I will. I should hurry. Where's the best place to buy a ladder?"

Val pinched Jamie's arm.

"Ouch. I was only kidding."

Val's laughter felt like a warm coat on a cold day. "I know. Don't forget." Val pulled Jamie back for one last kiss.

"I won't. I'll come back later. Love you."

***

Following her phone call to Kelly, Jamie tidied the house while she waited for the younger woman to arrive.

"Good afternoon." Kelly bent down to give Jamie a quick hug. "I brought us some muffins. After we work a little while, we can stop for a pick me up."

Jamie stepped back and opened the door wider for her guest. "I'm not sure what I did to deserve your help and kindness. I can tell you, though, without it I'd be in hot water." She pointed toward the kitchen table. "Do you want to sit down?"

"No. Let's get these boxes moved. The sooner we get them down here, the sooner you can get started sorting through them."

"You're right. Follow me."

It took Kelly no time to move the boxes from the attic to the first floor. After climbing the stairs and returning to the living room with Kelly who was carrying the first box, the two decided it would be best if Jamie sat down and started sorting. Kelly made trip after trip up to the attic, and finally, the last box joined the pile surrounding the older woman.

Kelly approached the painting on the wall opposite where Jamie sat. "This is beautiful. You have good taste. My mom was a photographer...quite a good one." She checked out the two smaller paintings nearby. "I settled on her house a week or so ago. I had to sell off most of Mom's work. I kept some of my favorites and all of her negatives. I'll dedicate a room to her work once I'm settled."

"Where are you moving to?"

"I'm not sure. I haven't found the perfect house yet. Kelly stepped around the boxes separating them and took a seat in the chair opposite her.

"Look." Jamie held up a picture. Her eyes had a faraway look, as her mind drifted back to the day it was taken. "This is Val and me, right after we first got together. I was probably about your age in this shot. That's our friend Sandy. Liz took the photo."

"You were a very attractive couple. You still are."

"Thank you."

"You mentioned your friends before. Where are they now?"

Jamie's face fell. "Oh. We still see them...individually now.

Unfortunately, they broke up years ago. That happens to the best of us sometimes." Jamie's eyes filled as she looked away and swallowed hard. She blinked a few times to clear her vision.

"You've been such an amazing help." Jamie placed the photo into the box in front of her. "Is there anything I can do for you?"

Kelly leaned forward and, with a twinkle in her eyes, she replied, "Well, now that you mention it, I hate to tell you this...my services don't come free."

"I see. I think I have some lovely muffins in the kitchen."

The unexpected comment drew a bark of laughter from Jamie's new friend.

"No. I'm going to drive a harder bargain than that. I'll take that as a down payment on your debt. You won't be paid in full until you tell me how to have a relationship like you and Val have."

"That's easy. Pick the right woman."

"I thought I had." Kelly sucked her bottom lip between her teeth. "I guess I was wrong."

Jamie leaned back in her chair and studied the woman across from her. "Do you want to tell me what happened?"

"I made a huge mistake. I told you I recently lost my mom. It took her six months to die. It was awful...painful for her and me. We were very close. I met Taylor about six months before Mom got sick. We were happy, thought we were in love...even talked about moving in together."

"And then?"

"When Mom got sick, I quit my job, closed up my apartment, and moved in with my mother. I was stupid. I didn't even discuss it with Taylor. I told her I wouldn't have time for a long-distance relationship, because I was leaving. We both cried. She asked me to rethink the move. I told her I only had a limited amount of time with my mother, and she had to come first. I left and moved here." Kelly ran her fingers through her hair and hung her head.

"I'm sorry." Jamie reached over and patted Kelly's hand.

Kelly raised her eyes to meet Jamie's. "I was incredibly stupid. I walked away from the best woman I've ever known."

"So you never gave her a chance to help you, to support you?"

Kelly shook her head. "Like I said, stupid. Instead of opening up and telling her how much I needed her help and support, I pushed her away and ran. The longer I'm away, the more I realize what I gave up. I still love her. It's hopeless though...there's no way she would ever take me back."

"Have you asked her? Or told her how you feel?"

"No. What's the use? What are the chances she's sitting there waiting for me? Slim to none?"

"Kelly? Are you asking me for advice?"

Using her sleeve, Kelly wiped an escaped tear from the corner of her eye and sniffed. "Is it free?" She grinned.

"One hundred percent, unless you count the muffins." They both chuckled. "You told me yesterday that you're on vacation. Why then, woman, are you sitting here? Go. Talk to Taylor and tell her exactly what you told me. Some flowers might not hurt. If you love her and you think she's the one, don't let her get away. If she's all you say she is, isn't she worth fighting for?"

Kelly shot to her feet like a piece of toast from a high-strung toaster. "Yes. Yes she is." She bent over and kissed Jamie's cheek. "Thank you."

Jamie followed Kelly to the kitchen, where she picked up her jacket and shrugged into it.

Jamie patted Kelly on the arm. "Go get her. I hope it works out for you."

"Me too. I'll call you when I get back."

***

The next two days sped by. Jamie worked in the mornings, sorting through the boxes. She made three piles: the keep pile, a toss pile, and a to-discuss-with-Val pile.

Val made good progress. For the end of her last day in PT, they asked Jamie to come in to learn her part in Val's care. Robbie came with her, thinking he might have to help them once Val was home.

The therapist put his hand on Val's shoulder. "Arrangements for Val's transport and care were all coordinated by the facility. She's ready to come home." He gave them a paper with all the information they'd need.

Before the ambulance team delivered Val to her home, Jamie asked Robbie and Mickey to help her clear a path in the boxes so they could get Val to the bedroom in the companion chair. They had the weekend to finish sorting and packing. "We'll see you on Sunday to help with the last of the preparations. The moving truck comes on Monday. Call us if you need us before that."

Jamie nodded. "I will. I made arrangements for Val at the cabin. Her visiting nurse and PT start on Tuesday."

***

Val and Jamie lay side by side in their bed in their craftsman cottage. Val's ankle was propped up on a pillow, and her head rested on Jamie's shoulder. "It's so good to be home."

Jamie sighed. "Don't get used to it. We move in a couple of days."

"Thank God we put the addition on the cabin, and moved from the loft bedroom to the first floor. Can you imagine me navigating those stairs with this ankle?"

"That was a hard decision." Jamie sighed. "I loved sleeping in the loft."

"Neither of us liked it much after we hit our sixties and had to make two or three trips down the stairs to the bathroom every night."

"I know. I think we started wearing divots in the stair treads."

Val yawned. "Are you as tired as I am?"

"I could sleep for a month."

"We can't. We have to push through till we move."

Jamie wrapped her arm tighter around Val. "Let's get some rest."

The two women had a restless night. Jamie got up several times herself to use the bathroom. She also had to get up each time Val got up, because she needed Jamie's help. The phone woke them at eight thirty.

"Hi Jamie. It's Kelly. I wondered if you needed some help today."

"I think we're in good shape. Robbie and Mickey are coming over. That doesn't mean I'd say no to an extra pair of hands." She tried hard not to make a noise as she yawned. "How was your trip?"

"I'll tell you when I get there. Want me to pick up something...muffins, bagels?"

"Oh, please. That would be great. I'm off to a slow start this morning."

"Okay. I'll give you an hour. Have the hot water ready. See you in a bit."

Mickey and Robbie rushed in around quarter past nine. They set to preparing coffee and tea and carried it into the dining room. They had already stacked all the boxes against the wall, so they had somewhere to sit. Mickey was busy reading the labels on the boxes. "Jamie, did you pack the spoons. I couldn't find them anywhere."

"I'll get them. I have some plastic ones." Jamie made her way to the kitchen and rummaged in the plastic bag on the counter. She noticed Kelly pull into the driveway, and couldn't resist the urge to see who got out of the vehicle. The driver's door opened first and Kelly jumped out. She went around to the passenger side door and leaned over. *Damn. I can't see what she's doing.*

"Jamie. Where are those spoons? The coffee is getting cold, and I need my sugar," Robbie yelled from the other room.

A breath of air pushed out through tight lips. "Hold your horses. I'm coming." She gave one quick look out the window, grabbed the box of spoons, and headed to the dining room. "Here, I have to go answer the door." Jamie returned to the kitchen and opened the door at the exact same moment Kelly was about to knock.

Strong arms wrapped her in a tight hug. "Thank you," she whispered into Jamie's ear. "You are a wise woman." Kelly stepped aside. "Jamie, I want you to meet Taylor...the most forgiving woman in the world."

"I'm not sure about that. Val may already hold that title." Jamie extended her hand.

Another giant woman stood next to Kelly. She grabbed Jamie's hand and pulled her close enveloping her in a warm hug. "I hope you don't mind the hug. I understand it's you I have to thank for this one finally coming to her senses." She tipped her head in Kelly's direction. "Oh, and I can't forget the flowers. They helped." She grinned and squeezed Jamie's hand.

Jamie looked up at the two happy faces. Taylor was almost as tall as Kelly. She was more slender, with finer features and a softer jawline. They were a beautiful couple.

"Come in, come in and meet the rest of the gang."

Jamie introduced the newcomers, and the group got to know each other over coffee, tea, and muffins.

Robbie stood up and patted his belly. "You'd better let us get to work before I fall asleep." With the extra set of hands helping, they finished sorting, stacking, and packing up the last of the items they were taking with them to the cabin. The boxes of donated items were on the covered porch, ready for pick up.

Jamie ordered takeout, late in the afternoon. Kelly volunteered to take her to pick up the pizzas and buy some beer.

"I can't wait to hear what happened," Jamie blurted, as soon as she clicked her seat belt into place.

"I did as you suggested. I threw myself on her mercy, and I was lucky enough to have her forgive me. It helped that she loves me and missed me as much as I love and missed her. As soon as we can work out where we want to live, we're going to move in together. I'm hoping our relationship will rival yours and Val's for longevity."

"If you're half as happy as we are, you'll not find that difficult."

At the end of the day, everyone bid each other good-bye. The boys promised they'd be there in the morning to help with the move on that end.

"How about Taylor and I drive Val up to the cabin and take care of things up there?"

Jamie glanced at Val, and then back to Kelly.

"I know you'd rather be with me, sweetheart." Val rolled her eyes. "Unfortunately, you're needed here and cloning isn't approved for humans. Anyway, what would I do with two of you?"

Jamie raised her eyebrows.

"Don't even say it, Jamie." Val looked in Kelly and Taylor's direction. "I think I'm in good hands. Kelly is an EMT. It doesn't get much better than that."

Kelly grinned. "Oh, but it does. Taylor's an emergency room nurse. That's how we met."

"Well there you go. I'm in your capable hands ladies. Robbie, Mickey...you're in charge of Jamie."

"Oh sure. We get the tough job."

Everyone was still laughing as they headed out the door.

***

Jamie gave her final instructions to the movers, as they finished loading up the small moving van with the last of the boxes. "Remember anything with a red sticker goes in the house. Everything else goes in the garage." The driver gave her a thumbs-up sign, as he pulled away. She made her way into the house for a final check. "Okay boys, it's all yours." Jamie extended a set of house keys to Robbie.

He draped a long arm over her shoulder. "Not until you get the check later this week."

"I'm not worried about it. I know where you live." They shared a good laugh.

"Let us know if you need help with those boxes."

"The girls are staying for a few days. I'm sure they can help us.

Thanks for offering though. You'll have your hands full here." Jamie's phone buzzed. "Hi, sweetheart."

"The girls just got me settled. I need a nap, so they're going to take a walk and scope out the neighborhood. Hey! Did Kelly tell you who her mother was?"

"No. She said she was a well-known photographer, though." Jamie's eyes widened and her mouth formed an O. "No kidding. She wasn't fooling when she said she was famous. She said she recently sold her mother's place in the city."

Val said, "Yes. That one and her place in the Hamptons as well. She told me she'd return every penny if she could have her mom back again."

"I'm sure. They were close."

Jamie looked at her watch. "As much as I enjoy talking to you, I'd rather do it in person. I'll see you in a couple of hours. I'm on my way."

"Drive safely, my love."

"Will do." Jamie punched the off button on her phone.

Considering that she had to stop for gas, Jamie made good time. She passed the moving van on its way home a few miles from the cabin.

Jamie walked into the cabin. Val was on the sofa, her foot propped and a bag of ice on it. She kissed Val on top of the head. "What's that heavenly smell?"

Taylor came out of the kitchen, wiping her hands on a dishtowel. "I'm making pasta for dinner. You are right on time."

Jamie got Val's wheelchair and helped her transfer from the sofa to the chair. She pushed her up to the table.

Taylor and Kelly served the meal.

"This is wonderful." Jamie dipped her bread in the rich tomato sauce. "I know this isn't considered polite." She shrugged. "I can't help myself."

"Val gave us directions to the little store. We walked up and got the things we needed for dinner. If you'd like, tomorrow we can drive over and stock up on food and whatever other supplies you need."

"That would be great. The fridge is a little bare, because we haven't been here for almost a month. Packing kept us tied to the house." Val touched Jamie's hand. "I can make a list for you."

"We love the lake and the neighborhood." Taylor wiped her lips with the napkin. "We met one of your neighbors, a Mr. Pederson. He told us he's planning on putting his house up for sale. He showed us through. His place is lovely."

Jamie glanced at Val. "Wonder when he decided to do that?"

"He and his wife are retiring, and they want to buy one of those big bus things. Their goal is to drive to each of the fifty states." Kelly plucked a piece of Italian bread from the basket and plunged it into the last of the sauce coating the bottom of her dish. She glanced at Jamie. "Good idea," she said with a twinkle in her eyes.

"Really?" Jamie assumed a straight face. "He's going to have trouble driving to Hawaii."

"No doubt." Taylor chuckled and then took a sip of her water. "Mr. Pederson told us he wanted to sell the place furnished. It's their second home, so they don't need any of the contents. He was working on taking out the last of their personal items today." Taylor looked at Kelly.

"Say hello to your new neighbors." Kelly opened her hands as if her next words would be ta da.

"No! You're serious?" Jamie and Val linked pinkies for saying the same exact phrase.

"We didn't get a chance to tell you about our plans. Jamie, you sent me off to apologize to Taylor and, at first, she was having no part of it. I begged, and after I threatened to jump off her porch if she wouldn't listen, she took pity on me."

"Oh stop!" Taylor grabbed her lover's hand. "The porch is on ground level. I live on the first floor."

"Anyway, I begged, and she finally forgave me."

"She's trying to take credit. It was the flowers that did it, Jamie." Taylor winked at the older woman.

"I'm glad my advice was good for something."

Kelly looked at Jamie. "I'm so grateful to you. If not for you, I'd be homeless and drifting." At Jamie's doubtful expression, Kelly reiterated. "I'm serious. I sold my mom's properties and was sleeping in a friend's guest room. Anyway, I told Taylor that I wanted to make it up to her for the time I'd missed with her. It's no secret that I did okay selling my mom's properties. I convinced her to take a leave of absence from work and take an extended vacation with me. I took leave too."

Taylor shrugged. "It sounds terrible. Like I'm a kept woman or something."

"I plan on keeping you right at my side forever, so in a sense, you are a kept woman. I'm hoping you'll be keeping me, too."

Kelly kissed Taylor's hand before she turned to Jamie and Val. "I know you might think it's a bit impulsive to buy the house up the street. It's not. He gave me a good deal on it, because I'm willing to pay him cash."

"We fell in love with your house and the lake the minute we saw it. Then, when we saw the Pederson's house, we knew this is where we want to spend at least some of our time." Taylor's eyes softened, and her lips turned up in a gentle smile, as she gazed at Kelly.

"He's having his lawyer draw up the agreement, and we'll settle as soon as we can get the paperwork signed. I gave him a very healthy deposit. He said as soon as my check clears, we can move in. He may call you for a reference."

By the time Kelly finished, Val and Jamie were sitting with their mouths open.

Jamie stood up and hugged her new neighbors. "I can't think of anyone I'd rather have buy that house. It's wonderful news."

"In the meantime, while we're waiting for our house, we'll help you two get this one straightened out. Agreed?"

Jamie clasped her hands together. "Where do we sign?"

•••

Later that evening, Jamie helped Val get into bed. She propped Val's foot on the pillow and slipped into bed beside her. Rolling onto her side, she cuddled Val next to her. "Welcome home, sweetheart. Have I told you yet today that I love you?"

"No, you've been so remiss."

They both chuckled at their routine.

Jamie nuzzled her nose into Val's hair and inhaled. "I've always loved the way you smell." She slipped her hand under Val's pajama top and cupped her breast.

"You'd better behave. We don't want the girls in the loft to hear us. Besides, I have a broken head and a broken foot."

Jamie chuckled and slid her hand around to Val's side and tucked it there. "Okay, I'll wait. We have the rest of our lives to make love."

"Have I told you that I'm so glad it's you?"

"You have." Jamie smiled at the love of her life.

"Are you glad it's me?" Val reached up and moved Jamie's hand back to her breast.

"I am. And don't ever forget it. I love you with all my heart." Jamie poured love into her kiss. She would have bet a million dollars that if her lips were not otherwise occupied, Val would have said, "Ditto."

About AJ Adaire

Let me tell you a little about myself. Twenty years ago, I wrote my first book just to see if I could do it. The novel occupied space on my bookshelf, unread for nearly twenty years until one day, while in a cleaning frenzy, I considered disposing of the neatly stacked but now age-yellowed pages. As I began to read the long forgotten work, I was surprised to discover that the story was enjoyable!

Editing and retyping the first book provided a new sense of accomplishment and additional tales followed. Completion of *This is Fitting* encouraged me to write five more romance novels all of which have been published. *Sunset Island*, first book of the Friends Series was released in September 2013. *Sunset Island* was quickly followed by the remaining books in the Friends Series: *The Interim (a novelette), Awaiting My Assignment,* and *Anything Your Heart Desires* and three stand-alone novels *One Day Longer Than Forever, It's Complicated, I Love My Life, and Journey To You.*

Now retired, there is all the time in the world to write. I live on the east coast with my partner of thirty years. Because we love a challenge, we provide a loving home for two spoiled cats instead of a dog. In addition to writing, any spare time is devoted to reading, mastering new computer programs, and socializing with friends.

Contact Information

If you want to be notified of future releases, please sign up for AJ's newsletter at http://www.ajadire.com/newsletters/

E-mail: mailto:aj@ajadaire.com
Website: http://www.ajadaire.com
Facebook: http://www.facebook.com/ajadaire
Desert Palm Press: www.desertpalmpress.com

Other books by AJ Adaire

Friend Series

Sunset Island
ISBN: 9781301136629

Ren Madison is certain her life couldn't be more perfect. She owns a private island with an Inn off the coast of Maine. She treasures her loving relationship with her older brother Jack, his wife, Marie, and dotes on her niece Laura. She has a passionate and supportive relationship with her partner, Brooke, and a successful business that doesn't require her undivided attention allowing her ample time to pursue her true passion, painting.

Ren's idyllic world crumbles when Brooke dies. Friends and family worry that Ren may never fully recover from her loss.

Dr. Lindy Caprini, a multi-lingual professor, is looking for an artist to illustrate the book she is writing comparing fairy tales from around the world. To make working together on the book easier, Lindy takes a year sabbatical and leaves friends, home, and boyfriend in Pennsylvania and moves to Ren's island. Ren soon discovers that the beautiful and mischievous Lindy is a talented author and a witty conversationalist. Their collaboration on the book leads to a close, light hearted, and flirtatious friendship. Will their collaboration end there?

The Interim (a novelette)
ISBN: 9781311099051

Devastated that her partner cheated, Melanie flees to a new job in Maine, where she meets Ren Madison. Ren is dealing with issues of her own after losing her partner Brooke in a plane crash

What happens in the interim after one relationship ends and you're really ready to love again? For Ren Madison, Melanie was what happened.

The Interim fills in the details of Ren Madison's life on Sunset Island after Brooke but before Lindy.

Awaiting My Assignment
ISBN: 9781310825248

Bernie was a liar. Amanda learned that much when she caught her lover cheating the first time. Upon discovering a second indiscretion, Amanda vows there will never be another. She leaves the relationship, fleeing to her friend Dana in New York State. While staying at Dana's home, Amanda meets and falls in love with a wonderful woman named Mallory.

Amanda is ready to move on. However, the consistently surprising Bernie isn't finished yet. Amanda learns of Bernie's rudest betrayal yet when she receives a package from her recently deceased ex-lover. A very surprising revelation and one final request are contained therein. The favor comes with a gift that delivers dramatic and life-altering changes, not only to Amanda's life, but to the lives of her closest friends and new partner as well.

Anything Your Heart Desires
ISBN: 978131163912

"Whoa—lesbians!" That was Stacy Alexander's first thought as she observes the group of women in the new shop across the street kiss each other in greeting. Stacy had been staring out her apartment window trying to think of a motive for the death of the character she'd killed off in her mystery novel. Ah ha—extortion! What could be a better reason for the murder of my heroine than being blackmailed because she's a lesbian? Now all I need is a lesbian to teach me about the 'lesbian lifestyle.'

That's where policewoman Jo Martin enters the picture. Jo has two rules by which she religiously lives her life: never get involved with someone already in a relationship and never, ever date a straight woman.

As Jo and Stacy collaborate on the novel, will Stacy want to gain a more intimate knowledge of the topic, and will Jo hold steadfastly to her rules?

Desert Palm Press

One Day Longer Than Forever
ISBN: 9781310847738

Dr. Kate Martin needs a vacation after a failed romance with her business partner nearly ruins her. Lee Foster is recovering from her first lesbian relationship that self-destructed when her partner moved several states away, leaving her behind.

Two failed romances, a double booked vacation cabin, and a blizzard—will fate intervene again and turn a passionate affair with a stranger, into something more?

Desert Palm Press

It's Complicated
ISBN: 9781311122964

Victoria Brannigham had a guilty pleasure. Every day she would take a detour, sit on the boardwalk, and wait. She tried not to covet what could never be hers. Beverly McMannis was lonely, until she discovered another lesbian on the island. Bev eagerly embraced the growing friendship with her neighbor. Victoria was honest with Bev right from the start; explaining that she wasn't free to explore their attraction. Bev promised to honor the boundaries. Love isn't always easy, sometimes it's complicated...especially when she doesn't know you're still being faithful.

Desert Palm Press

I Love My Life
ISBN: 9781311310002

Betrayal by her former partner sends Chris Baxter fleeing to Maine. To escape the monotony of staring at the four walls of her isolated cabin, she enrolls in a sailing class. A chance pairing with Stephanie Kincaid and her cohorts, Tina and Terry, offers an opportunity for new friendship. Their shared homework assignment might offer Chris the potential for more than just knowledge of navigation.

An urgent message interrupts the classmates' sailing vacation along the coast of Maine. While Chris rushes back to her twin's bedside, the others remain onboard to sail back to their homeport. Will the revelations from her ex, her sister, and her family, change everything in the new life that Chris has rebuilt?

Desert Palm Press

Journey to You
ISBN: 9781311571854

What do you do if you are one of the few who remain alive after a mysterious, flu-like virus claims most of the global population? This is a question Kim Robins and Peri Henderson have to answer when the world changes and society falls apart.

Violent gangs of looters make it unsafe to remain in the city. Hoping to improve their chances for survival, Kim and Peri decide to hike into the remote forest area of Maine.

Dangerous circumstances along the trail cause the women to join forces with another hiker and her dog. The longtime friends and their new companions set off on a daunting trek filled with both menacing and kindhearted survivors.

In this romantic adventure, the real question to be answered is, will this journey bring each of the women the happiness and safety she seeks?

Note to Readers:

Thank you for reading a book from Desert Palm Press. We have made every effort to edit this book. However, typos do slip in. If you find an error in the text, please email lee@desertpalmpress.com so the issue can be corrected.

We appreciate you as a reader and want to ensure you enjoy the reading process. We would like you to consider posting a review on your preferred media sites such as Amazon, Smashwords, Bella Books, Goodreads, Tumblr, Twitter, Facebook, and/or your blog or website.

For more information on upcoming releases, author interviews, contest, giveaways and more, please sign up for our newsletter and visit us as at Desert Palm Press: www.desertpalmpress.com and "Like" us on Facebook: https://www.facebook.com/DesertPalmPress/?fref=ts.

Bright blessing.